The
Last Line

The
Last Line

A MYSTERY

Scott Lyerly

NEW YORK

Published in the United States by Crooked Lane Books, an imprint of The Quick Brown Fox & Company LLC.

Crooked Lane Books and its logo are trademarks of The Quick Brown Fox & Company LLC.

Library of Congress Catalog-in-Publication data available upon request.

ISBN (hardcover): 978-1-63910-821-3
ISBN (ebook): 978-1-63910-822-0

Cover design by Amanda Shaffer

Printed in the United States.

www.crookedlanebooks.com

Crooked Lane Books
34 West 27th St., 10th Floor
New York, NY 10001

First Edition: July 2024

10 9 8 7 6 5 4 3 2 1

This one is for Olivia and Maggie:
Break legs, ladies

Cast of Characters

(in order of appearance)

Reginald Thornton IV: Lead actor in *Murder in a Teacup*.

Ellie Marlowe: Theater lover and owner of the Kaleidoscope Theater, living with Tourette syndrome.

Dana Nugent: Costume mistress at the Kaleidoscope.

Jerry Moynihan: Actor in *Murder in a Teacup*.

Kyra Bennett: Up-and-coming actress in *Murder in a Teacup*.

Merilyn Chambers: Director of *Murder in a Teacup*.

Steve Walker: Stage manager for the show.

Tony Roper: High school kid who runs the light booth.

Alex Hillman: The Thorntons' money manager.

Valerie Thornton: Reginald's wife.

Bill Starlin: Police chief of the town of Avalon, Massachusetts.

Turner Milton: Bill's only detective in the small Avalon Police Department.

August (Augie) Hoover: EMT with the fire department.

Bridget (Bindi) Falconi: Paramedic.

Det. Chuck Phelps: Detective with Massachusetts State Police.

Mike Marlowe: Ellie's husband.

Judy O'Loughlin: Ellie's nosy, octogenarian neighbor.

Darlene Starlin: Bill's wife.

Cast of Characters

Davis Whitney: Police chief of the town of Clifton, Massachusetts.

Paul Koehler: Theater reviewer for the local city newspaper.

Det. Jim Avery: Detective with Massachusetts State Police.

Jeremy Harding: Technician at the state forensics lab.

Alice Keaton: Assistant District Attorney for Worcester County.

ACT 1

"The sudden hand of Death
close up mine eye!"

Chapter One

On the last day of his life, Reginald Thornton IV was forty-five minutes late to call. When he finally decided to appear, he swung open the door to the Kaleidoscope Theater and strode into the lobby in the manner of a conquering emperor. He stood for a moment, seemingly waiting for those in the lobby to bask in his magnificence. When fanfare did not materialize, he resumed his course, entering the lobby filled with the murmurs of a crowd anticipating a show and the aroma of freshly brewed coffee drifting from the concessions area.

A corpulent man with a ruddy complexion, Reginald's commanding presence drew immediate attention the moment he entered a room. People could not take their eyes from him, a charisma he had parlayed into a reasonably successful career as a local actor. However, he had been known to bite the head off anyone who dared refer to him as an "actor." He was, should anyone ask, a finely trained and highly sought-after "thespian." Peerless and without equal, as he believed himself to be, he wore his disdain for those around him like a black velvet cape at a formal ball.

"You're late, Reg," said Ellie Marlowe as he breezed past, refusing to even offer her a glance of recognition. She used a nickname he hated purposefully, to show her displeasure. "Call was half an hour ago." She kept her voice low and her smile plastered on to avoid a scene in the lobby, which was steadily filling with patrons.

Reginald ignored her and continued his meticulous stride, peacocking for the patrons waiting for the theater doors to officially open. Most were older women dragging their husbands out for a bit of culture—what Ellie and the other board members of the theater referred to as the "blue-hairs," the bread and butter of the theater, the demographic that kept them afloat.

"Curtain is in thirty-five minutes. The house opens in five," Ellie said. He didn't acknowledge that Ellie had spoken, didn't turn his head in her direction as he passed her. She added, "I almost asked Dana to put Steve in your costume."

Reginald halted mid-stride. He turned toward her, cold gray eyes cutting a laser-hot line across the lobby to where she stood. Ellie held his look—not an easy task considering his intimidating glare contained a ferocity she had rarely experienced.

"You. Wouldn't. Dare." He spoke slowly. Something in his voice sounded strange to Ellie, slightly off. He swayed, and Ellie wondered if he was drunk. But he couldn't be. Reginald Thornton IV would never put his stage reputation on the line for a few drinks.

"Steve knows all the lines," she said. "He would be the perfect understudy."

"I will end this theater," he rasped at her. "I have more than enough clout in this area to ensure that you never put on another show. Ever."

Ellie tried to match the death-stare he gave her, but the tension grew to be too much for her. Her head bobbed suddenly, several times in quick succession, a staccato motion followed by a few grunts, a few sniffs, and a round of exaggerated eye blinks.

Her movements invariably drew odd looks and sometimes direct, if not indelicate questions from people: Was she okay? Was something wrong? Was she having a seizure?

"I have Tourette syndrome," she would answer, almost always followed by, *"This is standard for me. I've dealt with it for most of my thirty-two years on the planet."*

Normally her Tourette syndrome was simply something she lived with; she accepted who she was and tried not to worry about the things she couldn't control. But in this battle of wills, it mattered very much to her.

Nod-grunt-blink.

Reginald smirked as if he'd won some unspoken contest. And maybe he had, Ellie thought ruefully.

"We can talk afterward," Ellie said, trying to reestablish her authority. "It's opening night. Let's give them one they'll remember."

He cut her with his eyes a few seconds more, then turned sharply and strode away. Ellie watched him go. Tonight was the first performance of the theater's production of *Murder in a Teacup*. Publicly she'd made the usual noises about how enjoyable the experience of producing the show had been, but she would be relieved to see it wrap up. It had in fact been a miserable experience, and the reason was walking away from her as she spoke.

Reginald started through the side door that led backstage, pausing long enough to say, "It is always a show to remember when I'm involved, you twitchy bitch." Then he was gone.

Ellie's face flushed, her mouth a thin, bloodless line. She heard her costume mistress, Dana Nugent, mutter from behind the ticket counter, "Miserable prick." Ellie let go of the stranglehold on her tics, and they owned her for a few painful seconds.

She sighed, and once again questioned the casting decisions of the director, Merilyn Chambers. Ellie wished she had stepped in as the owner of the Kaleidoscope Theater and vetoed Merilyn's choice of Reginald for the star of this show. But theater owners who second-guess their directors develop bad reputations.

She took a deep breath, held it, and then she felt calmer. She picked up her phone and fired a quick group text to the rest of the cast and crew:

He's here.

Chapter Two

Jerry Moynihan got the text too late to avoid his nemesis. He knotted his bow tie for the fifth time, staring at it, tugging the sides, then pulling the knot loose and starting over. He tried to get the top of each end level with the other and, failing to do so with small tugs, finally gave up and pulled the damn thing apart to start yet again.

He ran through his lines in his head, his mouth moving, silently rehearsing the words. This show was taxing, and each night his routine never strayed, including disconnecting from every little ping and distraction. He placed his phone in Airplane Mode, as they always did before shows, and focused on getting into character. Every fragment of his concentration currently focused on the bow tie.

He caught his reflection in the mirror and frowned. He didn't have leading-man looks. His face was too long, his mouth was too wide, and his ears were too small for his head. Laugh lines pulled at the sides of his mouth, and his hair showed the beginnings of salt-and-pepper coloring. *What did you expect for forty-four?* But his eyes were still young— a deep blue, almost a royal blue, and bright. Easily his best feature. The new frown line between his bushy eyebrows, which drew attention away from his best feature, made him irrationally angry.

He yanked the tie out again, looking at his feet and shaking his head.

Deep breath. You can do this, he thought.

It had been a trying production. He'd started doing theater almost by accident fourteen years ago, when his then-girlfriend had dared him to audition for *Twelve Angry Jurors.* Surprising them both, he landed a part, and had been hooked ever since. Some roles had been better than others. Some productions were rocky, and some ran smoothly. But none had ever been like this one. *Shit Show in a Teacup,* as he had come to think of it. An infection in the production—an infection known as Reginald Thornton IV—had spread misery among the cast and crew. An infection nothing could alleviate.

Well, almost nothing.

When he looked up again, the mirror reflected a florid-faced man showing a repugnant smile. Jerry jumped and gave a little cry, inwardly cursing how he sounded. He tended to be jumpy by nature, and this asshole Reginald loved it. Jerry turned away from the mirror to face the pestilence.

"Very masculine, Jerry," Reginald said, his voice rich and warm as he spoke in the slow deliberate manner of a veteran stage performer.

"I'd appreciate you not sneaking up on me when I'm warming up."

"Do you always warm up by speaking to your feet? Or by tying a bow tie fifteen times in a row?" Reginald's speech was slower than usual, without his usual snap. Jerry looked in his eyes and saw the pupils were wide, much wider than he would have expected for a room full of light.

"I don't need costume advice from you, thank you very much," Jerry snapped.

"Perhaps you should let Kyra do it for you. I hear she likes tying things up."

Jerry's cheeks, already rouged with stage makeup, flushed. Reginald smiled in self-satisfaction, and waited. Jerry opened his mouth to respond but he couldn't find any words. His mouth worked, but no sound came out.

"Witty reply," Reginald said. "You're very masculine and very witty. The boys must eat you up." He winked at Jerry, blew him a kiss, and walked away.

Jerry stared at the older man's back, his hands shaking, his jaw clenched so hard his teeth hurt. *Someday,* he thought. *Someday that asshole will be dead, and I'll dance on his grave.*

* * *

Kyra Bennett caught the text out of the corner of her eye. She had set up her makeup on a little table in front of the floor-to-ceiling mirrors in the rehearsal space in the theater's basement. The space was marked by linoleum tile, laid to provide a surface on which to dance. There were several rooms off the dance space, some housing the costumes amassed over the theater's thirty-year history, some holding unorganized jumbles of small props. Kyra stood in front of the mirrors fussing with her hairpiece, fixing it in place with bobby pins.

At Reginald's insistence, and much to the annoyance of Dana, one of the costume closets had been temporarily transformed into a dressing room for him. The rest of the more reasonable cast each found a spot in the basement to call their own for the run of the play.

Kyra's setup was next to the remaining costume closet so she could use the mirrors. She tried to be ready and gone from the space before Reginald showed up, given his tendency to be late to call. But she had struggled with her period costume, and tonight her hair would simply not behave itself. Her phone dinged, she peeked at it, and without a second glance she threw all of her makeup back into its case with a sweep of her arm across the table. She slammed the lid shut and stood too quickly, knocking over her chair.

"What on earth—?" Merilyn Chambers, the play's director, started in her seat at the sound of the crash.

"You get the text?"

Merilyn shook her head and fished her phone out of her pocket. She read the text and sighed. Kyra grabbed the rest of her costume in one hand, her hairpiece in the other, and her makeup case under her arm. "Sorry, but I gotta find somewhere else to finish up. I can't be around that guy anymore."

"I understand," Merilyn said. She got to her feet, slowly—and to Kyra's eyes, painfully. Anyone could see that Merilyn was sick, and it hurt Kyra's heart to see her diminish day by day. She had wondered sometimes whether Merilyn would live through the end of the show's run, but the old director's toughness and determination was winning out over her cancer. At least for now.

Merilyn slowly reached down to right Kyra's chair. "Go. Find a safe place to finish up. I'll deflect him down here as much as I can."

"Thankyouthankyouthankyouthankyou," Kyra said, all in a rush. She vanished down the hallway and started up the stairs at stage right. Reginald usually came down to his "dressing room" via the other set of stairs on stage left. She turned, and turned again, and reached the top of the stairs.

Only to find herself face to face with Reginald.

Kyra had gambled and lost. For some reason, Reginald had changed his routine. She tried to control her face. Eyes wide, breathing hard, she tried to tamp down her revulsion.

"Oh, just you," he said dismissively. "Something thundered up the stairs, and I thought it might be an elephant."

Her lip curled slightly, and she said through clenched teeth, "Nope, just me."

"Well," he said, eyeing her up and down deliberately, letting her know he was assessing her. "You can certainly understand my confusion."

Kyra wasn't fat. She knew that. She worked out four times a week, splitting her workouts between a boxing club and a barre studio. She ran three times a week. At twenty-seven, she was in the best physical shape of her life. Her goal was to be a professional actress, and she knew she would stand no chance in Hollywood, or anywhere, if her body did not conform to a specific type. Standing five-six, she clocked in at 116 pounds. She could fit into anything she wanted, and all of her best girlfriends would die to be in her shape.

Yet something in the way Reginald looked at her, something in the tone of his voice, made her feel like the heaviest, least attractive woman in the world. The man thrived on being mean-spirited and vindictive. He held grudges. Everything he said was designed to cut. Just a little. A little cut here and a little one there. Death by a thousand pinpricks. Comparing her to an elephant was just another small cut. But its cruelty made her catch her breath.

Reginald spied the costume and a makeup case in her arm, the hairpiece dangling from her fingers, and said, "Looking for a place to get ready? You could join Jerry on the other side of the stage. He seems to be having trouble with his costume."

"I'm sure he's got his costume under control."

Reginald shrugged. "I think his bow tie would tell a different story. I told him to come find you. I figured you had experience tying things up."

Her mouth dropped open at the innuendo. Reginald added, "Nice pose. I imagine that's something Jerry would appreciate. You should definitely offer that. Though watch out you don't bruise your knees."

Her mouth snapped shut.

Reginald brushed past her and started down the stairs. As he descended, he said, "Assuming, of course, Jerry is straight. I think the jury is still out on that account."

Then he was gone, leaving Kyra dazed, unable to move. The blood had drained from her face, and now her cheeks prickled as the blood rushed back in. Tears stung behind her eyes as she repeated to herself, under her breath, "Don't cry, don't cry, don't cry." She didn't want to have to start her makeup over again.

Injury turned to rage, and her lips curled back to a snarl. She turned to watch Reginald descend the stairs.

Why don't you kill yourself, she thought at his back.

*   *   *

Merilyn watched Reginald reach the bottom of the stairs, wheezing and trying to hide it. He was a large man, and seemed to be having trouble catching his breath today. Standing at the bottom of the stairs, leaning against the wall, he huffed and puffed before spotting Merilyn sitting in a chair, watching him. He took a deep breath, stood, and snorted as she looked at him with tired eyes.

"The number of useless individuals in my life tonight expands," he said.

Merilyn, lacking enough energy for a full-fledged fight, merely smiled at him. She sat in an old, high-backed chair, a leftover prop from a previous show. She leaned heavily on an upholstered arm, legs crossed, and shook her head. Her body was thin, her skin fragile like parchment, with a sickly yellowish hue as if she was jaundiced. Her eyes were sunken, her face pale much of the time. She offset her sickly coloring with a bright floral scarf tied around her bald head.

"Good evening, Reginald."

"It will be when this train wreck of a show is over tonight."

"And here you are after demanding the lead."

"I expected you to bring vision to the show. That is what a director is supposed to do, wouldn't you agree? You should try it sometime."

She sighed. "Amazing you don't have more friends, Reginald."

"I have plenty of friends, you old bag."

"I know everyone you know. None of them like you."

He waved her off and headed across the linoleum floor toward his "dressing room." Her eyes tracked him without turning her head, which took almost too much energy to move.

"This is the last time you ever work with me," she said. "But I suspect this won't be a surprise to you."

He looked back at Merilyn, the first time he truly had seen her in weeks. Saw how far gone she was. No doubt she was down to mere days. A brief pang tugged in his chest, as if some invisible hand of his past fumbled for his heartstrings, feeling its way like a sightless reader along a book of Braille. Part of him, deeply hidden, remembered a younger time, a happier and healthier time. With her. He thought about the past and, for the first time since starting this show, was almost overwhelmed with regret.

Almost.

He recovered, then answered, "Judging by the way you look, Merilyn, I expect this is the last time you work at all."

In a previous lifetime, she might have been insulted, but she had come to expect the worst from him and didn't bat an eyelash. The benefit of a terminal sentence, she realized, was that she stopped caring about what someone said about her.

"And the last time you work in this theater," she said.

"As if this theater is worth working in."

"And," she said, continuing as if he had not spoken, "possibly the last time you work in the theater at all."

He halted as he crossed the room and turned a hard gaze on her. Eyes half-lidded, breathing hard, he said, "What are you jabbering about?"

Merilyn had seen that look before. Reginald was at his most dangerous when backed into a corner. He had been known to purposefully ruin careers over the tiniest of perceived slights, back when his influence reached farther than it did now. His opinion still carried weight, depending on the ear. But she didn't care. She thought about the peace and tranquility awaiting her on the other side of the curtain. Soon, she would be dead, and beyond Reginald's reach. Ruining him the way he ruined others would not be a moral thing to do before she died, she thought. It would be mean-spirited, and the repercussions might be more wide-ranging than she anticipated.

She should probably go to confession before she died. For several things.

"Reginald, you've been a jackass most of the years we've known each other. And you've only grown worse. The way you've treated this cast, this theater, everyone who volunteers here. For you to treat them like garbage has simply been too much. So the word is out. I've been doing this for a long time. I know lots of people. I'm making sure no one casts you in anything ever again. Not in this county, maybe not even in this state. If you want to keep performing, you'll have to pick up and move."

She used all her breath to finish talking.

Reginald stared at her, nose flaring. No one talked to him like that, not since he was a young actor struggling to make a name for himself in New York. He hadn't tolerated it then, and he certainly didn't plan to do so now. He took a step toward Merilyn, his hands clenching into fists. Merilyn didn't move, unafraid, watching with sad and tired eyes.

He regained control, lifted his chin, and turned his back to her. He stalked across the floor to the costume closet and, just before closing the door, said, "Like anyone would believe the word of an old whore like you."

The door slammed.

She smiled.

Chapter Three

"We have a gift basket we're raffling off, full of all kinds of wonderful things like gift certificates to Starbucks and Regal Cinemas, as well as gift certificates to Kaleidoscope Theater, Arthur's Restaurant, and Ned's Diner, plus some DVDs of our favorite murder mysteries . . ."

Ellie stood on the stage, lights shining down as she gave the curtain speech, a brief soliloquy where she tried to cover as much about the theater to the seated crowd as possible. Information about the raffles, upcoming shows, and concessions in the lobby, as well as encouragement to patronize the advertisers in the program, and other such things. She gave the speech before every performance and had it down to a science. *Cover specific things, don't go into too much detail, announce shows, suggest they sign up for the mailing list, don't forget to follow us on social media.* Start to finish, she could deliver it in under two minutes, which meant holding her tics back for two full minutes. No problem. Once done and back in the lobby, she would let go with a bevy of noises and twitches.

Steve Walker, the stage manager, stood in the wing off stage left. In his forties, edging toward fifty, he exhibited the good looks of an actor, and what Dana once described as the "hair of a god"—thick, blond, lustrous. Dana practically drooled over Steve every time he entered the room. Ellie once whispered to her, "Pace yourself, Dana. You'll give yourself a heart attack."

"Can't help it, Ellie. He comes into the room and I go weak at the knees."

"He's too young for you."

"You're only as old as you feel."

Ellie, still smiling, had shaken her head and left Dana to her fantasies.

Now Steve waited for Ellie to finish. When she did, she stepped off the middle of the stage into the audience, down the aisle that split the audience in two. As with many community theaters, Kaleidoscope was a "black box," primarily a room painted floor-to-ceiling in black paint to absorb the light, the stage just a few feet off the floor. The Kaleidoscope building had once been a small roadside mission church. Thirty years earlier, the congregation had outgrown it, and the church built a newer, larger building across town. The old building was sold and converted to a theater, with a stage built over the small raised dais where the altar once jutted. It traded hands twice more before Ellie bought it five years ago, walking away from her corporate job to fulfill a lifelong dream of owning a theater.

Ellie walked up the aisle to the double doors in the back. Halfway there, Steve pushed a button on his headphones and said, "Kill the lights." At the other end of the headphones in the light booth sat Tony Roper, a teenager who ran the lights and soundboard for the show. Tony had glommed onto Kaleidoscope as a high school freshman, and immediately declared he had found his tribe and was never going to leave. He hit a button and the theater went dark for a few seconds. Steve waited, watching under a black light bulb in the wings as the cast took their places. When the movement stopped, he pushed the button again, and said, "Okay, bring them up."

The curtain rose, the stage lit up, and the show began

Chapter Four

Alex Hillman had bought a ticket and slipped into the theater with the rest of the crowd. No one there knew who he was, which was how he liked it. He wasn't eager to draw attention to himself, being there for a single purpose. Well, two purposes, actually. The first was business. The second was pleasure.

He never introduced himself to the board of directors of the theater, or to Ellie, who owned it. He simply sent in a check every so often, a donation to help the little theater keep running. He loved theater, big or small. He had the burning desire to take the stage, give an amazing performance, and soak in the worship and adulation that came with being a star. He had the face for it, looking great despite being on the border of his mid-fifties. His body was trim and fit and athletic, and he had a fabulous head of iron-gray hair, ice-blue eyes, and a dazzling smile.

What he lacked was the courage.

Whenever he tried to rationalize his stage fright, he failed. He had been a hedge fund manager in Manhattan. He still did money management, though on a much smaller scale, from his "retirement" house in the country—at least that is what he called the little town of Avalon, Massachusetts. Despite its proximity to Worcester, a mere five miles and ten minutes away, he was living in a bucolic setting.

But while he had held sway over some of the most powerful people in board rooms in New York City, on a stage, he suffered from panic attacks.

So he chose to support the theatrical arts by attending and by anonymously underwriting, and it suited him beautifully.

Most of the time.

He was sitting near the doors, which he typically hated, but tonight he needed to slip out just after intermission and find his way backstage. He hoped to do it as quietly as possible, avoiding anyone who might ask him questions.

"Is someone sitting there?"

An older woman smiled down at him. Or rather, smiled at him, his face level with his, her back bent from old age. The feet of her walker were covered with tennis balls sliced open on the front to make it easier to slide forward.

"Not at all." He moved the program from the seat beside him and the old lady sat. She worked the hinges on her walker, got it to fold together, and left it leaning against her seat, protruding slightly into the aisle.

"Thank you so much," she said. "Such a kind man. And so good-looking." She smiled again. If she were twenty years younger, he thought, she would be coming on to him. It happened to him quite a bit. His leading-man looks often drew propositions from women, which he politely declined. Sometimes, he got them from men. Those he gave more careful consideration.

"Have you seen this play before?" the old woman asked.

"I have not, but I'm looking forward to it."

"I saw it years ago. Not many theaters do it. I remember enjoying it, even if I don't remember whodunit."

"I guess you'll find out with the rest of us."

She laughed, a thin, wispy sound like wind among reeds. "Yes, I guess I will." The lights came up, and Ellie took the stage to give the curtain speech.

The first act was enjoyable but mostly setup. No murder yet, which would apparently come later. He found himself transfixed by Reginald, marveling at how impressive the man was. The rest of the cast was also talented, especially the lead female, an actress named Kyra Bennett, according to the program. And the story itself was enthralling. He rather hated to leave his seat after intermission, but it simply couldn't be helped.

Alex got up and slipped past the old woman next to him, who dozed lightly.

He found the lobby empty except for two people cleaning up behind the concessions counter, and Ellie, seated behind the box office counter, head down, doing a final count of the concession money. No one noticed him as he slipped through the door to go backstage.

He threaded his way among the usual clutter found in the halls of a community theater: small props from previous shows, stacks of paper towels and cups for the concession area, costumes hanging on racks, stacks of dog-eared plays, and musical orchestration books. There was an old-fashioned bicycle, the paint flaking only a little, but with flat tires; an umbrella rack with various types of umbrellas, plus some canes, and a plastic sword; a set of milk crates resting on their sides and stacked one on top of the other, holding a mixed array of glasses, teacups, and saucers. Alex walked through all of this until he came to the basement stairs. Down he went.

Chapter Five

The show went smoothly, as Ellie suspected it would. Despite all the cast hating Reginald—and him loathing all of them in return—they were some of the best actors the theater had ever worked with. Murder mysteries could be fun, and the blue-hairs absolutely loved them. They had mostly small casts and, with the right director, could be put together cheaply and quickly. This one came together in only six weeks, a last-minute addition to the season. But with Merilyn at the helm, Ellie had never feared it would be anything but a success.

She stood behind the box office, bundling the cash from concessions, allowing herself to smile at the knowledge that, based on the first-night crowd and the concession money, Kaleidoscope was well on its way to climbing back into the black. And not a moment too soon. With federal grant money drying up, she needed to pack the house to keep her theater going. Musicals were always more popular but plays cost less. *Murder in a Teacup* was one of the cheapest plays she'd found available to license that wasn't garbage.

Her relief manifested itself in her tics. Her Tourette syndrome had begun to appear when she turned eight. Unleashing her tics was like relieving the pressure on a steam valve. The relief she felt popped like a bubblegum bubble when the door to the lobby opened and Valerie Thornton entered.

At sixty—fifteen years Reginald's junior—Reginald's wife was still a good-looking woman, tall and statuesque, a bottle blonde but from a high-end spa, so you'd never know. Valerie made a point of maintaining a ruthless vegetarian diet and an exercise routine Ellie privately thought was nearly sadistic. She had been surprised to learn that the two of them had been together for nearly twenty years. The surprise on Ellie's face must have shown when Merilyn told her this, because Merilyn added with wryness, "There must be some truth to the old adage, there's someone for everyone."

"It would take a lot of strength to be married to him," Ellie said.

"They were a hot item in their day."

"I'm not sure my marriage would survive two weeks if I were married to someone like Reginald."

Merilyn smiled, but it was a sad smile. Then she shook her head and said, "Ignore me. I'm lost in a memory."

Now Ellie turned to Valerie Thornton, who was approaching the counter. "Evening, Valerie. I didn't realize you were coming tonight."

"There is something I needed to deliver to Reginald." Her voice was the low, scraped voice of a former smoker, which Ellie thought made her sound a bit like Lauren Bacall. "He is backstage, I assume?"

"He is, but act two is underway. The show should be over in"—she glanced at her watch—"another half hour."

"I need to deliver this now." Valerie held an envelope in her hand.

"Can it wait until after the show?"

"No, I'm afraid not." Valerie's manner was chilly. Her reputation as a cold person preceded her, unless, supposedly, you got to know her. The cast referred to her as the Ice Queen. Ellie had asked Kyra about the nickname one day after rehearsal. "You'd be cold too if you went home to *him* every night," Kyra had said.

Ellie had gotten to know Valerie a little over the last six weeks, but never glimpsed under the icy veneer. In some ways, the woman could be as disdainful as her husband, but it seemed rarely directed toward individuals. While her husband repeatedly aimed at people and fired, Valerie Thornton seemed disdainful of *situations* rather than people. She never seemed to personally dislike Ellie, but Ellie always got the impression the older woman found the 200-seat theater unworthy of a talent such as her husband. It wasn't as if Valerie begrudged Ellie for operating the small venue, but rather that it was simply beneath her husband to perform on its stage.

Ellie had encountered this sort of attitude before, but she had reached a stage in her life where she was adept at allowing these things to roll off her back.

Valerie stood before the counter waiting for Ellie to answer. Before Ellie could speak, her tics betrayed her stress.

Nod-nod-blink-blink.

"Well," Ellie said after a moment, "if it's that important, I can sneak back and deliver it to him."

"No," Valerie said quickly. "This is something I must do. And I must do it now."

Ellie wanted to say no, that it would simply have to wait until after the show. But buried deep in Valerie's eyes, she thought she saw a hint of desperation, and so she took pity on the woman.

"Okay, I guess," Ellie said slowly, pointing. "If you slip through that door, you can access backstage on the stage left side."

"Thank you." Valerie seemed relieved. As she started to go, Ellie added, "Valerie, as quiet as you can, please."

"No one will know I'm there." She went to the door and slipped through, silent as a spirit through a wall.

Grunt-grunt.

Ellie couldn't wait to close this show.

Dana, who had been in the office behind the box office counter, joined Ellie, staring at the door leading backstage.

"What do you think that was all about?" Ellie asked.

"If that woman has any sense, divorce papers," Dana answered. Ellie put a hand to her mouth to suppress a laugh.

* * *

Merilyn dozed peacefully in a prop chair that was musty and old, upholstered in maroon crushed velvet going threadbare. Naps came more frequently now, sometimes whether she wanted them to or not. She would close her tired, tired eyes and wake up an hour and a half later. Things sped downhill fast. But that was the nature of this particular beast. Her doctor warned her it would be fast-moving—he'd used the term "aggressive"—and he had been right. In the last three weeks, she had gone from feeling sick from chemo to feeling as if each step was an uphill slog while carrying a backpack loaded with rocks.

She didn't mind the naps. She fell into them hard, usually hard enough to dream. Her doctor told her the chemo had been known to cause vivid dreams, and he wasn't kidding. Most people, he had told her, who experience vivid dreams usually have nightmares. For Merilyn, the opposite was true. Every dream was a blessing, each one lovely and green and verdant. She wasn't prone to religious beliefs, but she hoped desperately these were deliberately delivered glimpses of heaven.

She was walking through the gently waving grass at the edge of a white beach at sunset when a hand covered hers. She raised her face to the sky and awoke suddenly, looking up into ice-blue eyes. For a moment, she thought perhaps her cancer had finally overtaken her, that she was looking into the face of an angel. But she knew this face, recognized it, and realized she was still in the basement of the theater. She smiled, and Alex smiled back at her, his hand still covering hers. He took her hand in both of his, lifted it to his lips. He knelt on one knee in front of her.

"Hello, beautiful."

Merilyn smiled at the handsome man before her, wishing for one hot minute she was younger and healthy, and he was straight. The moment passed, and she was simply happy to see him again, at least one more time.

"Alex, my darling, darling, boy. So wonderful to see you."

"You too, love. How do you feel?"

She smiled, and in that smile he saw everything he needed to know.

"How long?"

She shrugged. "Tonight. Tomorrow. Next month. Who knows? I have to take each day as it comes and not worry about whether I've seen my last sunrise."

Their friendship covered a decade and had weathered some storms. But seeing his face now as he gazed at her—his gentle smile, his eyes filled with tears—Merilyn realized how deeply Alex loved her.

She changed the subject. "What are you doing here?"

He wiped the back of his hand across his eyes and *snurfed* through his nose. "I came to tell you I've destroyed the discs."

"What?"

"The discs. All three of them. Gone. And the original tapes as well. All gone."

Her smile faltered, replaced by concern. *Please let him be lying,* she thought. A white lie, for me, at the end of my life. But in his eyes, she saw his truth.

"But, Alex—"

"Everything will be okay, my love. It had to be done. I should have destroyed them a long time ago, but I was too concerned about myself. I was a miserable, pathetic coward. But no more."

Merilyn struggled to rise from the chair. But she didn't have the strength and sank back down.

"He'll ruin you. He'll absolutely ruin you, your career, everything you've worked for."

"I'm not scared of him anymore. It's time someone put a stop to his reign of terror. He terrorizes anyone and everyone he can. He needs to be brought to heel."

23

Merilyn only shook her head. He smiled, leaned in, and kissed her cheek. Her skin was dry and flimsy, and up close her perfume didn't quite cover the smell of her decay.

"Don't worry any longer, my sweet. Leave everything to me. It ends tonight."

He rose from his knee, held her hand for one more moment, a long moment where they regarded each other and so much that need not be said out loud passed between them. He left the room. Merilyn could hear the stairs creak as Alex climbed them, taking them two at a time.

She took a few deep breaths, then slowly, laboriously, lifted herself from the chair. It was an all-out effort to put one foot in front of the other. Only through sheer force of will would she be able to climb the stairs to stop Alex. Ellie had asked her at the beginning of the first show of the run why on earth Merilyn wanted to go down to the basement. "Won't getting back up be a challenge?" Ellie had asked.

Of course it would, but Merilyn loved being in the center of the actors as they prepared for the show. And when the curtain went up, she loved listening to the crowd as the sound came through the floor above. She would sit and listen, and when the cast completed the final bow, Ellie and Steve would help her back up the stairs.

But now she couldn't wait. She didn't know what Alex had in mind, but for the first time in as many years, she was terrified. She needed to do something, something drastic to help him.

Slowly, painfully, she started up the stairs.

Chapter Six

Reginald Thornton IV was not feeling well. He hadn't felt well since yesterday, but today was much worse. He huffed and puffed, trying to catch his breath, less like the Big Bad Wolf and more like an asthmatic trying to run a half-marathon during an attack. He wasn't a smoker, other than an occasional cigar. Cubans. He had long ago convinced himself they were the only ones he enjoyed. But they couldn't be gotten easily, so rarely did he enjoy one. No, smoking was not the issue.

Reginald loved food almost as much as he loved being onstage, and his girth reflected that. As much as he craved the adoration showered upon him on the stage, he harbored the same craving for fine dining. And despite whatever money troubles he might be having, he refused to scale back his epicurean tastes. His waistline gave testimony to his appetite.

But this was different. He had been out of breath before. A long flight of stairs could be particularly onerous. His wife had harped after him for years to trim down, get in shape. "I refuse to be with someone who treats themselves the way you do," she said. He snorted derisively. If she would not provide the basic comfort a woman provides a man, he could find it elsewhere.

He had before.

Reginald understood the feeling of being winded by basic exertion, or after eating too much. This didn't feel like that.

And he had never run out of breath onstage. Granted, he was beyond the age of singing or dancing, let alone both at the same time. But plays were his thing, having mastered breath control for his delivery. He held every confidence in his ability to be fit as a fiddle when the curtain went up. But this opening performance took its toll on him.

They began the final scene, which gave Reginald a bit of relief. He needed to get off this stage. It could be the theater itself. Maybe the space was too dusty. He couldn't understand why people who decided to go into community theater couldn't take better care of their space. Theaters always gathered dust, but some were worse than others. Though, grudgingly, he had to admit Kaleidoscope was relatively clean.

Or perhaps mold. That would be worse. He could pin the blame on Steve if he wanted. God knows the boy deserved more than his fair share of blame for a lot of things. Reginald loathed Steve, now more than ever, ready to be done with him and this theater forever. But the real blame for problems with a theater always went to the owner. And in this case, he figured the owner couldn't stop twitching long enough to get anything decent done around here.

Reginald tried not to become distracted while finishing the scene. He could deliver a knockout performance while simultaneously blocking out anything else happening around him. He prided himself on being able to burrow so deeply into a character that no matter what happened, he never lost his place. But as each breath became more labored, almost as if he were suffocating, his mind slipped out of character.

Mold. Had to be mold. A perfectly plausible explanation.

Finally, he reached the end of the scene, the end of the play, the penultimate moment where his character drinks the rest of the tea and collapses, dead on the ground. He slugged back the tea, some of the liquid missing his mouth and landing on the collar of his shirt. That had never happened before. He was too precise to let something like a stupid prop of tea in a cup spill. But at that moment he didn't care. Plus, the tea tasted awful, and he was glad not to have more of it in his mouth. His hands were shaking, which they should have been for his character, but he was no longer acting. He took his next step, then another, then his last. He sank to his knees, then to the floor of the stage.

Chapter Seven

J erry stood at the opposite end of the stage from where Reginald went down. The scene played out largely as expected. Jerry's performance was spot on, at least in his opinion. He went for understated, and that's exactly what he delivered. During rehearsals, he had conversations with Merilyn about how over-the-top Reginald could be, and what adjustments he should make.

"He'll always be over-the-top," Merilyn said. "That's who he is, who he's always been."

"But won't that be weird when we're up there, if one of us is over-the-top and one of us is—how should I put this?—*normal*?"

She put her hand on his arm. "Jerry, you'll have to trust me. As the director, I've got the vision for what I want to see, how I want the show to run. And you have to believe I will never let you make an ass out of yourself onstage. Okay?"

Reluctantly, he nodded. By the final dress rehearsal, he realized she was right. Something about how he played his character and the way Reginald mugged for the audience meshed. He didn't understand why it worked, only that it did.

Except for tonight. Tonight, Reginald was taking it too far. Jerry wanted to roll his eyes, and nearly did, but he managed to stay in character. He stole a quick glance at Kyra, but she was solid, never breaking character despite the overdone way Reginald acted his part.

When Reginald sank to his knees, Jerry dared a glance at his face. For the first time, Jerry forgot about what an asshole Reginald was. He found himself suddenly mesmerized.

Reginald clutched at his chest as if having a heart attack and collapsed forward.

Finally, Jerry thought.

* * *

Theoretically, tonight was the chance for a big break for Kyra. Like, a really big break. She had already made something of a name for herself doing local productions in the area, using everything she learned in school, pouring herself into every performance. Breaking into the business was never easy—she understood that, even as she worked on her performance degree. Within a few years, she had built an impressive local résumé.

She began reaching out to Equity theaters, trying to find work, even backstage work that might help her get her union card. Then she could become a *paid* actor. That would be game-changing. Once in the actors' union, she could turn her acting into a career rather than a hobby.

Tonight, on the opening night of the play, she knew that someone from the Foothills Theater, the only professional theater in the area, would be in the audience. If her performance were strong enough, she might just come away with a new hope for her future.

The biggest challenge to being "discovered" was standing out from the rest of the cast, especially opposite Reginald, who tended to steal every scene.

When Reginald went to his knees, the sound of his knees hitting the stage nearly startled Kyra out of her character. She fumbled her next line. But Reginald's pain looked so real, and in a moment of wicked pleasure, only for the briefest of moments, she broke character: she smiled.

* * *

More than anything, Merilyn wanted she wanted to close her eyes and go to sleep. But Alex. She needed to stop Alex before he cost himself everything.

The backstage was dark except for the one black light bulb. It produced enough light to avoid tripping over sets or props but still keep it from blinding the audience members in the seats with a slight view into the wings. Steve stood by the prop table, leaning, watching the show, finger on the buttons of his headphones. As Merilyn walked in, Steve whispered, "Cue the thunder." From the sound system came a crashing clap of thunder, followed quickly by him saying, "Cue the rain," and the sound of a storm emerged from the speakers.

He glanced back and saw Merilyn at the prop table, hunched over the teacups. Steve frowned and placed a gentle hand on her shoulder.

"You okay?" he whispered.

She nodded.

"What are you doing?" Steve asked her.

"Resting." She gave the same sad smile she gave to everyone these days, no matter the situation.

"You look—" Steve started to say but stopped.

"Terrible?" She finished for him.

"I wasn't going to say that."

"Sure you weren't." Her smile always brought a smile out in others. Steve was no exception, even if the smile was sad at seeing such a good person like Merilyn wither.

"Do you need something?" he asked.

"I need to see Reginald when he comes off the stage. I need to see him before he sees anyone else."

Steve looked back toward the stage, the current scene nearing its completion. The performance would end, there would be bows, and the cast would file off the stage. He knew that Merilyn would find a way to hang on even if she had to fend off the Reaper with a prop umbrella.

She heard Reginald give his final lines, and they sounded somehow different now compared to when she'd heard them so many times in rehearsals.

She heard him hit the stage when he went to his knees.

"Jesus," Steve muttered. "What a ham."

She closed her eyes.

* * *

Alex was back in his seat before the final scene. He slipped back into the theater and slid noiselessly into the seat next to the old lady. Her eyes were still closed.

It seemed to Alex that she'd drifted off. At least he hoped she'd drifted off.

The show appeared to be wrapping up. The butler had brought out tea, and everyone was drinking it.

Now a great deal of gesturing, the words becoming more frenzied, building to a crescendo, the climax coming. Alex thought he had probably missed something while down in the basement with Merilyn. Some of the things he was hearing in the play weren't making sense to him. Yes, he had definitely missed something somewhere. But he knew how the play ended—with the murder in the teacup.

He'd done what he set out to do, and now he knew that Merilyn would be free. He sat back and watched the show, knowing that whatever came next, he was more than prepared.

He'd been basking in the glow of self-satisfaction when Reginald went to his knees. The thunking sound stirred him as he watched Reginald slump over. The other actors reacted as if nothing unusual had happened. All part of the play, of course: Reginald's character was supposed to die.

It was, Alex thought, a perfect death scene.

Chapter Eight

Ellie stood just inside the theater doors with Dana as they both watched the final scene. Once the lights had gone down and come back up and the actors had taken final bows and moved off the stage, she would open the doors and watch the audience make its way out. She enjoyed many things about running a community theater, but this was one of her favorites: seeing the smiles on the faces of the audience members as they left, satisfied by the show they had just seen; hearing them murmur among themselves and say things like "Great job" and "Well done" to her.

The cast would always assemble in the lobby after a show so the audience could meet them and give their praise. And when it came to a man like Reginald, no amount of praise would ever be enough.

What an ego, Ellie thought. She wondered how he fit his head through the door. She had run across egos. Doing this for five years, she ran into people she would let be cast again in her shows, but only begrudgingly, and only if there were no other options.

But not Reginald. She would refuse to let him be cast in any show from now until she retired and handed Kaleidoscope off to the next generation. He was so poisonous, no amount of his talent would make him worth taking on again. The cast were at one another's throats, and the crew had threatened to quit, an especially onerous threat considering they were all volunteers. No one got paid for this, except the director. And Ellie usually tried to carve out a little stipend for the stage crew, which this time consisted only of Steve and Tony Roper, high school kid extraordinaire in the light booth. At least small-cast plays were easy to stage manage.

Reginald appeared to be barely holding on. He looked like a man, well, dying. Ellie supposed he might be making the final scene of this first performance memorable, but he seemed to be overacting to a degree she hadn't seen in rehearsal. Even in his death scene, he refused to be upstaged.

He hit the stage with his knees hard enough to make Ellie wince. Her own knees hurt at the sight, and she couldn't imagine the damage it did to his seventy-five-year-old bones. He clutched his chest with his hand and slumped forward.

"What an over-actor," Dana said, with an edge to her voice.

Ellie frowned. Something wasn't right. The scene finished, bringing the play to a close. In the light booth, Tony pressed buttons. The lights dropped, and the stage plunged into black. The curtain fell.

The audience burst into applause.

There was a long moment where nothing moved onstage while the audience clapped. Then, as if the pause was for dramatic effect, Tony pressed different buttons. The curtain swept away in a flourish and the lights came back up as the cast assembled onstage for bows.

Except for Reginald.

He remained face down and motionless on the stage.

Was he being overly dramatic? At any moment, Ellie expected him to leap up suddenly, to huge applause from the audience, and take a deep bow.

From the back, Ellie could see Jerry Moynihan cut his eyes at Kyra, who, still smiling, offered the slightest shrug. Jerry hissed something at the prone actor through his smile. He glanced down, but Reginald didn't move. Jerry bent down to shake Reginald's shoulder.

The audience watched with rapt attention. Was this part of the show? Was there some kind of coda to the show that only happened after it seemingly ended?

Jerry shook Reginald harder. The older actor didn't respond. Ellie watched Jerry place two fingers on Reginald's neck. Ellie shuddered at the thought of having to touch the sweaty, bloated neck of her leading actor.

The audience grew restless. Murmurs began to rumble through the crowd.

From where she sat, Ellie saw the blood drain from Jerry's face.

He stood up and shouted, "Somebody call 911!"

Chapter Nine

When Jerry put his fingers to Reginald's neck, Kyra had to hold her revulsion. When he started shouting for someone to call 911, her face paled and her mouth dropped open. She remembered her earlier thought toward the disgusting man, *Why don't you kill yourself?* She knew she should regret that thought now.

But she didn't.

*   *   *

Jerry tended to be nervous and fidgety to begin with. Reginald's melodrama and his refusal to get back on his feet during the curtain call had made it worse. He just wanted to be off this stage.

But Reginald refused to move, and Jerry began to wonder what kind of attention-grabbing stunt Reginald was pulling this time.

So even after taking Reginald's pulse, finding none, and yelling for someone to call 911, only one thought went through Jerry's mind:

Finally.

*   *   *

Steve had already begun to wash the teacups. He wanted to clean up and prepare for tomorrow's performance as quickly as possible. The sooner he started, the sooner he could go home and get away from the chaos of this production.

The teacups were nearly done, and he was thinking about what he'd tackle next, when he heard a shout from the theater, startling him so much that he nearly dropped one of the newly washed teacups. He bobbled it for a moment, like some juggling clown entertaining an audience, then caught it and set it down on the drying mat.

He poked his head back into the theater and saw Reginald face down on the stage, Jerry feeling his neck and shouting for help, and the audience mostly frozen and staring at the stage. Clearly, something had happened to Reginald, and the mayhem was centered around him.

The theater erupted in a buzz as the audience realized this wasn't an act. Above the noise, he could hear Dana shouting at Tony to close the curtain.

Steve tried to muster an ounce of concern for the prostrate actor and found he couldn't. He shrugged and returned to cleaning the teacups.

* * *

More than anything, Merilyn wanted to close her eyes and go to sleep. As the curtain came down, she made her way to the lobby and eased slowly into a chair, resigning herself to waiting until the show was over to catch up with Alex.

When she heard the initial shout, she managed to stand. Then the house emptied and she watched as the patrons streamed through the house doors, talking excitedly about the drama unfolding in front of them. Some were crying.

She needed to find Alex, to plead with him not to throw his life away. Not for her, at least. She was on her way out. He still had the rest of his life in front of him.

Except that he was not in the audience. She scanned the audience as it filed through the lobby and out the building doors. She couldn't find his face in the sea of people.

Where could he be? she wondered. At that moment, a police cruiser pulled up, lights flashing, and the officer jumped out of his car, grabbed an emergency bag from his trunk, and hurried through the lobby and into the house. Merilyn sighed heavily and shook her head, muttering to herself, "God, no, please, no."

She pulled out her phone and texted *What did you do?*

* * *

Alex Hillman had slipped out the side door the moment the play ended. Even before the curtain rose and the lights came up for bows, he was gone. It had been an emotional night, and he just wanted to go home. He'd done what he came to do. It was over. It was time to move on. And he didn't want to risk running into anyone he knew. He didn't think he could explain the expression on his face.

He arrived home and poured himself a drink. He sat with one leg crossed over the other, at ease, feeling the tension of the night drain away as he slowly enjoyed his scotch.

His phone dinged. He picked it up and looked at it.

What did you do?

He sighed and set the phone on the arm of his chair, face down, ignoring it.

Chapter Ten

On a Thursday evening, the last thing Bill Starlin, the chief of police in Avalon, wanted to do was leave the house. It was October, with football season well underway, and while football would never replace baseball as his favorite sport, it carried him through the fall and the first part of winter. The Patriots were on Thursday Night Football on ESPN, which he liked.

The game stretched into the third quarter, the Pats up by a touchdown, but with Miami surging. Third down and four, with four minutes left in the quarter. Bill was about to get up to fetch himself another beer. Not too many things would move him off the couch on a lazy game night. It really came down to three: another beer, an act of God, or a crime.

His cell phone rang, so he picked it up; it was Turner Milton, his one and only detective on the force. Turner would be calling only because of something big, which likely meant it was something big enough to take the police chief away from his TV. He sighed, pressed Mute on the remote, and answered the phone.

"What's up, Turner?"

"Sorry to interrupt the game, Chief. We got a situation at Kaleidoscope."

"The theater?" It didn't surprise Bill. He knew the average age of the audience often ranged in the late seventies. If he and his wife ever caught a show, they single-handedly brought the average age of the audience down by a good decade. It wasn't rare to have an EMS call to the theater for heart palpitations or someone passing out or something else age-related.

"What happened?"

"An actor collapsed on stage. Looks like a heart attack. That's what Fire is telling me."

"During a show?"

"Just as it was wrapping up."

Bill shook his head. *What rotten luck—and how terrible for Ellie and her theater.* "How long ago?"

"About twenty minutes ago. Fire tried to revive him, but then they called CMED and found out he had a DNR."

Bill paused a moment. CMED—Central Medical Emergency Direction—was part of Central Massachusetts Emergency Medical Systems, and all rescue crews communicated with the CMED team. And DNR, of course, meant *Do Not Resuscitate.*

"So he didn't make it."

"He did not," Turner said.

Crap, thought Bill. A death at the theater—Ellie's theater. This was *not* good for her.

"Thanks for letting me know, Turner. Keep me updated."

Turner didn't answer for a moment, then said, "I think you'll want to come down here, Chief. Maybe talk to the owner of the theater. Says she knows you."

"Yeah, we were kids together. We've known each other for going on thirty years."

"Well, she's kind of rattled. Asked when you'll be coming down."

Bill thumbed the remote off, and the game vanished. "I'll be there in fifteen minutes."

He took his empty beer bottle to the kitchen and popped a mint from the container he left by the sink for this very reason: in case he got a call after having one or two. He didn't want to smell like a brewery in front of his officers. Bill usually took evenings off, leaving other senior officers as watch commander. But sometimes, like tonight, he had to go to work. Turner wouldn't have disturbed Bill if he didn't think it necessary.

He slipped into his boat shoes as his wife, Darlene, came downstairs. Lithe and gorgeous, blonde with green eyes, most everyone in town who met her agreed Bill had married above his pay grade, a viewpoint he wholeheartedly agreed with.

"Work?" she asked in a sympathetic tone.

"Yeah," he said. "An apparent heart attack on the stage at Kaleidoscope. Turner's there now, but I need to put in a call to the ME and the State Police, see if either want to investigate."

Darlene saw his face and put two and two together. "Oh," she said quietly. "He didn't make it."

He shook his head. "The guy had a DNR, so Fire left him alone."

Darlene leaned into Bill and kissed him. They'd been married ten years, and she had grown up a cop's daughter. Her mother had been a detective with the Massachusetts State Police until her retirement seven years earlier. She was used to members of her family having to leave at odd hours or in the middle of a family event to go to work. "How long do you think you'll be?"

He kissed her back. "Don't know. I'll text you, but don't wait up."

She leaned in and gave him another kiss, a little one this time, a quick one that said *I love you* and *be careful*. "Go do your job," she said, followed by "Tell Ellie I said hi," not as warmly.

Bill heard the chill in Darlene's voice. Ellie was a touchy subject with his wife. Bill never thought of Darlene as the jealous type, but his nearly three-decade friendship with Ellie was not a topic they discussed much.

He clipped his gun to his hip and pulled a jacket over it. "Will do." He popped another mint for good measure, then, as an afterthought, shoved the whole tin into his jacket pocket.

*　　*　　*

Bill had been chief for nine years now. Most of that time had been quiet, which suited him just fine. The less to worry about, the better. Granted, no town was perfect, and quiet could be a relative term. Given where Avalon sat, at the intersection of two state routes, crime tended to drive up from Worcester on the east-west route and stop occasionally in his town. A rash of burglaries would crop up now and again, but they were easily stopped as soon as people started locking their doors. However, one of the state roads had earned the nickname "Heroin Highway" as mules ran from Worcester all the way out to Sudbury and beyond, and the number of opioid overdose calls his department received had become downright alarming. Junkies who picked up fentanyl or oxy in Clifton sometimes couldn't wait to fix and pulled off on the side of the road or into a gas station to shoot up. Bill's officers didn't carry Narcan in the squad cars; it had to be stored between 68 and 77 degrees, and a squad car could get well above that in the summer. But it was never more than an EMT truck away, and he had never seen an opioid overdose where it failed to bring someone back.

Sometimes Bill's department would be called in for an assault, usually a couple of drunken idiots who figured a fistfight to be the best way to solve an argument. Less frequent was the occasional domestic assault. He personally hated those—they made him physically angry. Once, after Bill had put cuffs on a wife-beater, Turner asked him why these calls filled him so full of rage. Bill supposed it was just how he was raised, his father being one of the best men Bill had ever known.

Only three other times in nine years had they dealt with a dead body. Old Betty Crumpton, age ninety-seven, found after a neighbor requested a wellness check. Bill took the call and found Mrs.

Crumpton had died in her sleep. The time before was a car accident of out-of-towners, so ugly they needed to bring all the body parts back together to bag them.

The time before that, little Jimmy Guftavson, age nine, jumped into the reservoir on a dare, thinking it shallower than it was. He didn't know how to swim. Bill had been chief for six weeks then, and Jimmy's death almost cost him his job. Bill had shut down, unable to function, give orders, or look at the body.

He saw his sister's face every time he tried.

He never realized how much he loved his sister, Ava, until she was gone. Before then, she was just a pesky kid sister, and Ellie had been her best friend. The two were inseparable, even when doing things they weren't supposed to. Not bad things, like smoking behind the shed or shoplifting. Just things like taking dips in the reservoir during the dog days of summer.

Except one day, Ava went under and never came back up.

At the scene of Jimmy Guftavson's drowning, Bill had sat in his car for thirty minutes, unable to get out, before he called the previous chief, Al Jensen. He asked Al to step in one last time, and Al, remembering the day eleven years earlier when he had showed up at Bill's parents' house—hat in hand, grim-faced, and shaking—to tell them their twelve-year-old daughter had drowned, said yes without a second thought.

And now a fourth body, in, of all places, Ellie's theater.

Chapter Eleven

B ill pulled up to the theater. Two of his officers already had both of their lightbars strobing, the chilly night awash in reds and blues. Two rescue trucks were parked there as well. Bill could see one was from the next town over.

He picked up the APD ball cap sitting on the passenger's seat of his car, pulled it down on his head, and got out. He said hello to Dennis Hassert, the officer standing by the door, and went inside.

Bill had been in the theater before, but not for a while. He went only on special occasions, convinced to go by his wife, who loved theater. He would inevitably surprise himself in one of two ways: how much he loved the show, or how much he hated it. He found no in-between.

He had not been inside since they finished building the addition, transforming the lobby into something far more spacious. Before, ticket holders had to wait outside for the doors to open.

He looked around, seeing the counter by the door near the box office, the window into the little office behind the box office counter, the concession area against the back wall, and the doors into the theater itself off to the left. Lots of light, very welcoming.

Through the office window, he saw a woman sitting. She had clearly been crying, still bringing a tissue up to her eyes every few

43

seconds. It took Bill a few moments to recognize Dana Nugent. He couldn't remember her function at the theater. Ellie had told him once, but it slipped his mind. Props? Or costumes? Costumes sounded right.

A second person sat in the office with Dana, her back to the office window. When he knocked on the door, the person turned, and he realized it was Ellie. She looked terrible.

"Bill!" she said, a bit louder and more excited than normal. She threw her arms around his neck and gave him a hug. She was always friendly and outgoing, but rarely came in for a hug so forcefully. His first thought went to Darlene; he was glad she wasn't here. He hugged Ellie briefly, and she broke away. He glanced away as she ticced, waiting for her to finish. Her random, uncontrolled movements were old news to him.

Nod-nod-grunt-grunt-grunt.

"Sorry," she panted. "I'm kind of frazzled."

"Heard you had quite an evening." He looked at her face, drawn tight, circles under her eyes.

Blink-blink. Sniff-sniff. "I've had better ones."

"Do you mind leading me to the body?"

"Sure." She nodded, though she looked like she didn't want to go.

"If it's too much," Bill said softly, "I can go by myself."

Ellie swallowed, took a deep breath, and said, "I'll be okay." *Grunt.* Bill thought she was trying to convince herself and might not be succeeding. She didn't move, and he waited patiently. He'd learned years ago that waiting, completely silent, for someone to speak could be more revealing than any conversation. In particular, waiting was what Ellie needed when she was struggling.

"It just . . ." she said, and then started again. "It just doesn't seem real."

"It never does when it's sudden," Bill said. "Had he seemed ill?"

Ellie shook her head. "He was . . . maybe a little off, overdoing his scene a little. Nothing huge." She wiped her eyes, took a deep breath, and got up. "Just that something feels off."

"Wrong how?"

Ellie shrugged. "I don't know. I guess I can't put it into words. Reginald never appeared to have health issues, despite his age and weight. But tonight, even when he came through the front door, he just seemed . . ."

"Off?" Bill finished for her.

She nodded. "Guess I already said that."

Bill smiled and said, "Okay. Let's take a look."

They went through the doors leading to the "house," where plays were performed. Bill followed Ellie as they moved down the center aisle and climbed up onto the stage. Her head bobbed as they went, and he could hear her sniffing and grunting. He couldn't remember a time when she didn't have these tics. Some kids had made fun of her, but not him. He never had the normal levels of cruelty other kids his age did. Neither did Ava, his kid sister, which is why he suspected she and Ellie became such fast friends. The best of friends, until—

He shook his head to clear the memory. He needed to be clear-headed now, not lost in a past tragedy.

Turner Milton stood downstage left, next to a large person-sized lump covered by a sheet. Turner was a tall man, younger than Bill or Ellie, with close-cut light-brown hair a smidge too long to be considered a buzz cut. Ellie thought he might be slender, but couldn't quite tell with the vest and all the bulky gear he wore. Two emergency responders stood with him, chatting casually. Turner waved Bill and Ellie over.

Bill reached the trio and recognized August Hoover, a highly freckled, red-haired kid, whip-thin and laconic, an EMT with the town fire department. Bridget Falconi, a tall girl built like a wrestler, was a paramedic from the next town.

"Chief," Turner said. "You know Augie and Bindy."

Bill nodded at them in greeting.

"So here's what we have," Turner said, gesturing at the sheet. "Mr. Reginald Thornton, deceased, seventy-five years of age, had just finished the play. We talked to a couple of people who were still here when we arrived. Most say Mr. Thornton looked as if he didn't feel well at the end of the show. One castmate"—he consulted his notes—"Jerry Moynihan, said Mr. Thornton hit the floor of the stage particularly hard."

"Hit the floor of the stage?" Bill repeated.

"Part of the show," Ellie said. "Reginald's character dies at the end of the show, going to his knees, then slumping to the floor. Come to think of it, I thought he hit the stage awfully hard too."

"Harder than normal?" Bill asked.

"Yes, definitely."

Bill turned to Bindy and Augie. "What did you guys find?"

Augie answered. "Dennis and Turner had already started trying to revive him. We took over, Ambu-ing him, hooked him up to the AED and zapped him, but nothing."

"No heartbeat when we hooked him up," Bindy said. "And no heartbeat after the shock. At that point, we learned he had a DNR."

"Hospital didn't want you to bring him in?" Bill asked.

Augie shook his head. "Davey Parker was still in the truck, phoned it in, then got the info on the DNR, so we stopped. The doctor at the hospital told Bindy she could call it, being the paramedic on the scene."

"We tried zapping him once more, just to be sure, but then I called the time of death."

Ellie shuddered. *Blink-blink-blink.*

Bill bent down and lifted the sheet. He looked at the face of the deceased actor, noting how swollen the face looked. But there was something else, something that nibbled at the back of Bill's mind.

Bill lifted the sheet further and looked at the man's fingertips. Then he pushed open one of the eyelids and stared at the eye. He replaced the sheet and stood. He turned to Ellie. "You said he seemed off today. What did you mean by that?"

Ellie seemed caught off guard. "I guess if I had to pinpoint it, when I talked to him when he came in, he seemed, well, maybe a little tipsy."

"Any chance he could have been?"

Ellie shook her head. "I can't imagine him jeopardizing his performance. He was an ass, but a fine actor. Being onstage meant everything to him."

"And during the play? How'd he seem?"

"Kind of like when he came in. A little off. A bit lethargic, stumbling here and there. Spilled some tea on himself in the final scene."

"What are you thinking, Chief?" Turner asked.

"I'm wondering if this was a drug overdose."

"What?" Ellie practically shouted.

Bindy and Augie looked at each other. Bill caught the look.

"I'm not blaming you guys," he hastened to say. "I think it definitely presented as a heart attack. But the blueish tint around the lips and fingertips, very faint, but it's there, and how enlarged his pupils are—plus him seeming drunk earlier, and maybe confused, it seems like it could be a benzodiazepine overdose."

"Yeah, maybe," Augie said.

Bill looked at Bindy, who hadn't spoken. "If he was that far gone, odds are he would have been DOA at the hospital. Narcan doesn't work on a benzo overdose, you know that, and with his heart stopped for that long, the ER wouldn't have been able to revive him."

Bindy remained silent, but she nodded.

"Thanks for sticking around," Bill said.

"You need anything else, you know where to find us," Augie said.

They packed up the rest of their gear and hauled everything up the stairs and out of the theater. Bill turned to his detective.

"You call the state police?" Bill asked Turner.

"They're on their way. Should be here shortly."

"How about the ME?"

"They're waiting for feedback from MSP. If it's just a heart attack, they'll probably pass, but if the state takes it on, the medical examiner will at least do a tox screen."

Bill frowned. He knew it would be an uphill push to get someone interested in an investigation when the evidence was as thin as tracing paper. This really could just be an older, overweight guy dropping from a heart attack. But something felt itchy to Bill. Itchy in a way that needed scratching. He held out hope that MSP wouldn't just rubber stamp it.

"Where does this guy live?" Bill asked

"Couple towns over in Clifton, according to his driver's license."

"Okay, I'm friendly with the police chief over there, Davis Whitney. Good guy. Give him a call, ask him about notifying next of kin."

"Already called him," Turner said. "He's on his way to the victim's house."

Bill nodded. "Anyone go through his personal items yet?"

Turner shook his head.

Bill turned to Ellie. "Where do the actors keep their personal things?"

"The basement," Ellie said. "That's where the costume closets are, the workshop for props, stuff like that."

"Can you lead us down there?"

Bill and Turner followed Ellie through the back hallways of the theater while Hassert stood guard over the body. They descended stairs and landed in wide space bathed in fluorescent light.

Ellie brought them to one of the costume closets. "Reginald made us empty the closet so he could have a private dressing room."

"Bet that didn't go over well with your costume mistress," Bill commented.

"Dana was pretty steamed. It's not a good idea to tick off the woman responsible for dressing you in a show."

They opened the door, and on the floor next to a small table and folding chair sat a small leather messenger bag. Turner pulled on a pair of gloves and began to go through it. In a moment, he made an *aha* sound and held up a prescription bottle.

"Valium," Bill noted.

Ellie looked startled.

"Yep," Turner said. "Assuming he took some, we don't know how many pills."

"Can we figure it out from the date of the prescription and how many pills were prescribed?" Bill said.

"Valium is something you take only when needed," Ellie pointed out. "It's not a one-pill-a-day kind of thing."

"Which means it could have been prescribed three months ago, and he might have taken only one pill so far."

"In this case," Turner said, turning the bottle over in his hands, "the med was filled six months ago."

"Okay," Bill conceded. "What else?"

Turner dug through the rest of the bag. "Looks like that's about it. Change of clothes, keys, wallet, but nothing else."

"I didn't know people could overdose on Valium," Ellie said.

"A fatal benzo overdose by itself is rarer than an opioid overdose," Bill said. "It can happen, but it's not like an opioid. There's also a pretty long run-up time to a benzo OD and, once detected, abusers usually end up in the hospital. But mix a benzo with something else—"

"Opioids or booze," Turner interjected. "Or both."

"Then it's lights out, no pun intended. Your respiratory system shuts down. If enough booze or opioids are added to the mix, say good night."

"So he could have essentially poisoned himself accidentally, if he had Valium and something else?" Ellie asked.

Bill nodded.

"Or it could be suicide," Turner said.

"No chance," Ellie said without even thinking.

"What makes you say that?" Turner said.

She cleared her throat. "Reginald was not a pleasant person. But he was an actor, and a good one. Theater was his life. Everything important to him was tied up in his reputation. He would never have done anything to risk his performance, including drinking any time close to a performance, or taking opioids."

Bill's mouth folded down into a grimace. He trusted Ellie's judgment. He didn't want to jump the gun, but her opinion counted for a lot.

"If something was used to speed up his death and he took it unknowingly," Bill said, "and we assume he wasn't drinking liquor, then what was it?"

"Something else, maybe, something slipped into a drink somewhere," Turner said, looking around. "Did he have a water bottle he was using?"

"Tea," Ellie said absently.

"Sorry, did you say 'tea'?" Bill asked.

She nodded. "The show is called *Murder in a Teacup*. They're constantly drinking tea. It's a real drink, and they were really drinking it. Someone could have spiked his tea."

"Who prepped the teacups?" Bill asked.

Grunt-grunt-nod-nod-nod. Sniff.

"I did," Ellie said.

Grunt.

Chapter Twelve

The next three and a half hours were a chaotic swirl of police activity and a lot of waiting. Ellie had never been in a situation like this before and was thankful Bill was in charge—she trusted him, and she didn't need to worry as much as she might have if someone else had been managing the scene.

Bill left Turner with the body and took Ellie back to her office. "What happens next?" she asked.

"Massachusetts State Police sends out a detective. Any unattended death—that is, a death without a doctor present—gets a visit. The detective will take a look at the scene, talk with us, and determine whether or not an investigation needs to be opened."

"Will they?" Ellie asked.

"Open one?" Bill shrugged. "They make the call. A benzo overdose isn't terribly exceptional. If the state decides the death looks wrongful, they'll open a case, but if the state decides it's accidental, then that's probably the end of the story."

As they spoke, another man entered the lobby from outside, tall and rangy, with a leather car coat and his badge clipped to his belt. He saw Bill and walked over.

"Starlin."

Bill acknowledged the brusque greeting and turned toward Ellie. "Ellie, this is Detective Chuck Phelps. Phelps, Ellie Marlowe, owner of the theater."

Phelps extended his hand, his manner noticeably softer with her than with Bill.

"Evening, Miss Marlowe. I'm with the state police. I've come to take a look at your dead body."

Ellie shivered at the words "dead body" and pointed through the doors toward the house. "He's in there. Up on the stage."

"He unattended right now?"

"One of my guys, Turner Milton, is in there," Bill said. "I'll be in in a sec."

"Oh goody," Phelps said, pushing past Bill and going through the doorway.

Ellie looked at Bill with concern. "What was that about?"

Bill sighed and looked at his feet for a moment. Then he said, "My leaving the state police force wasn't exactly mourned. A few of the detectives and I have some bad blood. Phelps wasn't part of that, but he wasn't on my side either."

Ellie knew Bill's time with the state police had been a problem for him, but he never said why, and now wasn't the time to ask.

"What should I do?" she asked.

Bill led Ellie into the lobby office. Dana was in there scrolling through Amazon on the laptop.

"Dana, what are you doing?" Ellie asked.

"Unless they're going to strip Reginald before they haul him away and give me his costume, I'm going to need some replacement pieces. And Amazon delivers next day."

"We don't even know who will replace him. Or even if we're going to," Ellie said.

"Gotta be ready in case we do."

"Dana," Bill said. "I need the office for a few minutes."

Dana looked him up and down, then stood. "Fine. I'll go see what I can slap together from our closets, then order the rest."

She left, and Bill closed the door.

"I'm going to need a statement from you, and we might as well do that now," he said. From an inside pocket of his jacket he pulled out a notepad, spiralbound at the top, and flipped it open.

Ellie took a big breath. "Okay."

"You prepped the teacups, and set them backstage?"

"Yes."

"But anyone could have accessed them, is that right?"

"Yes."

He nodded. Ellie stared at her hands, clasped in her lap. She looked exhausted, her eyes red and her mouth drawn. He realized this was a difficult situation for her. But something else was bothering her, he could tell.

"You okay?"

"Not really."

"Because if you want to talk about anything, you know I'm here to listen. Is there something about this death I should know?"

"You don't think I would ever . . ."

He looked at her and placed one hand over both of hers. "Ellie, I've known you for almost thirty years. I know you could never do something like this."

"I have Valium," she blurted out. Bill pulled his hand back.

"What?"

"Valium. I have some. I keep it in the medicine cabinet at home. Almost never take it."

"The same drug that Reginald had."

She nodded. He sat on a corner of the desk and looked down at Ellie, who appeared to have shrunken before his eyes.

"Why do you have it?" he asked gently.

"It can be used as an anti-seizure med, Bill." A split second of confusion, then he understood. "Sometimes I just need a break."

"Ellie," Bill said with a gentle smile, "I'm pretty sure I can rule you out as the source of the benzo. And there are plenty of people who have or have access to Valium, and obviously Reginald had his own."

"What about the tea we used for the props?" Her eyes were red, her vision blurry. She felt miserable. She'd already wept once, sharing a cry with Dana after word came upstairs that Reginald had died. Now she felt like she was on the verge of crying again.

"It's only a theory," Bill said. "We can't prove it because we don't have any of that tea to test. Steve dumped it and cleaned the teacups already."

He stood. "Why don't you stay in here for now? I've got to get back to the stage and deal with Phelps. He may want to ask you some questions, though I doubt it. But just hang out in here until I can clear you to go home."

"What about Valerie—is someone notifying her?" Ellie thought of Reginald's wife, so austere and emotionless. Surely this would devastate her.

"Yes, the police chief of the town she lives in is headed over there," Bill said.

"Oh!" she said. "Which reminds me, she was here tonight."

"His widow?"

"Yes. She insisted on seeing Reginald while he was in the middle of the play."

Bill wrote in his notepad. "What did she want?"

"Said she wanted to give Reginald something, but didn't say what."

"Did she stay till the end of the show?"

"I didn't see her leave, but she wasn't in the audience either. After, you know, after he . . ."

Bill nodded, made another note, then closed the notepad. "Okay, that's good to know. Granted, it's a still a heart attack as far as anyone is concerned, but if it turns out it wasn't . . ."

"Then maybe you need to talk to her?"

"I'll want to talk to her anyway. Thanks for letting me know."

She nodded, and Bill headed for the stage.

Ellie sat there, wondering what would come next. She tried to not let her mind whirl in circles, thinking of the cast and crew, the audience, and what this news would do to her little theater, which was barely squeaking by as it was.

Chapter Thirteen

When Bill returned to the stage, he sensed the tension in the air. Phelps was wandering around the body in what little space the costume closet offered. Turner stood off to the side, his arms folded across his chest and his mouth a thin, bloodless slash. He cut his eyes toward Bill, and the police chief could feel the unspoken grievances Turner felt toward the state detective.

"So," Bill said, trying to keep his voice neutral and professional. "What do you think, Chuck?"

Phelps didn't answer and didn't look up. He knelt, felt around the body, made a note, stood, took some pictures with his phone, stepped over the body, and repeated the cycle. Bill understood it was a power play, that Phelps wanted Bill to know who was the top dog, even in this little corner of Massachusetts.

Bill waited. He stood a little ways from the body, while Turner stood at the far side of the stage and brooded.

When Phelps stood for the last time, he peeled off his blue latex gloves and shoved them in his coat pocket. He closed his small spiral-bound notebook and tucked it into an interior pocket. He turned to Bill and said, "Heart attack. Done and done."

Turner unfolded his arms and took a step forward, mouth open to speak, but Bill stopped him with a raised hand.

"I'm assuming my detective filled you in on our suspicions?" Bill said. "There are some indications that it might have been a drug overdose. He did have a Valium prescription, which can be fatal, alone or with an opioid or alcohol. I've spoken to Mrs. Marlowe, and she assures me he wouldn't have been abusing something that might inhibit his performances."

"She live with him?" Phelps said.

"No."

"Good friends? Buddies?"

"It was more of a professional relationship," Bill said.

"Did you know I collect Pez dispensers?" Phelps said.

"What?"

"Pez dispensers. I collect them. Did you know that?"

Bill frowned. "No, I did not."

"'Cause we're not buddies, and we don't live together. The same way Mrs. Marlowe likely has zero idea what went on in the deceased's life."

Bill rubbed the bridge of his nose with two fingers. He felt a headache coming on.

Phelps shrugged. "I can order a tox screen. Maybe it shows he OD'd, maybe it doesn't. But even if it does, there's nothing here to indicate it was anything other than accidental. Unless you have something else for me?"

Bill shook his head. "Just a feeling."

Phelps chuckled. "Yeah, I can't do anything about a feeling. You interview any of the cast or crew? Get statements or anything like that?"

Bill looked at Turner, who shook his head. "When everybody thought it was a heart attack, they mostly took off. Nobody wanted to stay and watch."

"We wouldn't usually need to gather statements for a man who had a heart attack," noted Bill.

Phelps shrugged. "Guess you don't got much else to go on, then."

"That's it, then?" Turner asked.

"Unless you got something else hidden up your sleeve. I'll order the tox screen, but even that's a stretch. So, yeah, that's it."

A tense moment of silence passed between them, then Phelps brushed past them both to head toward the lobby.

"I'll get a copy of the report to you, Bill," Phelps said as he left. "Feel free to take some statements if it will make you feel better. But do yourself a favor: try not to be you when you start talking to people." And then he was gone.

"What the hell just happened?" Turner said when Phelps was out of earshot.

Bill's face felt hot and his teeth were grinding together. It was all he could do to open his jaw to speak. "We go back, me and him," he said. "Me and the whole MSP, apparently."

"And because of that they're just gonna let this go without a second thought?"

Bill shrugged his shoulders to loosen them and rotated his head to stretch his neck. He needed to bleed off some of his anger. Then he sighed deeply, and that seemed to do it.

"Yeah," he said. "Except for the tox screen, they're just gonna file this one away."

"Which means we won't hear anything for two weeks, at best, if they rush it."

Bill waffled his hand in the air. "Maybe not. I got a buddy in the lab company the state uses for toxicology. He might be able to help."

"In the meantime, what do you want us to do?"

"Let's go plan out what we'll do next."

Chapter Fourteen

Ellie had decided to try to get some theater work done but was too distracted to concentrate. Everything she started she abandoned. She was rummaging through her small desk when Bill popped his head into the office

"We're going to wrap up soon. Why don't you head home and get some rest?"

"Are you sure?"

"Completely. We've got this covered."

The thought of finally going home to her own bed should have perked her up. Instead, she sagged, suddenly more tired than perhaps she had ever been. She had held back a series of tics, which had been building up pressure before they'd faded with nothing more than her wrinkling her nose twice. The only other time she remembered being nearly this tired was when she'd woken up five years ago and decided to quit her job. A job she hated.

"Honestly," she said, "I want nothing more than to curl under the covers and sleep for the next two months. I'm so tired, I'm tempted to sleep on the floor behind the box office."

Bill smiled a tired smile of his own. "I know what you mean."

They stepped toward each other and hugged, taking brief comfort in each other's company. It made Ellie remember when they had been through death together before, and they broke apart. She wiped her eyes, tried to make it look like she hadn't been crying, and blew her nose. She grabbed her jacket and her purse.

"I'll leave you the keys to the theater. Can you lock the doors when you go?"

"You bet."

"Thanks." She turned to Dana, who was still red-eyed but no longer crying. "Do you need a ride home?"

"That would be great," the older woman said. "Stan will be too distracted by the Pats losing to be any use to me now."

"They lost?" Bill said. "Dammit."

They both said good night to Bill, and together the two women left the theater in silence, crossing to the parking lot, and climbed into Ellie's car. They closed the doors, and Dana immediately said, "Something going on with you and Bill?"

Ellie, drained and running on fumes, was doing everything she could to keep her eyes open. Dana's question woke her like a slap to the face.

"What?"

"You and Bill. Anything going on between you two?"

"Jesus, you can be so tactless sometimes, Dana."

"That a yes?"

Nod-nod-nod.

"No! That's a no."

"You sure? 'Cause it seemed like—"

"Dana." *Grunt-grunt.* "No. We're friends. For decades." She put the car in reverse, pulled out of the parking spot, dropped into drive, and pulled onto the street. The evening was clear, the new moon all but invisible in the night sky. The road was empty of everyone but them. The police cruisers' lightbars were off now, the red and blue carnival shut down for the night. "Bill and I grew up together."

"He's older than you, but you seem close."

"We are. Were. Are." Ellie couldn't quite make up her mind. "I grew up with his sister, Ava. She was my best friend."

"Oh." Dana made a disappointed face. *A sixty-five-year-old busybody*, Ellie thought. Ellie wondered sometimes why she put up with Dana—but she was an amazing costume mistress. She could turn a roll of felt and a spool of thread into something out of *Gone with the Wind*. Dana also kept up with town gossip, which meant that Ellie was always up on, if not the truth, at least the rumors of the town. Dana was right about half the time, but it never failed to be entertaining. Except when the gossip radar aimed at her.

"I didn't know Bill had a sister. She live close by?"

Ellie took a deep breath. She considered telling Dana the story but thought better of it. This was not the time for that conversation, not the time to rehash past hurts.

"No," she answered, simply and with finality. "No, she doesn't."

Even Dana could tell the conversation was over, and they rode in silence.

Chapter Fifteen

After dropping Dana off and making sure the older woman got inside her house okay—something Ellie worried about as Dana struggled with the lock for several minutes before finally opening the door—she pulled into her own driveway. She unlocked the door and slipped inside. She closed and locked the door again and took her shoes off by the door. Ellie and her husband, Mike, lived in an old house, built around the turn of the century, with high ceilings and the original creaky hardwood floors.

Trying to avoid the creaky spots as much as possible, she stepped lightly. The house was quiet, at least in the foyer, and she wanted to hold on to the quiet as long as she could after the chaos of the theater—and of her own body.

Faintly, distantly, the noise of the TV came from the family room. Although they didn't yet have kids, Ellie still thought of this big room, with the gas fireplace and stacks of books along the broad windowsills, as a family room, the place where she would want to raise her future family.

She padded into the room and found Mike on the couch, TV on, a book on his chest, and apparently fast asleep. The book rode the gentle wave of his breathing, his chest rising and falling. She picked up the remote off the couch beside him and clicked off the TV.

"I was watching that," he said sleepily, low and gentle. Ellie jumped at the sound of his voice and dropped the remote. He sat up, drowsy, his face contrite. "Sorry. Didn't mean to scare you."

"I thought you were asleep."

"You can tiptoe all you want. The hardwood never lies." He yawned.

"I didn't mean to wake you."

"Eh." He shrugged. "I've been up and down anyway."

"Everything okay?"

"Software upgrade for the financial system is going in tonight. I'm on call in case it goes sideways."

She sat down next to him and said, "Mm-hmm," which she often said when Mike talked about his work.

"Late night," he commented.

"Yeah." She let out a breath, a long, slow release as if letting all the night's stresses out through her mouth. She felt a brief urge to tic, but the feeling passed.

"What happened?"

She took a deep breath and told him everything: the show, Reginald, and the police afterward, trying and failing to keep the story short and succinct. She had texted him only that there had been an EMT visit for someone in the cast, and that she would fill him in when she got home. She hadn't wanted to explain the whole thing in texts. Now home, it all came spilling out of her.

"That's bonkers," he said when she finished. He was awake now, sitting up straight. "I mean, could it be any more dramatic? Having an actual heart attack right there during your death scene?"

"Assuming it was a heart attack."

"From what you described, the evidence for an overdose is pretty thin."

Ellie picked up his hand and twined her fingers through his. "The state police passed on opening an investigation. They think it's a heart attack too. But Bill managed to get them to agree to a tox screen. The whole thing seems a little off to him."

"Sure it's not Bill who's a little off? I mean, assuming it does turn out to be an OD, it's not like overdoses are all that uncommon."

"Opioid ones, sure. But no one thinks Reginald was using opioids."

Mike shrugged. "Still doesn't mean he wasn't. You've been telling me stories of what an asshole this guy is for the last six weeks. A drug habit could certainly turn a guy into an asshole."

"Or," Ellie said peevishly, "if you're an asshole long enough, maybe it could make someone want to kill you."

"You have that same 'something is off' feeling, then?"

She gave Mike a look. He held up his hands in surrender to a fight he didn't want to start.

"Sorry. I don't mean to sound like a jerk."

"Mm-hmm."

"It's just you throw yourself into anything you do full throttle, no brake pedal. You did that at your old job, and you've done that with every show since buying the theater. For the last month and a half, I've heard nothing else except how much you can't stand the lead actor and you wish Merilyn hadn't cast him."

Ellie leaned into her husband, her head on his shoulder. Her eyes drooped. On the couch, curled against Mike's body, the fireplace on, and the evening wearing on, she began to nod off.

"So what's next?" Mike asked.

"Geez, I haven't even thought about that. I guess the next thing is to find a replacement for Reginald," Ellie said sleepily, her head bobbing gently twice.

"Ah. The show must go on."

She smiled, and Mike shifted and put an arm across her shoulders, pulling her closer. She shifted into his embrace, snuggled against him, and for the first time all night, felt normal.

The Last Line

*   *   *

The next day, Mike was up and ready for work by eight. The software consulting company he worked for was located in Manhattan, but he worked remotely. Mostly, he did project management, as easily done on a phone in Massachusetts as in New York. He drove down to the city once a month for a few days, an easy trip to make in exchange for working at home the other three and a half weeks per month.

Despite having woken in the middle of the night on the couch, climbing up to their bedroom, and trying to fall back asleep, Mike was out of bed by six. His internal clock woke him at the same time every day whether he wanted it to or not. When they'd first moved in together, Mike's sleep pattern used to drive Ellie nuts. Together in a small apartment, she would wake every time he rose. He apologized nearly every morning but was powerless to stop it. And to Ellie's initial annoyance, and eventual resignation, her body adjusted, and now she woke at six every morning as well.

They woke and slowly rolled out of bed, stretching and shuffling down the stairs to the kitchen. Mike started the coffee maker and Ellie got the mugs. The coffee maker started gurgling, and the coffee dripped into the carafe. No single-serving pods for them. Ellie and Mike mutually agreed on the superiority of an automatic drip-brew.

They sat at the kitchen island, sipping and talking—one of the things Ellie loved most about their marriage. Early morning talks over coffee. Even if the talk lagged and silence stole in, few things compared to sitting across from her best friend, drinking coffee before the world woke. This morning, though, the death of her lead actor was on both of their minds.

"So, Reginald made an enemy of everyone in the show?"

Ellie nodded. "He had a way about him. Managed to alienate everyone. Honestly, murder wouldn't really surprise me."

"Married?"

"Yes. His widow got the news last night."

"She hate him too?"

Ellie didn't know the answer. Before last night, she might have said no, Valerie Thornton loved her husband. She'd had only a few conversations with the woman. For Ellie, a few conversations usually gave her enough of an impression to form an opinion. Ellie had always possessed what Mike sometimes referred to as her "Asshole-o-meter," being able to tell within an interaction or two if someone was little more than a preening phony. Valerie registered as cold, but not as an out-and-out bitch. Her nickname might have been the "Ice Queen," but she never gave off anything close to a murdering vibe.

"No, I think she loved him. Or, if not love, then she tolerated him. More than once, she defended him to me or Merilyn, the director."

"What was she doing there?" Mike asked.

"No idea. She showed up, claimed she needed to give Reginald something, and slipped backstage. I didn't see her leave either."

"Think she did it?" Mike asked.

"Technically it's not a murder."

"So what's your plan?"

"Me? What makes you think I have a plan?"

Mike stared at her, lids half-closed, and she blushed a little. "I was born at night," he said. "But not last night."

Ellie sipped more coffee and thought about what she might do next. Her default was to start making lists. A lifelong list maker, she lived her life off Post-It notes, slips of scrap paper, and the backs of envelopes and receipts. Sometimes she plugged her lists into her phone, but she found something satisfying in the process of pencil to paper. To-do lists, grocery lists, lists of things to be done for the shows, lists of material to acquire for making the props. There was no end to them.

This morning, the lists were mental, full of items she never expected to make. Lists of suspects, of motives, of opportunities and alibis. If Reginald hadn't died accidentally, who would have wanted him gone? With a character like Reginald Thornton IV, there was no shortage of people he had wronged or irritated. She meant it when she told Mike everybody seemed to have a reason to want Reginald out of their life. But the more she turned the situation over in her head, the more she realized the question wasn't where to start and how to narrow the list down.

The question was whether she should start at all.

"I'll probably visit Reginald's wife, Valerie."

"Why?"

"To give her my condolences."

"Please don't get like you do," Mike said.

"What?"

Mike looked at her with raised eyebrows and a don't-give-me-that-crap expression. "Remember why you left your old job? The inability to let things go? The obsessiveness?"

She shrugged. "This is different. It's my theater; one of my actors died."

Mike looked into his coffee cup and sighed. Then he raised his eyes to her. He leaned in and kissed her on the forehead. "Just, please, don't let it take you over."

She held up two fingers. "I promise."

Chapter Sixteen

Mike was well into his phone calls when Ellie, freshly showered and fueled by a second cup of coffee, strode out her front door. She walked along the short path to the driveway, surveying her front yard. The summer had been hot and dry, and the leaves changed colors earlier than usual. The two trees that flanked her house burned golden and crimson, shedding more leaves by the day. October came in drizzly and gray, as if trying to make up for the lack of water in the summer. But today the clouds had cleared, the sun shone down, and the air carried the crisp smell of leaf piles and chimney smoke.

Despite yesterday, Ellie felt surprisingly good. She took in her house, a lovely old home she and Mike had repainted slate-blue a few years ago. White trim, and ornamental scrollwork along the cornices. She loved her house and the autumnal landscape.

"You killing people at that theater of yours now?"

Ellie looked past her driveway to the other side of the fence separating her property line from that of her neighbor, all five-foot-nothing, one hundred pounds soaking wet, of cantankerous old woman. At eighty-seven, Judy O'Loughlin lived as if she were eight years old. She seemed to have virtually no verbal self-control, speaking whatever came to her mind. She lived alone but never seemed lonely. She went out with several "gentleman callers," as she labeled them.

As sweet as Judy could sometimes be, she could be sharp-tongued and wicked. Her demeanor was mercurial, her moods as changeable as New England weather.

"No," Ellie answered. "We're not killing people at the theater, thank you very much." *At least as far as I know,* she thought.

"What the heck happened up there?" Judy stood in a bathrobe and slippers on the other side of the short picket fence that separated the driveway from Judy's lawn, slightly out of breath, as if she had been waiting inside for Ellie to emerge before dashing outside.

Ellie said a silent prayer, hoping Judy had something on under the robe. "Our lead actor passed away," she said.

"Onstage."

"That is true."

"Heart attack?"

"That is what they listed as the official cause of death," Ellie said, hoping to curb the gossip. "Who am I to argue?" But if Judy had spoken with Dana, gossip containment would be nothing but a pipe dream.

"But they're doing a tox screen anyway?" Judy said.

Ellie couldn't contain her surprise. "Where did you hear that?"

"Oh, honey bunch, it's the talk of the town. Someone talked to someone else who said something about the state checking for drugs. So now people are saying he OD'd. And"—she lowered her voice conspiratorially—"some are even wondering if someone else 'done 'im in.'"

"Judy, really!" Ellie tried to keep the alarm off her face. "Who is saying that?"

"It's all over Facebook."

Ellie's brow furrowed in puzzlement. "You're on Facebook?"

"What, am I too old to be on Facebook? I'm up on things. I'm not some old biddy who stays inside all the time and watches the soaps."

"I never said you were. But what are people saying online?"

"It's in the town group, of course. Best place to go for a front row seat to the decline and fall of civilization. Local town Facebook pages. The townies eat themselves alive."

"What are they saying?" Ellie said, trying not to sound impatient. *Blink-blink. GRUNT.*

"That the lead actor died in a smack-fueled bender last night, and the local keystone cops finally called in the professionals from the state homicide unit."

Ellie cleared her throat. "None of that is accurate."

"And that the cops shut you down, taped off the place as a crime scene, dusted for prints, all the usual stuff."

Ellie rubbed her hands over her face. "Good Lord. Anything else?"

"Only that the actor was a jerk and his death isn't the worst thing to happen in this town." She rubbed her hands together gleefully. "I love a good conspiracy theory. Makes for great true crime podcast stuff."

Oh boy. "He was a difficult personality sometimes," Ellie said precisely. *Nod-nod-nod.* "But that doesn't mean he deserved to die."

"We all gotta go sometime, honey bunch. No one gets outta here alive."

"Thanks for clueing me in on the town gossip, Judy." Ellie started to leave.

"Where you going today? Isn't the theater still closed?"

"I'm not headed to Kaleidoscope. I have another errand." She wasn't about to tell Judy she was going to call on the widow.

"You can't fool me. Go get 'em, tiger."

Ellie shook her head and climbed into her car. The conversation took a moment to sink in, and her body twitched and convulsed with frustration. Then it passed, at least for the moment, into the glorious stillness between spasms. She turned back in time to see Judy wandering around her yard, still in her bathrobe.

The Last Line

Judy's neighbor on the far side came out and barked something at her, and the old woman sniped back at him. The long-simmering feud between the two neighbors did not appear to be abating anytime soon. More words were exchanged, until finally Judy had had enough, opened her robe, and shook her body at her neighbor. Horrified, he darted back inside while Judy laughed.

Ellie thanked whatever deity might be listening that Judy's back was to her. She started the car and pulled out of the driveway before she got pulled into the squabble.

Chapter Seventeen

Bill's alarm went off far too early for his liking. He swung his legs to the floor and shoved his feet in his slippers. He shuffled downstairs to start some coffee, trying not to wake Darlene as he left.

He set coffee to brew, the smell alone helping his eyes stay open. While it brewed, Bill thought over what he had learned last night. He broke things down into facts and assumptions.

The facts were simple. The lead actor, Reginald Thornton IV, collapsed onstage and died. While the cause was still to be determined, every hair on the back of Bill's neck pointed to a drug overdose. The toxicology report would have the final say.

When it came to assumptions, Bill conceded to himself that there were a lot of them. An assumption it was an overdose, and an assumption it was a benzo. An assumption it wasn't an accident? Maybe, but not yet. All he had to go on for that was Ellie's assertion that Reginald would never allow himself to be too far gone to be effective onstage. If that were true, it made a case that the OD was deliberate, and deliberately done to Reginald. In other words, murder.

Granted, that assumption, based only on Ellie's opinion, was razor-thin.

If someone gave Reginald, who, by all accounts, was a grade-A jerk, a benzo, how would they have done it? Crushing a pill or pills and mixing them in something Reginald would drink would be the easiest way. All the actors drink something as part of the play. Ellie had prepped all the drinks before the show started and set them backstage so they would be ready to go when the scene called for it. Which meant anyone with access to the backstage area had access to both the potential murder weapon, and the means to use it.

The coffee dripped, then stopped. Bill poured himself a cup. It was strong and black, and he added half a packet of Equal to it, just to take the edge off the bitterness.

Something else nibbled at him about this case.

Sure, benzos could be fatal in large doses, and that alone *could* cause Reginald to stop breathing. But it would have needed to be a really big dose. An extra nudge to push him over the line would be more efficient.

For example, an opioid dissolved in the preset drink.

He needed to call the ME to talk this through.

But first, he wanted to get an appraisal of the widow. He pulled up the number for Davis, the Clifton police chief, and dialed.

"Morning, Bill. Awfully early, isn't it?"

"Hi, Davis," he said. "It is, but this thing last night is nibbling at me. You talk with the widow?"

"Yup."

"How'd she take it?"

Whitney paused on the other end of the phone, giving Bill enough time to wonder why he would need to pause before answering.

"So, not as I would've thought. Kinda inconsistent."

"Inconsistent how?"

"She started out stone-faced, for one, then almost *elated*. Then she burst into tears and sobbed for a solid minute. Then she was done. Like a summer squall or something."

Bill considered this. "What's your impression, Davis?"

"Honestly, I got the impression she was both happy *and* sad that her husband was gone."

He thanked Davis, then called his one and only detective.

"Turner, I want you to take that list of names of the cast members, along with DOBs and socials, and start running Triple I background checks on all of them."

"You got it. It will take me a couple of hours, depending on how deep we dive. Anybody I should spend extra time on?"

"See if anybody has a history of substance abuse. See if you can find out if anybody has been through rehab, is in AA, what medications people are taking, what other connections they might have to the victim."

"That won't be easy. Lots of privileged information there. Getting medical records without a warrant or exigent circumstances is close to impossible, but I'll see what I can dig up. Anything else?"

Bill hesitated. He hated having to do this, but if he wasn't thorough, if this somehow slipped through his fingers and he was accused of favoritism, he might be out of a job the next time his contract was up for renewal with the town selectmen.

"Yeah. Run Elizabeth Marlowe with the rest of them."

Chapter Eighteen

Ellie drove, taking a right, north on the state road that ran through Avalon. She loved her town, a hidden gem in the hills of central Massachusetts. Originally named Jacobston for one of the town's founding fathers, the town rechristened itself Avalon when the state seized the wide valley on the northwest side. They cleared the homes and people and farms, paid fair money for the land, and sunk the valley under sixty-five billion gallons of water. The resulting reservoir watered Boston via a series of large pipes and aqueducts running over and under the land to the east. The valley vanished, except for Apple Hill, a lone rise of land remaining above the waterline after the reservoir was complete.

The hill became a symbol for the town. Every fall, the town selectmen would choose a few residents, and together they would motor out to the little island and harvest apples from the few apple trees that remained and snap photos for the paper. Two years into it, following popular sentiment, the selectmen added a motion to the town warrant to rename the town Avalon, a reference to Arthurian legend and the Isle of Apples.

This tradition was now closing in on ninety years old.

Ellie drove out of the town, her GPS chirping at her every so often until she pulled up to the Thornton house twenty minutes later. She marveled at what a beautiful home it was, constructed to resemble an old stone English cottage. Sitting on several acres, much of the land was finely manicured and leaf-free despite the many trees and autumn wind. Behind the house, the property became a wave of gently undulating hills that made Ellie think of the English countryside. She had a sudden inexplicable desire to walk those hills with a border collie.

She went up the slate path to the front of the house and took a deep breath.

Nod-sniff-sniff-sniff. SNIFF.

Grunt-grunt-blink.

Get it all out now, she thought, though she knew Tourette syndrome didn't work that way. She ticced some more, some elaborate ones that affected multiple muscle groups—contract and release, contract and release. Finally, it felt like the last one had passed. Her shoulders sagged with exhaustion.

Sometimes she hated her body.

She took a deep breath and knocked on the ornately carved wooden door and waited, her tics cycling through one more time.

She half expected a butler in coattails and an English accent to open the door, but no one answered.

She rolled her shoulders back, then repeated the action. She wondered if this would develop into a new tic, then wondered which one this potential new tic would replace. Her Tourette syndrome always seemed to follow that pattern: a new one popped up, and an old one vanished.

She knocked again. It had been a long night for everyone, and for Valerie Thornton that included being told her husband was dead. Ellie wouldn't have blamed Valerie if she swallowed a couple of Ambien and chased them with a highball of scotch.

Ellie raised her hand to give it one more try when the door opened.

Dressed as if for a cocktail party, Valerie Thornton stood before her in a pale-pink button-down blouse and a black pencil skirt. Her makeup was perfectly applied, highlighting her natural beauty. At her throat lay a string of pearls, a complementary string of pearls on one wrist and a petite gold watch on the other. Ellie suddenly felt under-dressed and tried to hide her embarrassment. She reminded herself that this was Valerie's standard look.

Except that her eyes were bloodshot and puffy.

"What can I do for you, Ellie?" No hi, or hello.

Nod.

"Hi, Valerie. I wanted to come over and say how sorry I was about Reginald, and see how you were doing."

"How do you think I'm doing?"

Nod-nod. "I would expect not well."

"Of course not."

They stood for a few awkward moments, Ellie beginning to think she'd made a terrible mistake, and Valerie standing like a linebacker blocking for the quarterback.

"Is there anything I can do for you?" Ellie asked.

"What could you possibly do?"

Blink-blink-nod-grunt.

"I don't know. I'm offering whatever I can. Is there anything you need?" Ellie remembered Ava's funeral and the immediate aftermath, how the community rallied around the Starlin family. "We could have people bring over dinners, or get groceries, or run errands for you?"

Valerie eyed Ellie up and down, taking her in in a way that made Ellie feel completely inadequate. Reginald's wife sighed, turned, and walked back into the house, leaving the door open, which Ellie took as an invitation to follow. Her tics let loose, and she grunted and twitched for several solid seconds before she was able to take a step inside the house.

Once inside, she closed the door. Valerie moved toward the inte-rior of the house, seemingly oblivious to someone following her. Ellie attributed the dazed state to shock, the mind-numbing blow of being so suddenly without your partner of twenty years. She couldn't imagine what it would be like if Mike were suddenly gone. Gone not just physically, but emotionally, spiritually, sexually. Sure, he left town for half a week every month for work, but they still talked on the phone. A sudden death made it all disappear, like a black magic spell.

Ellie had never been here before—the house was beautiful, as well put together on the inside as it was out. It seemed a mirror of the woman who walked ahead of her: meticulously planned, beautifully executed . . . and cold as ice. They entered the living room, lavishly decorated with furniture and bookcases. Something about the decor reminded Ellie of New York City during the Gilded Age, but as if in a museum rather than a place where someone lived.

A baby grand piano sat in one corner of the room, covered with pictures. At a glance she could see that most showed Reginald; only one or two were of Valerie. None of them together.

Valerie sat on one of the sofas and motioned for Ellie to sit on the other. Ellie sat. She tried to fill the awkward silence.

"Reginald was excellent in the role," Ellie said. It sounded stupid and hollow in her ears. "He will be missed."

Valerie stared at her for a long minute before speaking.

"Our town Chief of Police came by last night," she said. "A man named Davis Whitney. He said Reginald died onstage, from an apparent heart attack."

"That's my understanding."

"Resulting in no investigation into his death," Valerie said. Not a question.

"I think that's still to be determined," Ellie said uncomfortably.

"By whom? I made some phone calls this morning. I was told the state decides whether to investigate. And in this case, they are treating it as a *medical incident*."

"The state police are. But our town's police chief is following up, just to be sure."

Valerie fixed Ellie with a gaze that made her feel like a bug under glass. Worried Valerie's next question would be "Following up with *what*?", Ellie blurted out, "Do you know if Reginald could have taken too much Valium?"

"I beg your pardon?"

Ellie stammered. "We . . . I mean, the police . . . there was a prescription bottle of Valium among his personal items last night."

Valerie's stare didn't lessen in intensity. It may have actually become sharper. "Are you suggesting my husband overused drugs?"

"No, I was just wondering—"

"You think he died of a drug overdose?"

"He seemed, well, a little off yesterday, as if he were dizzy or didn't feel well."

"As he would if he were about to have a heart attack," Valerie said, sitting stock still.

Ellie bumbled on. "Well, yes, I suppose that's true. However, the police aren't sure, and the state police have ordered a tox screen—"

"Reginald was many things," Valerie said, her voice tight and cold. "But he was not a drug addict."

"Are you sure?"

Valerie gave Ellie a withering look.

"What I mean is, everyone has secrets. Sometimes little, sometimes big. Personal things we don't want to share, or maybe that we feel like we can't share. I'm wondering if Reginald had any and if this might be one of them."

"Then I wouldn't know about it, would I?" Valerie said bitingly.

Ellie paused, then tried again. "Did you have any reason to suspect he was hiding something?"

"No. But perhaps I was a fool this entire time."

Ellie nodded. Then nodded again. And again. And again. Twice more. Then she was done ticcing. For now.

"But he *did* have a prescription for Valium?"

Valerie looked at her as if to say *How dare you ask that?* But instead she asked, "Do you?"

Ellie gave a small, embarrassed shrug. She hadn't been prepared to have the spotlight shone on her. "I do, actually. It's sometimes helpful for people with Tourette syndrome."

Valerie made a face like she heard an off-key note. "The condition where people shout swears in the middle of conversations for no apparent reason."

Nod-nod-nod.

STOP! Ellie shouted at her brain. *Just stop. For a moment. Please.* Her body obeyed, if only for a moment. She took a breath.

"In reality, that's much rarer than you might think. TV shows tend not to do the condition justice."

Ellie pivoted. "Valium is a benzo, and they are highly addictive. I'm only wondering if you had any reason to suspect Reginald was hiding a pill addiction."

Valerie looked out a window as she spoke. "Why are you here?" she asked icily. "Trying to save your theater? Worried about its reputation?"

"No," Ellie said, with some surprise. Of course the thought had occurred to her that this could destroy her theater. Maybe it already had. *Damage control needed to be done.* She started making a mental list, rapid-fire, in her brain. She almost fell down the rabbit hole but pulled out at the last moment.

This was about the people. How could this have happened at Kaleidoscope? In a way, she felt like she had some responsibility for Reginald's death. Either he had problems and an addiction she wasn't aware of, or someone had reached a breaking point or hated him enough to kill him. She failed to recognize how toxic the environment at the theater had been with him there. No matter how much she disliked the man, she owed it to him and her theater to learn the truth about what happened.

Her concentration wavered, the strength of holding back her tics faltering, and she bobbed her head twice in quick succession, short bobs, followed by rapid blinking. She managed to pull herself under control as Valerie stared at her.

"This is about a performer in my theater," she said. "A performer who, by being in the production, became part of the Kaleidoscope family." Family was a stretch, but maybe not. "And I'm very protective of my family."

Valerie surprised Ellie by laughing. The laughter gave way to crying, and for a brief moment, Valerie Thornton sobbed, wiping her perfectly made-up eyes with a tissue that appeared as if by magic in her hand. As quickly as it started, her sobbing stopped, leaving her eyes wet but her waterproof mascara flawless. It reminded Ellie of a thunderstorm in Orlando. A few minutes of downpour, then sunny skies.

"*Family*. How rich."

"Did I say something wrong?"

"The thought of Reginald and a family." She paused as if searching for the right phrase. "Family wasn't ever a priority for him."

"You and Reginald didn't have children?"

"No," Valerie said with an air of disdain, and perhaps a pinch of sadness. And something else Ellie couldn't pinpoint.

"I'm sorry."

"Don't be. I made my choice and resolved to be happy regardless."

Ellie sat with that for a moment. *Happy regardless*, Valerie had said, but the beautiful house, neat as a pin, supremely decorated, and as cold and quiet as a mausoleum didn't spell happiness to Ellie. It held none of the laughter or chaos of a full, happy life, with or without children. Airless. Happiness differed for everyone, she realized, but this house closed in on her like a tomb. And she suspected that tomblike quality had existed before Reginald's death. Nothing about the space felt joyful.

It was time for Ellie to leave. There didn't seem to be anything else to say. She hadn't really learned much, and it didn't seem like she'd been any comfort to the widow. She looked at the piano, with its parade of pictures on the closed lid.

"Do you play?" she asked.

"I do." Valerie's face changed. It was happier, or perhaps more at ease. Ellie thought it almost wistful. "I used to play quite a bit."

"Did you study formally?"

"Yes. I graduated from the Peabody Conservatory."

"In Baltimore," Ellie said, her face surprised.

"Yes. I grew up in Baltimore."

"Would you play something?" Ellie asked on a whim.

Once she said it, she almost wished she could take it back, but the woman—legs crossed at the shins, stone-faced, closed off, the Ice Queen the cast knew—changed before Ellie's eyes. It was like watching a flower bloom in a time-lapse video. One minute Valerie was folded in on herself, and the next she unwound herself from the couch and crossed over to the piano.

She moved with the grace of a performer, an elegance Ellie had not noticed in her before. Perhaps Ellie failed to recognize it, but maybe this Valerie, this true elegance, seldom emerged. Perhaps no one had asked her to perform in a long time, and even an audience of one drew the flower out of its bud.

Valerie opened the piano and sat on the bench, placing her hands on the keys. She took a breath and, with a bow of her head, began a piece that was slow and soft and sad. Ellie marveled watching her, the sound of the piano rich and clear, filling her with a sense of longing and heartbreak. Her tics, which she had been holding back with sheer force of will, settled in with her to listen to the music, and she no longer had to fight them off. She gazed outside for a few minutes, and the music seemed to draw her attention to the glorious windswept day, sunny to start. But then a cloud seemed to pass over the sun, and the bright slants of sunlight were now hidden by a smudged sky. A great sadness infected her.

Just as Ellie thought her heart could bear no more, Valerie suddenly stopped playing. The silence jarred Ellie back to the living room and to the widow before her.

It took a moment for Ellie to speak. "That was one of the most beautiful things I've ever heard."

"Chopin. Prelude in D minor."

"Do you perform? Publicly, I mean?"

Valerie sighed, as if at a lost memory. "I used to. I gave it up when I married Reginald."

"Why?" Ellie knew the question was blunt, but it had to be asked.

Valerie hesitated, answering slowly, and only after some thought. "He didn't want me to perform. Said he wanted to be able to support us with the money he made from acting, said the need to support us made him hungrier. But that was all bullshit." Her voice turned bitter. "He didn't want the competition."

"Do you act as well?"

"No. Nor sing. Only the piano."

Ellie was puzzled. "Then how could you be competition?"

"Ellie," Valerie said, not unkindly. "It didn't matter if I played the piano instead of acted. If I ever drew a bigger crowd or bigger applause as a performer of any kind, his ego never would have recovered. That's the kind of man Reginald was."

Nod-nod-nod.

Valerie went on. "And when I tried to return to performing, he blocked me at every turn. He called up venues I had booked and forced them to cancel. All to keep me second, behind him. Always."

Ellie watched Valerie as she spoke, watched her face turn from sad to angry, with flashes of rage, only to land with finality on exhausted.

Ellie could well imagine how tired Valerie must be. Twenty years of marriage to Reginald, twenty years of being pushed down, having the thing you're good at, possibly brilliant at, shoved down so that no matter what you did—no matter what instrument you played or where you played it—you'd never be better than him. Ellie tried to picture Mike telling her to set aside everything she loved because his ego wouldn't tolerate it. But she couldn't imagine it.

Something else, though, cut through the strange pain and sadness—could it be relief? It flowed like an undercurrent through the house. Ellie tagged it for mental examination later. She knew she would be rolling this conversation around in her thoughts for a while.

And despite the enormous empathy she now felt for Valerie, she realized that the woman had at least one motive to want to get rid of her husband, perhaps more.

"I should probably get going," Ellie said, standing. "Your playing was beautiful."

"Thank you."

"Can I ask you one more question?"

"I don't suppose I can stop you." Valerie attempted to return to her previous imperiousness.

"What was so important that you had to deliver it to Reginald last night before the show ended?"

Valerie's eyes never left Ellie, but they became hard and unfeeling. "I don't see how that is any of your business."

"It's not," Ellie admitted, chagrined. "But I'm just trying to figure things out."

Valerie cut right to it. "Figure what out?"

Ellie blinked. "Why Reginald died. Right now it's a heart attack. If the tox screen comes back showing a lethal level of drugs, then it might be considered an accidental overdose, or suicide."

"Suicide?" The word slipped out in a harsh whisper.

"Hopefully not," Ellie hastened to say. "And there's no indication of that. I don't think most life insurance policies pay in the event of suicide."

"There was no life insurance."

"Really?" Ellie tried to keep the surprise from her voice but suspected she'd failed. Given the lavishness of the house, and her assumption their lifestyle was equally so, it seemed odd to leave his wife with the funeral bill. But maybe Reginald had money tucked away.

"No, we did not have a policy." Her voice was ice-cold and dangerous.

"I'm sorry," Ellie said, and she was. "I truly came here to give my condolences and to see if there was anything I can do for you. I'm trying to understand what happened. I know that sometimes I ask too many questions."

Valerie made a sour face and said, "I lied last night."

"Pardon?"

"I lied," Valerie repeated. "I didn't have anything to deliver to him. I went to confront him."

"Confront him?" Ellie was confused. Had Valerie decided to stand up to her husband, or to leave him?

"About his philandering. About his acting like a Lothario."

"He was unfaithful?"

Valerie raised an eyebrow that suggested Ellie was perhaps the stupidest person on the planet.

"The envelop?" Ellie asked. "The one you held up when you came to see him backstage?"

"A prop."

Ellie had a thought. "Do you think he and this person were, um, popping pills?"

Valerie's face became dangerous. "Ask that miserable bitch of a lead actress of yours," she spat.

Ellie, blindsided, stood at a loss for words, unable to fully process what Valerie had just said.

Blink-grunt-grunt-blink.

She hated how ticcy she became when nervous or stressed. Valerie had surprised her, and she tried to hold back the tics but couldn't.

Grunt-sniff-grunt-grunt-nod-nod-nod.

"I'm sorry, what?"

"Your lead actress. Ask her."

"Kyra?"

"Does your constant and consistent inability to control your own body also make you hard of hearing?" Valerie sneered.

Ouch. Ellie caught herself before she gasped, but it was a near thing. She tried to remind herself that Valerie had just lost her husband and that she was mourning, grieving somewhere deep in her heart.

"I'm sorry," Ellie said, and hated herself for apologizing for something over which she had very little control. "Sometimes my tics get away from me."

Valerie rolled her eyes. Ellie was considering prodding her to continue when she spoke.

"Talk to that gold digger. She had an eye for Reginald. And he for her, but she couldn't leave well enough alone, had to pester him at every turn, Too bad, really."

"Too bad?"

"That he died, and not her."

Chapter Nineteen

When his cell phone rang, Bill glanced down and saw Ellie's number. He answered.

"I'm headed to Ned's for some breakfast," Ellie said. "Want to meet up and talk about last night?"

Bill's stomach rumbled. He hoped she didn't hear it through the phone. "Sure. I could use more than a muffin. I had Turner start pulling records for the cast and crew. So far, nothing much to write home about. Maybe you could fill me in on things I won't find in the RMV database. Like what you hear through the grapevine, that kind of thing. I gather the theater world can be small, and rumors can travel far."

"I can't begin to describe how much of an understatement that is."

"So, yeah, that kind of stuff. Scuttlebutt."

"Sure," Ellie said. "And I want to tell you about a conversation I just had with the widow."

Bill sat upright in his chair and leaned forward, elbows on his desk, voice with a sudden edge. "Ellie, you didn't."

"I wanted to offer my condolences."

Bill sighed. "Ellie, we don't even know if there's anything to look into. I don't want you playing amateur detective."

Nothing but silence from the other end of the phone for a few seconds before Ellie spoke. "I genuinely wanted to express condolences for her husband's death—and to get a feel for her since I don't know her all that well. And there were a few surprises," she added.

Bill massaged the bridge of his nose, his eyes squeezed shut. He felt the beginnings of a headache behind his eyes.

"I'll meet you at Ned's in fifteen," he said.

* * *

Ned's Diner, a small place on the side of the road leading out of town and into Worcester, was one of the last diner cars made by the Worcester Lunch Car Company before the company folded in 1957. It had the distinctive barrel-shaped ceiling of the WLCC lunch cars, the heavy porcelain enamel exterior panels, the marble counter with stools fixed on metal stanchions, and a kitchen behind the rear wall of the counter area. Along the front wall sat booths that fit four almost comfortably.

When Bill entered, he saw Ellie was already in a booth toward the far end of the diner. He went over, waving hello to Cheryl, the waitress, before sitting down.

"Wow, you look tired," Ellie said.

Cheryl came over and poured their coffee to start. Ellie ordered two poached eggs on wheat toast, while Bill ordered eggs, bacon, home fries, and three pancakes.

"I eat when I'm stressed," Bill said when Ellie's eyes widened at the size of his order.

"I would take stress-eating over stress-ticcing any day." As if to back up her statement, her head bobbed up and down several times, then side to side as she tried to crack her neck.

"Fair point," Bill said.

The food arrived quickly, and Ellie filled Bill in on what Valerie had told her about the apparent affair with Kyra, how controlling Reginald was, and the lack of life insurance. When she finished, Ellie sat back and took a drink of coffee.

"There's an awful lot there to unpack," Bill said.

Ellie sipped more coffee. Cheryl came over and cleared their plates, came back and poured more coffee, then moved away again.

"I don't know what to think, honestly," Ellie said. *Blink-blink-grunt-grunt.* "But, Bill, I just don't buy the idea that Reginald was using. Even if he was, his reputation as an actor was everything to him, maybe more important than his marriage. I can't see him risking anything when he was about to perform."

She put down her coffee cup and leaned forward. "I know you're waiting on the tox screen to confirm if Reginald had taken anything. And maybe he took a Valium and forgot and took another, or stopped on the way to the theater and had a vodka or something, and it was all too much."

She leaned closer and lowered her voice. "But what if he didn't?"

Bill put down his fork. "What do you mean?"

Ellie chose her words carefully. "You saw indications of an overdose, slight but definite. So, most likely, it wasn't just a heart attack."

Bill nodded, watching her.

"There are any number of people among the cast and crew who were not fond of Reginald. Like, all of them. And his wife seems to have felt the same. Not that they are the only ones who may have felt that way." Ellie knew that people who are that nasty in one venue as well as, apparently, at home are seldom pleasant the rest of the time.

"You know I love my theater, Bill," Ellie said, fighting off the compulsion to bob her head. "I love it all: the plays, the crowds, the cast, the crew, my little theater family, however dysfunctional it is. Reginald died on my watch, Bill. He died on my theater stage, in front of people who bought tickets to the play." Now she fought for words, fought to control the rising emotion in her voice, and said the words they may have both been wondering since last night, since the first hint this was not a heart attack. "What if someone in the theater poisoned him?"

Bill ran his fingers through his hair. "I really hate that idea."

"Not as much as I do, believe me."

"Let me ask you something," he said. "Do you think anyone in your theater is capable of murder?"

Ellie sat back so suddenly the booth seat moved. Her eyes were wide, and her face was pale. Then she leaned back in.

"Maybe," she said. "I hope not, but maybe. And if so, we can't wait for tox screen results in what, a week or two? We need to find out who was where when, and what everyone saw and heard, before time passes and people's memories get blurred. Accidentally on purpose, you know?"

Bill nodded. "So," he said. "Kyra, for instance. Was she near the costume closet last night? Could she have messed with his things?"

Ellie blinked. "They all were. Every night. They all go back and forth backstage, multiple times, during the show. There are a couple of times where each of the actors is offstage for several minutes. Costume changes, scene changes, intermission. Valerie didn't arrive until near the end of the show."

"In theory," Bill said, thinking, "his wife could have slipped him a dose of something the day before."

"Then she went backstage and slipped more into his drink to help him along?" Ellie said.

Bill shook his head. "Or she knew that he might take a Valium before performing, and would have a good chance of dying while she was back at home."

"Jeez," Ellie said.

"Where does Kyra work?" Bill asked.

"Out in Framingham."

"Let's take a drive out there. Ask her a few questions about the things Valerie said."

Ellie sighed but agreed. She knew it would be awkward to question one of her actors, especially about something as nasty as Valerie's accusation. She and Bill would ride together and try to catch Kyra around lunch, when she would have free time.

Cheryl came over and set the check on the table. She stood a moment, looking at Ellie through her cat-eye glasses, and said, "Heard you had some excitement at that theater of yours last night."

"News travels fast," Ellie said as they paid the check and got on their way.

In the parking lot, they paused.

"Ellie," Bill said, causing her to look at him. "This could get messy."

"Phelps practically told you to go ask questions and get statements," she pointed out.

"Getting statements is a lot different than interviewing people about a murder that, quite frankly, at the moment exists only in our imaginations."

"At the moment," she said. "We just don't know."

Bill shrugged. "My point is, this is something for Turner and me. You don't have to get involved. As it is, we're walking a fine line. We might take a bad step and get ourselves in hot water."

"What are you saying?"

He paused for a moment. "I'm asking, are you sure you want to be involved? You could get people upset with you. Or you might get in hot water for being involved in an off-the-books police investigation that had no business starting up in the first place."

Ellie looked at him steadily. Her tics, normally amped up during stressful situations, had vanished. She spoke firmly.

"Bill, this happened in my theater. Love them or hate them, these are my people. I owe it to them—Reginald especially—to figure out what happened. And if someone did kill him, then I owe it to all of my people to help bring that person to justice, if I can."

Bill nodded. He understood exactly how she felt.

"All right, then," he said. "Let's do this."

ACT 2

"Let me have a dram of poison."

Chapter Twenty

Outside of Ned's, Ellie's phone started to ring. She pulled it out of her pocket and held it up.

"It's Steve," she said.

"The stage manager, right?" Bill said.

She nodded. "Hi, Steve. How are you doing this morning?"

"Tired," came the voice on the other end of the phone. "And you sound a lot more chipper than anyone should after somebody's died in their theater."

"Ned's coffee. Cures anything. What's up?"

"Wondering what the plan is for tonight. We doing a show or not?"

"Oh my God," Ellie said. "Tonight. The show. Believe it or not, I totally forgot about the show."

"We're going to have to find someone to step into the role."

Ellie rubbed her forehead. She felt the pressure of her tics building up.

"Hold on a sec."

She pulled the phone away from her ear and covered the microphone. She didn't know why she did—a holdover from her teenage years when you covered the receiver when you didn't want the person to hear something.

95

"Everything okay?" Bill asked.

"We have to figure out how we're going to cover for Reginald tonight," Ellie said. "Actually, for the rest of the run."

"You're not going to shut down the play?"

"Can't afford to. Not if I want to keep the theater from going under. And it's not really fair to the rest of the cast and crew, I think."

Bill made a shooing gesture with his hands. "You better go, then."

"Steve?" Ellie said into the phone as she climbed into her car. "Meet me at the theater in fifteen."

She pulled up to the theater at the same time as Steve. Together, they entered the lobby to the sound of someone yelling—Dana. A phone slammed down, and they heard cursing.

"Dana?" Ellie called out.

Dana emerged from the office, shaking a fistful of papers.

"We need to replace that damn printer!" she said. "I can't get any of the online reservations to print properly, and the guy at Staples was no help."

Ellie grimaced. "There's no money for a new printer right now."

Dana glanced at Steve with a smile and said, "There will be."

"What do you mean?" Ellie said.

"I logged on to TicketStage this morning to check out what had come in since last night," Dana said. "We're almost at capacity tonight already."

"What?" Ellie couldn't hide her shock. Her head jerked, and she blinked rapidly, then grunted. "Just since last night?"

"Yep. I guess people become interested in theater when they think they might see somebody die onstage in real life. And not just tonight. This whole weekend is sold out, and next weekend is nearly sold out."

Ellie's breath grew short. The news hit her hard, relief and guilt at the same time. *Her theater would survive.* The publicity from last night had spurred enough morbid curiosity that people had started buying tickets to the play where the lead actor had just died. Some probably wanted to see how the theater would adjust without their lead. Some doubtlessly wanted to see the play where someone died onstage. Others, she thought, may have just wanted to support the theater during a tough time.

No matter the reason, the jump in ticket sales would ensure that Kaleidoscope could hold on at least until *White Christmas* in December, which, if they made enough on this show, could be big and splashy.

And this good fortune came at the expense of one of her cast—as a result of his death. Her theater had been saved by one of the actors literally dying.

She had to sit down.

"Ellie?" Steve said. "You okay? You look pale." She could hear the concern in Steve's voice, even as gray spots danced at the edge of her vision and her ears seemed full of wool. She thought she might pass out.

He helped her to a chair, and she sat clumsily.

"I'll be okay," she said. "I'm a little overwhelmed, I just need a minute."

"When you're done playing the ingenue," Dana said, "get over here and give me a hand. We've got to process these reservations, and we need to get Steve up to speed on the part."

"Steve?" He blinked, looking puzzled. "Get Steve up to speed on what part?"

"Congrats, kid, you're now the leading man," Dana said.

"You want me to replace Reginald?" Steve asked. He looked as if he might be the next to nearly pass out.

"That's brilliant," Ellie said, turning to Steve. "You're the stage manager. You already know the show. You've got the lines mostly memorized."

"And you're a hottie, as the kids say," Dana added.

Steve blushed. "Um . . ."

"Don't let this old woman alarm you," Ellie said, shooting Dana a look that said *Control yourself*. "But, she's right. You have leading-man looks. Which is good, because now you're the leading man. And I have no doubt you can perform this role."

Steve swallowed hard and asked, "Should we maybe shut down for a night or two, out of respect?"

Dana gave Steve a glare that suggested he was surely the stupidest person she had ever met. "We'll lose the theater if we do that," she said.

"But won't it look like we're profiting from his death?" he protested.

"We don't keep doing shows, the whole theater dies."

Ellie put her fingers to her temples and began to rub in slow, gentle circles. The discussion was driving her crazy. She wanted to go back home and crawl under her covers. Except she couldn't. She needed to manage her show. That realization gave her strength. The fuzzy gray wool that had flooded her ears a few minutes before began to recede. She started to feel normal again.

"Ellie," Dana said. "We need to make a decision about the rest of the show. You need to make it. It's your theater. Are we pausing the production out of respect for Reginald, or should I keep processing reservations?"

"We keep going," Ellie said without hesitation. "We'll issue a statement of some sort. I'll work on something. I'll talk to Reginald's widow, explain that we want to honor him somehow at tonight's performance."

"That should be a fun conversation," Dana said. Ellie nodded, thinking of her visit to Valerie and the haunting piano playing.

"Has anyone heard from Merilyn?" Ellie said.

"Not yet," Dana said.

"Okay," Ellie said. "I'll get on the phone with her. It's her show, so she should have a say as well. I don't know if she'll make it to the show tonight, but I'll clue her in and get her input. You"—she pointed at Dana—"keep processing those reservations. You," she said, pointing at Steve, "run *your* lines. I'm going to get a quick breath of fresh air."

Steve opened his mouth as if to protest one more time, but Dana cut him off. "Let's go, you. Times a'wastin'." She spun him by the shoulders and pushed him toward the house. "The stage is in there. Let's get to rehearsing."

Ellie watched them go, wondering if she was making the right decision. But what other choice did she have? She pushed through the lobby doors to go outside and leaned against the building, nearly hyperventilating.

* * *

Ellie headed home. She needed to find a place of quiet solitude. Too much was bouncing around her head, too many balls in the air. She needed a moment to sit quietly and organize them.

She got out of the car and headed up the walk to her front door. Ellie fumbled with her keys, looked up, and gave a little cry. She dropped the key ring and ticced violently for a few seconds.

In a dark corner of the porch, on what appeared to be a pickle bucket, sat her elderly neighbor.

"What're you doing, Judy?" *Nod-blink-blink.*

"Keeping out of the wind."

Ellie picked up her keys and flipped through them until she found the house key. *Nod-nod.* She put it in the lock.

"Did you need something, Judy?"

"Came by to bring you this." She stood and kicked the bucket gently with her shoe.

"Why did you bring me a bucket of pickles?" Ellie knew to limit the conversation to one direction so she could bring it to a halt and go inside her house.

"'Cause I thought you might like 'em. There's a lot of pickled things in there."

"I think there might be something pickled on my front porch," Ellie muttered to herself.

Judy continued. "Cukes, bell peppers, asparagus, just to name a few. Got my own pickling spice recipe too. These babies been fermenting for about six months. Probably good and ready. Perfect for summer."

"It's October."

"So what?"

Ellie blinked rapidly, then smiled. "Well, thank you, Judy. It's a very thoughtful gesture."

"You're welcome. I'll let you go. Say hi to Mike for me. And to that cute police chief."

"Judy!"

But Judy was already walking away. Ellie watched her go, then opened the door and went through. She closed the door behind her and leaned on it. Her body stayed still for a moment, then the tics started. She stood, back against the door, twitching, waiting for the feeling of completeness, as if she had crossed some invisible threshold and now her body was satisfied. In another thirty seconds, she crossed that elusive finish line, panting.

She thought about what Judy said. Sure, she and Bill were close, close in the way shared tragedy brings you close. But they had gone separate ways, led different lives, married different people. He had a family now, which was awesome. In truth, she was a little jealous. She and Mike had been trying for a few years, but so far, nothing.

She shook her head. No, not nothing. They had lots of fun in the trying. They kept a regular schedule, a rhythm her body demanded they act on, lest they lose the opportunity. And when it came to sex, her tics receded, sitting on the sidelines as the pleasure mounted. But nothing ever stuck, and after a year of unsuccessful attempts, the trying became less pleasurable. It became something they did, something they put in their planners and made sure to be home for, sex rendered rote.

And then, one night, a tic made an appearance. Only one, a head nod. But it was a tic nevertheless, and where one lurked, others congregated. That was a tough day for her, for each of them personally but also for their relationship. That became the day they decided they would stop putting pressure on themselves. If a baby happened, it happened. If not, so be it.

But, like so many other days when her tics and thoughts were constant, unwanted company, once she started thinking about children, she couldn't get the idea out of her head. Even though they decided to stop trying at such a regular and unromantic interval, she still thought about conceiving when she should have been enjoying herself. She realized she was getting in her own way.

She could hear Mike upstairs, talking on the phone. She thought again about the fun of spontaneity. She glanced at her watch. She wasn't meeting Bill for another hour.

She had time.

She went upstairs. At the top of the stairs, she kicked her shoes off. She walked slowly into Mike's office. He was finishing up, saying thanks and that he would talk to them later. He hung up the phone, turned, and saw Ellie in the doorway.

"Hi, babe. How'd it go?"

Ellie walked across the carpet, put her arms around Mike's neck, and kissed him slow and deep. He pulled back, brow furrowed but with half a smile on his face. He saw the sly smile she sometimes wore. He put his arms around her waist and leaned into the kiss.

* * *

After, Ellie pulled her jeans back on while Mike lounged in bed.

"That was nice," he said.

"Sounds like you mean unexpected." She smiled.

"That too."

"I actually came home to organize my thoughts, but I thought this would be a nicer way to spend the time."

"I like the way you think."

"And by being relaxed, and spontaneous, I thought, maybe—"

"You wouldn't put so much pressure on yourself?" Mike said.

"Something like that." She pulled her shirt over her head and leaned down to kiss Mike again. "I'm sorry to run."

"Meeting up with another man already."

She gave him a smile and another kiss, then left. Mike put his hands behind his head, leaned back on the pillow, and gazed at the ceiling for a while.

Chapter
Twenty-One

Around noon, Bill and Ellie walked into a biotech firm in Framingham and came up to the counter. Initially, Kyra couldn't identify them. The sun shone brightly into the front lobby, making anyone coming into the building little more than a silhouette. As they neared, their faces gained definition, and Kyra was stunned—but perhaps not surprised—to see Ellie Marlowe and another man. He looked familiar, but Kyra was still a little hungover and too tired to place him.

"Ellie. What brings you in here?"

"Hi, Kyra," Ellie said. *Nod-nod.* "You remember Bill Starlin, the Chief of Police of Avalon?"

Ellie saw the look of recognition come over Kyra.

That's where I know him from, Kyra thought. Her heart beat faster and she shifted nervously in her seat.

"We're following up on some stuff from last night," Bill said. "We have a couple of questions to ask you."

"Sounds awfully official." Kyra smiled. Bill didn't smile in return, so Ellie smiled for both of them, but weakly, followed by rapid blinking and a bobblehead movement. Kyra had almost grown used to Ellie's tics.

Kyra's defenses came up. "I already talked to one of your officers."

"I've read your statement. But we'd like to clarify a few things."

She looked at them. Ellie seemed uncomfortable, but she was trying not to look it. Bill remained unreadable.

"Am I in trouble?"

"No," Ellie cut in quickly. *Blink-grunt-blink.* "No, we're trying to piece some stuff together. I was talking with Valerie Thornton earlier today, and your name came up."

"My name? With Reginald's wife?"

"Widow," Bill corrected, which did little to put Kyra at ease. Ellie put a hand on Bill's arm, apparently a reminder to keep him from becoming too official. What surprised Kyra was how intimate the gesture seemed.

"Kyra," Ellie said. "Can you talk to us? Take a break? We figured this was around lunchtime."

"Um," Kyra's eyes flitted from side to side. The last thing she wanted to do was talk about Reginald or his death. The most positive thing about working with the man was his death. She would just as soon celebrate, put everything behind her, and move on.

Bill and Ellie stood there, looking at her.

"Yeah, okay. Sure." Kyra picked up the phone and pushed a button. She spoke into the phone briefly and hung up. A minute later, another employee appeared.

"You mind if I do lunch now?" Kyra asked the other woman, who looked at Ellie and Bill, and said, "Sure," drawing the word out. "How long you need?"

"Not long," Bill answered.

Kyra walked outside with Ellie and Bill. It was a beautiful day for a walk, sunny and crisp, the October chill nipping gently at their ears. Kyra tried not to think about having to talk with a police officer about the death of a man she despised.

"Kyra, first off, I want you to know Reginald's death was ruled a heart attack by the state police. However, that might change, pending the toxicology report," Bill said.

"Toxicology? You think he was poisoned?"

"Interesting," Bill said. "You jumped right to poisoned instead of accidental overdose?"

Kyra frowned. "Yeah, I guess I did. I've only ever heard of toxicology reports on cop shows, where they're always trying to solve a murder."

"It could very well be an accidental overdose."

"But we're not completely convinced." Ellie seemed hesitant to Kyra.

"What? Are you saying—" Kyra paused and continued in a whisper. "Are you saying you think that someone really did murder him?"

"That's what we're trying to figure out."

She stopped walking and looked at Ellie and Bill. She studied the expressions on their faces. This was bad.

"Kyra," Ellie said. "We're not here to accuse you. We're trying to understand the dynamics."

"Dynamics?"

Ellie waited expectantly, without twitching or grunting, which Kyra found unnerving. *Can she control it?* Kyra wondered. If so, jerking movements and guttural noises would be quite a way of getting attention.

Eventually, she couldn't take the silence.

"You mean the dynamics between the actors, is that right? Or maybe between me and Reginald?" There could be no mistaking the bitterness in the last part of her words.

"Was something going on between you and Reginald?"

"Ew, my God, no. You've seen the man. He was disgusting."

"Some women found him handsome."

"Yeah, women my grandmother's age. Yuck. No. Gross."

"Why might his wife think you and he had a relationship?" Bill asked.

"Is that what she said? What a miserable bitch."

"Then you've met her?" Bill said, nonplussed.

"Yeah. She came into rehearsal one day and yelled up a storm about something. I thought she was putting on a show at first. Right up until she got in my face."

"Valerie interrupted a rehearsal?" Ellie asked.

"Yeah. To yell at me. You were at that Worcester Cultural Council gala thing."

Bill spoke up. "Why did Valerie yell at you?"

"She had it in her stupid bottle-blond head that I was banging her husband."

"What did you say?"

"I told her I thought her husband was disgusting, and that if he was the last man on Earth, I'd screw a tree branch before I would screw him."

Ellie chose to overlook this. "Was Reginald there at the time?" she asked.

"Of course. And you should have seen the smile on his face. Loved every minute of it. Loved watching two women getting into a fight about him. As if I'd ever fight to get him." Kyra made a vomit sound to emphasize her point.

"Why would Valerie think you and Reginald were sleeping together?" Bill asked.

"Knowing him, he probably told her he was. Or if he didn't tell her outright, he probably dropped all kinds of hints."

"To boost his ego?"

"Exactly."

"Kyra," Ellie said, taking the younger woman by the arms. "Why didn't you tell me? I would have done something about him. I know you guys had issues with Reginald, but I didn't know it was this bad."

"It was worse than that," Kyra said.

"What do you mean?" Bill said.

Kyra bit her lip and didn't answer. She looked away, and Ellie saw tears forming in her eyes. Bill glanced from Kyra to Ellie, his face questioning. Kyra was an actor, after all. But the tears seemed real.

"Kyra," she said. "Did something happen?"

Kyra took a deep breath that rattled in her chest. She shook her head and closed her eyes, and the tears overflowed. She wiped at her cheeks with the cuff of her blouse sleeve.

"You remember the day when Reginald came in with a bandage on his face?"

Ellie nodded. "He said it was the cat."

"You talked to Valerie?"

"Yes."

"At her house?"

"Yes, but—"

"You see a cat?"

It took Ellie a moment to realize what Kyra was saying. Bill beat her to it.

"What happened?" he asked, gently.

Kyra wrung her hands. The tears flowed freely now, and she hated herself for losing control like this. She thought maybe she shouldn't be talking about this, that it would only make her appear guiltier than she already did. But she didn't care. She wanted them to know she hurt him, that you don't do that to her and get off scot-free. In a way, she was proud.

"After rehearsal one night, I was packing up my stuff, which I had stashed downstairs. Reginald came down after me. We were alone. Everybody had left except Merilyn, who was in no shape to help. Besides, she was upstairs and wouldn't have heard me. Reginald comes over and corners me. Starts saying how pretty I am, how *alluring*. He used that word, 'alluring.' If I never hear it again, I'll die happy. I'm getting creeped out, so I say thank you and try to finish and get out of there as fast as I can. But he corners me and starts telling me he knows I like him, that I think he's sexy. As if I could think that. And then he's on me. Groping, kissing, his hands were everywhere. For an old guy, he's fast and strong when he's horny. And that's when I scratched him."

"The Band-Aids," Ellie said. Her body began to ache, desperate to tic, to run free with twitches, grunts, and involuntary movements. She held them back.

"He told everybody at the next rehearsal that his cat scratched him. I don't know if anyone believed that, but that's what he said."

Bill crossed his arms and stared at his shoes in thought. He looked up again. "I wish you had come to me with this, or one of my officers. You could have filed charges. At the very least, we would have pulled him into the station for a chat."

"I didn't want to make waves. I just wanted to do the show and be done. And I didn't want anyone to know about it."

"This isn't the kind of stuff you should let go, Kyra," Bill said. "It's assault. Sexual assault."

Kyra scoffed. "It's he said-she said, no matter what."

"Sometimes pressing charges scares people enough to make them behave themselves."

Kyra's face showed her doubt, and she kept wiping tears away with her cuff.

"Your body is yours, and not someone else's," Ellie said. Her own body begged to differ, like a cardboard dam trying to hold back the Nile. "You don't have to take that kind of thing from people. I am so sorry this happened to you."

Kyra sighed and nodded.

"Did he ever try again?" Ellie asked, concerned.

"No," Kyra said, "but he just got nastier and nastier—the things he said, how he spoke to me." At this point, she let go and sobbed into her hands. Ellie moved over and rubbed her shoulders and murmured to her.

She caught Bill's eye over Kyra's shoulders. This all had the ring of truth, but it also meant that Kyra had a motive.

Holding, holding.

The pressure, the pressure.

Ellie fought to tamp it down.

Kyra's tears eventually dried. Her face was pale, her mouth shut tight, her lips a bloodless line across her face. "Are we done?"

"Yes. Unless you have anything else you want to tell us," Bill said.

"I have to get back to work." She pushed past them and stomped toward the office building. She paused, turned back, and said, "You should talk to Jerry."

"Why?" Ellie said.

"Because he was the one who actually told Reginald he was going to kill him." She turned back and continued walking away.

Chapter
Twenty-Two

"Do you believe her?" Bill asked.

Without pause, Ellie said, "Yes, I do."

She sat in the passenger's seat of Bill's cruiser, staring out the windshield. After Kyra walked away, Ellie let the stranglehold on her tics go, and twitched and convulsed and made clicking and grunting noises all the way back to the car. She had explained to Bill long ago that she could hold her tics in for only so long. Eventually, they would have their way with her, and she simply had to allow it.

She rolled down the window, and the wind pulled her hair in all different directions.

Sometimes when Bill looked at Ellie, he felt a slight pang as well as curiosity. What if he had stayed home instead of joining the army? They might have dated eventually, though he was five years older. Five years is a sizable difference at fourteen and nineteen. But as they moved into their twenties, the difference became less pronounced.

Other times, he remembered what she was like as a little girl, running around with Ava, the two of them inseparable, until—

There it was again. He pushed the thought out of his head. All these years later, it remained too painful for him to focus on. His sister's death caused him to join the army. He essentially ran away from home. From the pain. Leaving his parents to grieve the loss of their

110

daughter, transplanting their grief into fear for the safety of their son. In his second tour in the desert, it struck him how selfish he had been and how much his parents probably needed him just as he bailed on them. Like a coward. He was overseas when his mom passed away. And now his dad had lucid days, but mostly he didn't remember he even had children.

He squeezed his left hand into a fist, fingernails digging in his palm to force him to focus on the problem in front of him. Not the past.

"You don't think she's telling the truth?" Ellie said.

"I think she's telling the truth about Reginald's assault on her. But was there more?" He shrugged.

"Where does that leave us?"

Bill shrugged and rubbed his chin with his left hand, the half-moon dents his fingernails had made sensitive to the stubble. He brought the unmarked car through the center of town, a town he'd explored every inch of since elementary school. Avalon slid past the windows at thirty miles per hour, fast enough to get somewhere but slow enough to enjoy the view.

Avalon had been described in a lot of ways: quaint, picturesque, quintessential, but also rural, backward, and the boonies. The town exuded charm with its old buildings and new businesses. He had felt blessed when the selectmen hired him as Chief of Police, his hiring sandwiched between getting married and putting his father in a home. To him, it was a changing of the guard, the next generation taking over for the previous one. He never wanted to let the town down.

"I think we keep asking questions. If we talk to everybody, we may uncover some ugly secrets, but at least we'll know the truth behind his death."

He pulled into the police station lot where Ellie had left her car.

"So, what do we do next?" she asked.

"I need to check in with Turner to see how the background checks are going and put in a call to the ME to see when the tox screen comes back." He sighed. "In the meantime, I have an unpleasant house call to make to the widow to see if I can get her permission for a full private autopsy. Just in case."

Ellie winced. "Good luck."

"And you," he said, "have a show to prepare for this evening."

"I do. Steve is going on for Reginald. Right now, he's trying to make sure he knows all the blocking and every line."

"Sound like a lot of pressure."

"Actually, the most dangerous thing for him will be Dana chasing him around with a pincushion," she said with a wan smile. "She'll be trying to alter some of the costumes so they fit."

She drove away, winding her way back through town. When she passed Brewed Awakenings, the local coffee shop, she saw a man sitting outside at one of the patio tables. He sipped from a mug radiating steam and thumbed through a newspaper. When Ellie saw the newspaper, an idea clicked into place. She turned the car around and took the road out of town, toward Worcester.

Chapter
Twenty-Three

The theater reviewer for the Worcester *Telegram & Gazette* sat back in his chair, put his hands behind his head, and stared at his computer screen. Paul Koehler closed his eyes for a moment and replayed some of the key moments from the previous day's show in his head. A tiny community theater forty-five minutes northwest of Worcester had put on *Jesus Christ Superstar*. They jumped on the rights after a live broadcast of the same show on TV, no doubt hoping to capitalize on the sudden increased interest. But one of the things he'd learned over the years of reviewing shows was that just because you could obtain the rights to do a show doesn't mean you should put it on.

Reviewing community theater productions was only one of the things Paul did for the *T & G*. In this dwindling age of print circulation and money, newsrooms asked more and more from their staffs. Weekday circulation at the *T & G* had fallen from roughly a hundred thousand in 1999 to approximately twenty-two thousand. Everyone got marching orders to double or triple their reporting responsibilities. As one of the primary arts editors, he covered community theaters, local bands, art openings, museum exhibits, as well as managed incoming book and movie reviews by freelancers. It kept him busy and gainfully employed, but sometimes he wished he could take a deep breath and hit Pause. Reviewing *Jesus Christ Superstar* was a perfect example. He needed to come up with something to say, and he wanted to be supportive of local theater, even with significantly flawed productions, but he had to spin the review just so. At the moment, the words eluded him.

The phone on his desk rang, and Paul opened his eyes and sat forward to answer, lifting the old black handset. "Paul Koehler."

"Mr. Koehler?" It was Janice, the woman who ran the front desk. "There's someone to see you. Mrs. Ellie Marlowe."

"Send her up."

The *T & G* offices were on the fifth floor of the Mercantile Center building on Front Street, a tower rising nineteen stories above Worcester. In the city of one hundred thousand people, it was the third tallest building in the skyline. Despite the paper's name being emblazoned on the top of the building, the actual staff occupied only one floor of the building, and even then, it did not take up the entire floor.

The elevator dinged, and Paul rose from his desk and walked toward the elevator bank as one of the doors slid open. A woman stepped out—a brunette in her thirties, statuesque and stunning. Paul always appreciated how beautiful Ellie Marlowe looked ever since he met her at the first show she produced at Kaleidoscope. The show itself underwhelmed, a black box version of *The Sound of Music*, chosen to draw a crowd. The production told everyone Kaleidoscope was back and better than ever, not afraid to try big things. And *The Sound of Music* was a big show, with lots of actors, singers, and children.

Paul had squirmed his way through the performance, though the audience around him loved it. He met Ellie after the show and talked with her a bit, not revealing his role at the *T & G*. He had been genuinely impressed by her, if not a little smitten. He went out of his way to say something nice about the show and gave it two stars, at least one more than it deserved.

The Last Line

Two years later, Ellie put the name to the face. She could have been angry that he deceived her, but instead, she chose to understand the tough position he was in. Navigating the dynamics of the theater community in the greater Worcester area and being fair and honest in his reviews without trashing theaters or performers required a delicate balance. She put a hand on his arm and said she appreciated what he did for their community. At that moment, he sprang past smitten and fell hopelessly in love with her, despite being nearly double her age.

He stopped reviewing her shows, choosing to pass them to another staff writer. But he still came to Kaleidoscope to show his support, and to talk with Ellie afterward.

That she was here now he found both strange and exciting.

"Ellie, my goodness," he said, hugging her. "What good fortune brings you to my dominion?"

"Paul," she said with a smile. "I'm here to talk."

"Be still, my beating heart. Be gentle. I have a pacemaker."

"I'll keep it clean, I promise."

"You may feel at liberty to break your promise at any point."

He led her back to his desk, pulled up a chair from an unoccupied desk, and offered it to her with a gesture. She sat first, and he followed suit, his hands twined together and resting in his lap. He watched her head bob involuntarily for a few seconds, followed by some exaggerated eye blinks. *Something is bothering her,* he thought.

"How are they treating you these days?" Ellie asked.

Paul shrugged. "I'm still around. More than I can say for a lot of folks who used to be here."

"The paper still making cuts?"

"Paper cuts." He smiled. "Funny." His tone changed. "I figure I'm safe for a bit longer. You lay off one of the only persons of color on the staff, you appear to have a racial problem."

"Instead, they'll just make life difficult until you resign?"

He nodded. "You catch on quick."

His eyes locked on her face, and his balding head gleamed under the overhead florescent lights.

"So, tell me, what do you want to talk about?"

She leaned in conspiratorially, though the floor was mostly empty. The news staff was out following up on local items, city hall stuff, or local police blotter items. The sports staff wouldn't start hammering out copy until the games ended in the evening.

Ellie, voice low, ticced twice, then said, "You must have heard what happened at the theater last night."

Paul nodded. "I did. Tragic, really."

"You knew Reginald, right?"

"Oh, yes, for many years. Way back."

"How far?"

"Oh, goodness, let's see. Back to New York City, at least. Trying to remember if I knew him before that. He was a local boy who headed south to make his name in the Big Apple."

"What can you tell me about him back then?" she said.

"When he moved to New York City?"

Blink-blink-blink. "About his past in general."

"What would his past have to do with his death?" Ellie didn't answer for a beat, and Paul filled in the empty space. "Wait," Paul whispered harshly, "are you saying Reginald's death was, shall we say, not accidental?"

"I don't know. Right now the official cause is a heart attack."

"That's what I heard. Collapsed right there onstage."

"He did. But some things feel weird about it. It may have been drug induced.."

"Wouldn't that be ironic?" Paul chuckled mirthlessly. "Reginald's final scene is an actual death scene. A final bit of stagecraft."

Ellie nodded. "And listen, you can't go spreading this around. I'm asking people some questions to make sure we cover all our bases."

"We?"

Ellie kicked herself mentally—she didn't want to mention Bill's near-official interest—and ticced her frustration. "Well," she said slowly, "two of us who are not happy with how this went down."

He noticed that she didn't say who, but he let that go and went straight to the point. "If it's suspicious, why isn't the state investigating?"

"They took a pass. They believe it's medical. We're following up on our own. And I decided to dig into Reginald's past a little more. That's where you come in."

Paul untangled his hands and raised them in a gesture that was nearly a shrug. It told Ellie little, other than Paul would play the innocent with her.

"What can I say, Ellie? I didn't know him very well. More than a few of us local boys went to New York City at that time, the heady days of the seventies. Reginald was older than I by a good decade. I knew him by reputation more than anything else. We met at parties occasionally, but we were never what you might call close."

"Any idea why he left New York?" *Grunt-grunt.*

Again, he gave an almost-shrug with his hands. "Other than a lack of success?"

"I thought he was successful in New York."

Paul gave her a look as if asking how naive could she be. "Why would anyone successful in a grand city like the Big Apple leave such a wondrous place and return here?"

"Paul," she said, "I'm trying to figure out what happened. Nothing about Reginald struck me as a pill popper. This whole thing has set my little hairs on edge."

"What kind of pills?"

"He had a bottle of Valium." *Nod-nod. Blink.*

"You checked with his doctor?"

"I haven't. Since it's not listed as a wrongful death, I don't know if the doctor will tell us anything."

"Yet you don't think this was an medical emergency. Or even an accidental overdose."

"I can't say it wasn't either. A third option is suicide. Did Reginald ever strike you as the type to kill himself?"

"Hardly."

"You see my dilemma."

Paul leaned back in his chair and sighed. "If it wasn't an accident, and he was poisoned, you got a real-life *Curtains* on your hands, don't you?" he said.

"I do," Ellie agreed. *Grunt.*

He paused for a moment before answering. "I wish I could help you, Ellie, I really do. But I don't know much about Reginald's past, other than he was born and raised in Worcester, left the city, and eventually came back. Not unlike myself. And as far as his past is concerned, nothing I can think of would lead to him being murdered. At least, nothing outside of him being a monstrous prick."

Ellie sighed and stood. "Okay. Thanks, Paul." She didn't sound like she meant it. "If you change your mind and decide to talk about what you don't want to talk about, give me a call."

Paul's jaw dropped open. He tried to come up with a witty response, but Ellie was already stepping into an elevator.

The truth was, he and Reginald had known many of the same people in New York City, and most hadn't cared for the man. Reginald had been arrogant before going to New York, and downright detestable since returning. If coerced, Paul would probably admit he didn't mind that Reginald was dead. Yes, there were things he could tell Ellie, but sometimes the past should stay in the past. If he started talking, other people's secrets might come out, things better left uncovered.

Chapter Twenty-Four

Bill was back at the station, dealing with paperwork that was part of the job. He hated paperwork, but if nothing else, he had to sign off on timesheets. When Turner ducked his head into Bill's office, Bill felt relieved to have an excuse to postpone the administrative stuff.

"Got a sec?" Turner said. He was holding a sheet of paper.

"Sure. What's up?"

"You'll love this one."

Bill sat back in his chair. From Turner's tone, he expected that he would most definitely not love this one.

"Finished the criminal background checks on all the names you gave me. There was a recent criminal complaint against one Gerald Moynihan, the same Jerry in the show at Kaleidoscope. An assault complaint. Apparently, Jerry punched somebody."

"Who'd he hit?" Bill asked.

Turner handed the sheet of paper to Bill. "Reginald Thornton IV."

Bill jolted forward, took the paper and scanned it, then looked up at Turner with a hopeful expression.

"Turner, where can I find Mr. Moynihan at this moment?"

* * *

Jerry Moynihan was packing up his messenger bag and getting ready to head out to an appointment when a knock at his office door made him jump. Agnes, the office admin, stood in the doorway. Someone lingered behind her.

"Jerry? There's someone here to see you."

"Me?" He rarely got people coming in to see him. Mostly, he did his work over the phone or in the field. Which was fine. Offstage, Jerry wasn't much of a people person.

Agnes stepped aside, and Bill stepped into the office. He stuck out his hand.

"Jerry? Bill Starlin, Chief of Police in Avalon. I don't know that we met in the craziness last night."

Jerry tentatively took Bill's offered hand.

"I don't think we did," Jerry said. "I talked to one of your officers, slim guy, short hair. Can't remember his name."

"Detective Milton."

"No, that's not it. It started with a T."

"Turner?"

"Yes," Jerry said. "That's the one."

"That's his full name. Detective Turner Milton."

"Oh. Well, I have to say, this is a surprise. Your detective indicated he'd call me to arrange for me to come in and give a statement about last night."

"Do you need anything else?" Agnes asked. Jerry shook his head, and Agnes went back to her desk by the front door.

"Do you have a few minutes to talk to me now?" Bill asked.

"Only a few. I'm heading out for an appraisal."

"You work as an appraiser for an insurance company, is that right?"

Jerry nodded. "Fender benders keep me busy."

"Us too," Bill said with a smile.

"This is about Reginald's death, I assume?"

"It is."

"What's the word on that?" Jerry asked.

"The word is that he's dead, and the cause appears to be a heart attack, but we're also looking into possible respiratory failure caused by an overdose of a prescription med. But that is still to be determined." Bill watched Jerry carefully as he spoke.

Jerry shrugged as if to say, *oh well.* "Can't say I'm sorry. He was . . ." He didn't finish, so Bill finished for him.

"An asshole?"

"I was going to say something like 'difficult,' but yeah. Asshole fits."

"Do you think he got what he deserved?"

"Does anybody deserve a heart attack?"

"I meant more broadly," Bill said. "Do you think he deserved to die?"

Jerry's head tilted to one side, and his eyebrows went up.

"I'm sorry, Chief. Why are you here?"

Bill waited a moment. He let the silence edge toward uncomfortable before continuing. Jerry watched him.

"Jerry," Bill said. "Did you get into a physical altercation with Reginald?"

The question flustered Jerry, who shifted in his seat and turned red around the tight collar of his shirt. He straightened and smoothed out his tie before answering.

"Why would you ask me that?"

"We're running background checks on all the cast and crew. Reginald made a complaint against you for assault."

Jerry shifted again as Bill waited a beat before continuing.

"You want to tell me about it?" Bill asked.

"Not particularly," Jerry said. He no longer held Bill's eyes, looking down at his hands now.

Bill waited.

Jerry smoothed his tie once more. His leg started bouncing up and down.

"I'm just trying to fit puzzle pieces into a picture, Jerry. Why'd you hit him?"

Jerry shifted in his chair again. He started to stand, reconsidered, and sat down again. "Do you know what that man is like?"

"Was," Bill corrected.

Jerry squirmed uncomfortably but didn't take the bait. "You hadn't met Reginald before, had you, Chief? You never saw it. You have no idea how awful he was."

Bill kept his eyes on Jerry. "I'm learning more and more each day."

"Awful doesn't begin to describe it. He was miserable. To everyone. He thought he was God's gift to acting. Which he wasn't." Jerry stopped abruptly, but it seemed like he wanted to say something else. He finally said, "I will admit he was a very good actor, though."

"Ellie has told me the whole cast is very good."

Jerry's smile was wan.

"He had a magnetic charm. Sometimes." Jerry almost sounded wistful now. "When he turned it on, he was unstoppable. Do you know, I almost asked him for an autograph? Honest to God. The first time I met him. I had seen him perform before, and followed his career. But then he opened his mouth. What a prick." He practically spat the last word.

Bill remained impassive. "Jerry, can you tell me anything about Reginald's death?"

"He terrorized more people than just me. Do you know he tried to force himself on Kyra one night? You should talk with her."

Bill was careful to not show a reaction. "Miss Bennett is on our list to speak to," he said. He watched Jerry closely, gauging the man's reactions. Jerry seemed to be genuinely fond of Kyra, almost protective.

"He tried to sexually assault Kyra in a closet in the basement. I wanted to kill him for that," Jerry said. "But of course I didn't. Because I'm not a murderer."

A thought hit Bill. It might explain a few things. "Jerry, are you and Kyra dating?"

"What?" *Fidget, fidget, shift, shift.* "Dating? Of course not. She's at least fifteen years younger than I am."

"Age is just a number, and lots of people have relationships with people whose age difference spans a decade. Or more."

"Not me." Jerry opened his mouth, and Bill thought he wanted to say more, but he closed it again.

Bill tread cautiously. "Fair to say, though, you are fond of her? Not necessarily romantically," he added as Jerry was about to protest. "More like in a protective manner. Like you grew fond of her as a person, and you want to protect her."

Jerry looked everywhere but at Bill. "I would consider her a friend," he said at last.

"And as a friend, if she were hurt in some way, or put in danger, you would want to protect her. As a friend."

"That's what friends do. They stick up for each other."

"And when you learned Reginald tried to force himself on her, you bristled. Why wouldn't you? Like you said, you wanted to kill him for hurting her. And as a friend, you saw the need to defend her."

"And perhaps," Jerry added acidly, "before I blew up at him, he bragged about already 'having' her, as he put it, in front of everyone, though we all knew he was lying. You could see the disgust on her face. The horror and revulsion. And that fat prick grinned the entire time. So possibly he and I had words, and possibly he was quicker with words than I am, so perhaps all I could do was tell him I would kill him if he ever went near her again."

"Did Kyra storm out before you did?"

"Yes. I followed her to comfort her, yelling at Reginald as I went. When I went back inside, he was laughing. I became so enraged, I hauled off and punched him. Right in the side of the head. Know what he did? He looked up at me and smiled. A nasty, cruel smile, like this was what he'd been going for, and now he could ruin my life."

Bill rubbed his chin in thought. Multiple people appeared to have a reason for wanting Reginald dead.

Jerry's agitation final got the better of him. He stood and shouldered his bag.

"I'm sorry to cut this short, Chief, but I really have to go. I have some appraisals to finish today and then I have to be at the theater for call. I have no idea how we'll go on tonight, but if I know Merilyn, she'll find a way."

Bill stepped out of his way and watched Jerry go.

What a mess this whole thing is, he thought.

Chapter
Twenty-Five

Bill spent his afternoon digging through online records for each of the cast and crew. He trusted Turner's research, but he needed to see it all for himself. He was in the middle of reading about Merilyn when his phone rang.

"Chief Starlin."

"Bill? Jimmy Avery."

Bill sat back slowly in his chair. The nasally voice with the underlying disdain—Mass State Police Detective James Avery, a former coworker from Bill's time with the MSP. A flash from the past, and not a good one. Bill knew that this conversation would not be fun.

"Jim," Bill said, trying to sound neutral. "To what do I owe the pleasure?"

"Well, I called to give you some bad news."

"Bad news."

"Yeah. You saw Phelps last night, right?"

Bill's heart sank. The only reason Jim would be calling instead of Chuck Phelps would be to throw cold water in Bill's face. No love lost between them. Jim would always blame Bill for getting their colleagues tossed from the force because of the overtime scam five or six years ago. Jim hadn't been scamming, but he had buddies that were, and wouldn't roll over on them. Bill had a harder stance. You do bad shit, you suffer whatever consequences you got coming to you.

Jim was a big part of the pressure applied on Bill before he decided to quit the MSP. And the only reason Jim would be the one calling was to twist the knife.

And it almost certainly meant Reginald's death would not be reconsidered.

"Yes, Phelps came out last night," Bill answered. "Felt like there might be some follow-up work for him to do."

"But he agreed with the EMTs at the scene. Heart attack. Start and end."

"True, he did, but I hoped he might reconsider—"

"Did you think we'd simply say yes because this time you said pretty please?"

"We have some concerns," Bill started.

"Good for you. But this doesn't rise to the level of investigation. I've read the report. Nothing at the scene indicates homicide. I know you didn't last long as a state dick, but if you had some more experience, maybe you'd see that."

"Jim—"

"We're not adding a case just 'cause you asked nicely."

Bill closed his eyes and brought his free hand to the bridge of his nose and massaged it. He'd known the moment he picked up the phone and Jim Avery's voice came buzzing down from the other end that the case had been shit-canned.

"Sure," Bill said. "There are clearance rates to consider."

"I don't think I like what you're implying."

"Hey, Jim," Bill said, smothering his rage. "Been great catching up. But listen, I gotta go."

Before Avery could answer, Bill slammed the phone down in its cradle.

He sat at his desk for a full ten minutes, deep breaths in and out of his nose, trying to calm his fury. He should call it a night, but needed to make a stop first. He rubbed his eyes with the heels of his hands.

When his cell phone chirped, he considered ignoring it, but duty got the better of him.

"Chief, it's Turner."

"What news do you have for me, Turner?"

"Not much, I'm afraid. I went to Clark Brothers. They took possession of the body from the state. Took another look, but there wasn't much to find. I asked the guys here if anything appeared off to them, and they said no. They couched it with the usual 'we're not experts' baloney, but they know their stuff. If the body showed signs of bruising or something, like if pills were forced down his throat, they'd notice the bruise marks."

"And be required to report them to the state."

"Exactly."

Bill added this to his notes.

"Funeral or cremation?" he asked.

"Cremation. The body will be headed out tomorrow."

A furrow in Bill's forehead appeared as he frowned. Tomorrow. Not a lot of time. If they wanted to get anything from the body, a private autopsy was the way to go. If they could get consent.

"Anything else you need from me out here, Chief?"

"I think that's it for today, Turner, thanks."

"What do you want to do next?"

"I'm going to speak with the widow."

"You going to try to convince her to agree to an autopsy?"

"I'm going to give it the old college try."

"I don't expect that to fly." Turner chuckled.

Bill shrugged. He knew that the town selectmen wouldn't look kindly on the Chief of Police using part of the department budget to fund a private autopsy for a person who, for all appearances, simply had a cardiac event. "Money is a secondary problem. First, I have to convince the widow an autopsy is necessary before we can figure out the funding. No signature, no scalpel."

"Let me know if I can help," Turner said. "In the meantime, I have a complaint to take care of about someone letting out the Jansons' pig every couple of nights."

Bill smiled and shook his head. *Small-town living.*

"Well, you better get on that, Turner. I'd hate for this department to be accused of not caring about the residents' pigs."

Turner laughed and ended the call.

Bill sat in his chair, lost in thought for a few minutes. It had been a long day, following a long night. His exhaustion was nearly absolute, and he wanted to go home, eat some dinner, and crash. But if he didn't push on this case—even though there was no formal case—he knew it would fade away to nothingness, leaving regret in his soul.

He thought briefly of Robert Frost. *Yeah,* he thought. *I got miles to go before I sleep, too.*

He picked up the phone and dialed his buddy at the lab where the toxicology analysis would be done. It was answered on the first ring.

"Jeremy Harding."

"Jer. Bill Starlin."

Jeremy chuckled. "I was just thinking to myself, Bill hasn't called yet, he must be developing some patience in his old age."

"Middle age, bozo. And having kids will definitely teach you patience."

"Don't I know it. I just put my last one through college."

"Listen, I don't mean to push, but I could really use some good news on that toxicology report."

"Well, I guess it's a good news/bad news situation."

Bill closed his eyes. "Let's have the bad news first."

"Tox screen isn't done, and won't be for at least another week."

"What's the good news?"

Bill thought he could hear the smile in Jeremy's voice when he said, "We're moving on to liquid chromatography with your sample."

Bill's head came up. "Officially?"

"Lord, no," Jeremy laughed. "I'd like to keep my job. Totally off the record. But yeah, the gas chromatography picked up a positive for substance, so your sample has been passed on to the liquid chromatography analysis to separate the pieces and figure out what they are."

Bill's heart raced. Ellie's hunch was right. Something *had* been off with Reginald.

"Which means. . ."

"Which means your vic had drugs in his system."

Bill told Jeremy he owed him a good bottle of scotch, and hung up the phone. He leaned forward, snatched his keys from his desk, and walked out of the office. He checked in on his dispatcher, which he did every night before leaving. Ruthie Cardoza was on the night shift.

"Headed home, Chief?"

"Got a stop to make first."

She picked up a piece of paper from her desk and handed it to Bill.

"Margot asked me to give this to you. Said you asked her to draft it, but then she couldn't find you."

Bill took the paper, scanned it, and nodded. It was exactly what he was looking for, and just in time for his next stop. He folded the paper and tucked it into the back pocket of his jeans.

He left the building, climbed into his car, and pulled out of the police station lot. He headed out of town, down along Route 70, traveling two towns up toward Clifton. He plugged the address into his phone, the GPS app guiding him through the small-town roads. Twenty minutes after he'd left the station, he pulled into the driveway of the Thornton house.

Bill sat in his car in the driveway for a few moments, taking slow, deep breaths and quieting his heart rate. He got out of his car, walked up the perfectly laid slate walkway to the front door, rang the bell, then knocked for good measure. When he received no answer, he repeated both. From inside, he could hear movement. The door opened. An older woman, striking and handsome, stood on the other side.

"May I help you?"

"Mrs. Thornton? I'm Bill Starlin, Chief of Police in Avalon. Do you have a minute?"

Valerie looked over her shoulder, turned back, and said, "Certainly. Come in." She opened the door wider and stepped to the side. Bill entered, eyes sharp and appraising. The home was lovely and clean, if perhaps a bit sterile. Then again, compared to the chaos of his own home, any home felt sterile.

But why the glance over the shoulder?

"What can I do for you, Chief?"

"I spoke with the Massachusetts State Police again this afternoon. I asked them to reconsider investigating your husband's death. They declined. They feel it was a medical incident, and there's not enough to warrant an investigation."

"Meaning?"

"Meaning they don't believe it was anything other than a heart attack."

She sat slowly and gently on a chair that looked like it was more for decoration than sitting. She gazed up at him, her eyes scrunched and suspicious. "And what do you believe, Chief?"

Bill answered carefully. "I think this is something that should be investigated further. There isn't enough evidence to convince the state police or the medical examiner to devote resources to it. Both are stretched for time and money, so something presenting as a heart attack won't get a closer look. But I have unofficial confirmation that there were drugs in your husband's system."

"Unofficial?"

"The toxicology analysis won't be complete for at least another week. However, the lab doing the analysis has moved on to a secondary test. It's a test they run only if the first test shows a positive."

She frowned. "Do you know what kind of drugs they found in Reginald's system?"

"That's what the next test will tell us."

Valerie took a deep breath and dabbed a Kleenex at the corners of her eyes. Bill missed the moment she pulled one from her pocket. Like magic, one moment her hands were empty, then abracadabra, the tissue appeared. He wondered whether she kept it up her sleeve, like his grandmother used to.

He said, "Do you think your husband was a habitual drug user, or that he accidentally took too many Valium?"

He looked at the widow and she looked at him, long and hard. Finally, she shook her head. "No," she said. "I do not. Nor do I think he would do so deliberately."

"I'd like to know definitively what killed your husband, and the best place to start is with an autopsy."

"The state won't do one now?"

Bill shook his head. "I was hoping you would sign a release allowing the town to arrange for a private autopsy to figure out the cause of death." He pulled out the paper Ruthie had given him, unfolded it, and handed it to Valerie.

She read through the paper slowly, finished, and looked up at him. Her eyes were bright and furious. "You want my permission to let some person with a scalpel and bone saw cut into my husband?"

Bill felt a twinge of nervousness. "Not how I would have chosen to put it," he said, "but essentially, yes. A highly trained man or woman who would treat your husband's body carefully and do what is necessary to determine what killed him."

Valerie returned to the paper, her eyes flicking back and forth as she read. She folded it back up and handed it back to Bill. "No."

"No?"

"No," Valerie repeated.

Bill fumbled around for words until he managed to say, "Do you mind me asking why not?"

"I do."

This time his recovery wasn't as quick. "Mrs. Thornton, I might not have explained this well. You see—"

"Are you going to—what's the term?—'mansplain' this to me?"

"No. I wanted to see if I made myself clear."

"You did. I understand it perfectly well, Chief Starlin. The state police have decided Reginald's death doesn't meet the criteria to be classified as suspicious, and as such, they will not be performing an autopsy. But you suspect they may be wrong and would like an autopsy done, yet you can't without my permission. Which I don't give. Do I understand you correctly?"

Bill's face reddened, but he kept his voice cool. "You do. And you don't owe me, or anyone, an explanation for your decision. But I'm going to ask for one, because if nothing else, I'm intensely curious and, admittedly, surprised."

"Curiosity killed the cat."

"The cat wasn't murdered."

Valerie pursed her lips and folded her hands together. Still seated on the decorative chair in the foyer, she struck Bill as someone used to getting her way. The word "regal" came to mind. "Chief, what do you think an autopsy will tell you?"

"Cause of death, and hopefully—"

"Let's say you are right. You find evidence of benzodiazepine and some other substance. What exactly will that tell you? Will it tell you who killed him? Will it give you any more information than you have right now? Knowing the substances will not identify the sources, unless my research is very much mistaken. All it will do is validate your guesswork. You don't need to cut into my husband to confirm what you think you already know."

"If we don't confirm the cause of death, we'll never—"

"You assume this was a murder. But you must also admit you could be wrong."

She said this with such final assuredness Bill thought she must know more than she let on. As if her husband was killed, but she either didn't care, suspected who did it and wanted to protect them—or was herself involved in his death. Something was wrong here.

From deeper in the house came a noise, the kind of sound that might be made by a person moving about.

"Mrs. Thornton, is there someone else in the house?"

"No."

"Sounds like there is."

"It's the cat."

She was playing with him, and he knew it. "Mind if I have a look around?"

Without raising her voice, she said, "I most certainly do. If you feel the need to search my house, I will insist that you return with a warrant."

Bill observed her carefully as she spoke, but she revealed nothing. Finally, he said, "Mrs. Thornton, do you know something about Reginald's death you are not telling me?"

Valerie Thornton rose from her chair and opened the front door. "Good evening, Chief. Thank you for making the trip."

Chapter
Twenty-Six

On his way home, he called Ellie and told her about his call with Jim Avery, his call with Jeremy Harding, what he asked Valerie Thornton, and what her response had been, including the last part of the conversation, almost verbatim, and the noise inside the house.

"You think she was covering for someone?" Ellie said.

"Felt like it."

"Well, maybe the ME will step in now that you know Reginald had some level of drugs in his system."

"That's not official yet." He sighed. "I'm going to call it a day and start again tomorrow."

"I've got a show to stage, so I have to run. I'll call you in the morning."

"Okay."

He hung up the phone and kept driving until he reached the center of town. He stopped for a red light, his eyes roving around the town center, the liquor store on the corner, and the post office on the opposite corner. Arthur's, the best restaurant in town, was in the brick building on the other side of the street, and across from it was a woman's clothing boutique. He knew all the proprietors and liked them all. All of this within a stone's throw of Worcester.

His face changed, and he caught the reflection in the rearview mirror. A cloud had fallen on Avalon, on this town he loved. He wished he could take a deep breath and blow it away.

He turned and drove along the side streets, winding through the neighborhoods lined with Bradford pear trees and dogwoods, until he came to his home. It was a modest little house, what the real estate agent had described as a California bungalow. He didn't know what that meant, nor did he care. All he knew was he loved his house and had never felt more at home than he did now.

Inside Bill was greeted by the usual chaos. His wife, Darlene, was yelling at their son, Aiden, to stop running through the house chasing the dog, while their daughter, Emma, was crying because Aiden had broken her doll. The detritus of the children's school day was strewn in the foyer: coats fallen off pegs, shoes abandoned in the middle of the floor, backpacks unzipped and papers falling out. Bill stood for a moment by the door, eyes closed, listening to the noise, and smiled. Then he came into the house, bellowing in the low, deep voice he used when pretending to be a giant: *"What's all this noise?"*

Both children ran over and gave him a hug. Darlene looked on, a little annoyed at how easy it was for Bill to get the kids to simmer down. Both kids tried to be the one to tell their father about their day, and the effect was that they each told a little piece before being cut off by the other like verbal ping-pong. When they finished, he hugged them again and shooed them off to go wash their hands before dinner.

He came into the kitchen, the smell of sauce, cheese, and meat bubbling in lasagna washing over him and filling him with gladness. He kissed his wife on the cheek and said, "Hello, beautiful." Darlene rolled her eyes but smiled.

"How did it go today?" she asked. Bill told her, which was basically a lot of pieces that didn't connect. Yet. "So, what's next?"

"Tomorrow we continue poking around. I have some calls out, and some more to make. You would think everything would be online by now, but it's not. Sometimes good ol' fashioned police work does the trick."

"Do you expect anything to pop?"

He shrugged. "I don't know. But something's pinging me about the widow. Something is off with her. If someone possibly killed me, would you block their investigation?" Darlene didn't answer but made a point of showing him a large chef's knife. "Presuming you weren't the killer," Bill added.

Darlene turned to the teak cutting board and brought the knife down on a cucumber. Bill's stomach rumbled. He hadn't realized how hungry he was.

"Didn't you tell me the number one thing they taught you in police school was to avoid preconceived judgments?" she said.

"'Police school'?" He smiled. "I don't recall that lesson, no."

"You must have missed that day," she said. She added the sliced cucumber to the salad and went to work on a red bell pepper. "Get all your facts, then narrow it down."

"Since when do you know so much about police work?" But he knew the answer.

"Remember, you're a small-town cop without the authority to investigate, and it's not a murder. Just use your intuition. Don't let it get the better of you."

Always good for keeping me in my place, he thought. *Someone has to.*

"I won't," he said, smiling.

"Don't let Ellie get the better of you either." Darlene's tone was flat, and Bill knew not to push too hard.

"I won't." He came over, wrapped his arms around her waist, and kissed her lightly on the cheek. "I promise."

Bill helped her finish preparing dinner, spreading homemade garlic butter on a large piece of toasted Italian bread sliced open lengthwise. Then he corralled the kids, and together his family ate dinner.

Chapter
Twenty-Seven

The next morning dawned overcast, with rain in the forecast for later. Ellie rolled out of bed early enough to pull on a pair of running shoes and hit the pavement before Mike dialed into work. She padded lightly along the streets, her form nimble and athletic. She wasn't the kind of runner who pounded the pavement. She had been running for years, enjoying the solitude of the world around her as she passed by at a pace of her choice. Sometimes she pushed, sometimes she loped.

As she started out, her usual tics and twitches invariably plagued her: sniffs, grunts, blinks, and nods. Her throat squeezed itself in rapid succession as if fighting against the oncoming exertion.

One foot in front of the other, slowly at first, then picking up speed and settling into a sustainable pace, she quickly left her tics behind her. The athletic effort quieted her body and gave her peace and quiet for the better part of an hour. She didn't know why this happened, and she didn't much care. She loved the inertness of her tics as her body carried itself forward. When she completed her run, her tics would stay at bay at least until she finished her shower.

She wound her way in and around the quiet center of town, staying mainly in the street rather than on the sidewalks. The town had not yet come fully awake. Brewed Awakenings's door was open, with one or two people inside. Everything else would sit lifeless for another hour or two.

Ellie ran through the town center and started up the road that would take her alongside the reservoir. As she ran, her mind tended to grow clearer as her relentless tics faded into the background.

She turned the situation over in her head. She didn't want to believe any of her actors could be capable of murder. Or anyone on the production staff, for that matter. But she might have to talk to everybody. Good Lord, did she just think "murder"? Was Bill's intuition rubbing off on her?

But . . . what if it was murder? She hated that thought. Hated it with every ounce of her being.

She planned to talk to Jerry today anyway. She would start there and move on to the next person, depending on what he said. Would she talk to Merilyn? Probably. And if so, then soon. Merilyn was not well. And if it turned out Merilyn had a hand in Reginald's death, what would she do? Turn her in? Merilyn might not live to see the arraignment, much less the trial.

Part of Ellie hoped it would turn out to be Valerie. She hated that she thought that way, but Valerie seemed filled with a quiet, bitter rage that Reginald caused. How many murders had begun with a slight? Enough slights could build into a seething anger.

If Valerie was angry enough, might she have killed him?

Ellie felt certain that the cold fury Valerie held inside was not enough to make the woman a killer. The resentment was long-simmering, a pot that never boiled over. But if money had been involved, it could have put her over the edge. Only, was money a factor? It would be easy enough to check.

Jealousy was a much different matter. Anger and jealousy mixed together? Maybe a toxic combination.

Which fed into a sadness that lay deeper within Ellie, a sadness that took longer to run out than just her normal route. A sadness knowing that someone involved in her theater, someone she knew, murdered Reginald. She hadn't been lying when she told Valerie that the people in the theater were like her family. She believed that deeply, and knowing that one of them had killed another was like a dagger to her heart. Yes, Reginald had been the most difficult person she'd dealt with by far, and she had looked forward to never working with him again. He was an infection she couldn't wait to put behind her. But she had never wanted him dead. The idea that someone might have murdered him killed a piece of her soul. She needed to find the truth, if only to find some measure of peace for herself.

Before she realized it, Ellie was practically sprinting. She eased off for the last quarter mile, finishing her run gently and stretching in her front yard before heading upstairs to shower. She stripped off her damp clothes as she went. She walked by her husband naked, who raised an eyebrow and followed her, coffee in hand. She turned on the shower, leaving the bathroom door open.

"Good run?"

"Very."

She pulled back the shower curtain, got in, and before she closed it, she peeked over her shoulder and winked at him. He smiled and put down the coffee mug.

* * *

Freshly showered and feeling satisfied, Ellie drank from up a cup of coffee downstairs while Mike dressed. After a bit, Mike came downstairs to the kitchen to warm his coffee. Ellie handed him her mug to warm as well.

"Where to today?" he asked.

"To talk to Jerry."

"The guy who played the butler?"

"That's the one."

Mike had met him once and hadn't been all that impressed. "A cold fish," he'd told Ellie at the time, and, if he was being honest, Jerry seemed like a wimp. "Struck me as a jumpy guy when I met him."

"He is, no doubt." The microwave beeped, and Mike handed her the coffee mug. Ellie took a sip of her coffee, then gave him a thumbs-up as he put his mug in to heat it.

"You really think it's in his character to do something like that?" Mike asked.

"His character?" she said.

"Not his butler character, but his character-character." She smiled at him, and he frowned and said, "You know what I mean."

"I do. I'm just teasing you."

Mike shrugged and sipped his coffee, slightly miffed at being teased. He got up to put his coffee back in the microwave.

"Honestly, I don't think it's in his character," Ellie said. "But I wouldn't have thought any of them could have killed him. I mean, there was a lot of tension in the cast, but I relied on Merilyn to manage it. At various points during the rehearsals, I think they all wanted Reginald dead. But wanting him dead and actually killing him are very different things."

Nod. She sighed. *Here we go,* she thought. *Nod-nod. Blink.*

Mike tested his coffee, found it satisfactorily heated, and sat at the kitchen island across from his wife. "I'm glad I never met Reginald," he said. "Sounds like it didn't take much to despise him."

Ellie sighed. *Sniff-sniff-sniff. Blink-blink.* "Reginald had that effect on people. He could make them mad enough to want to kill him. And while I think Jerry is too mild-mannered, he's also pretty high-strung. Who knows what his snapping point is." *Nod-nod.*

Mike nodded like it made sense to him.

"Be careful," he said. "I don't want you getting so caught up in this thing that it puts you in danger."

"In this town? Doubtful."

"We've already had one person killed here."

Nod-nod-nod. "Touché. But it may not have been a murder."

Mike's eyes narrowed. "If that is the case, why are you interrogating people?"

"I'm not interrogating people, and shut up." She smiled. He smiled back and reached down to give her another kiss before heading upstairs to his office. Ellie drained her mug, ticced several times, then grabbed her keys and wallet.

Chapter
Twenty-Eight

Jerry Moynihan stopped at Shannon's Bakery every morning to
get a cup of coffee and a cheese Danish on his way to work.
Today would be different. Today he would stay at the bakery, waiting for Ellie to join him. He was surprised when he'd gotten her call
asking if they could meet and have coffee. And talk. He wondered.
Did this have anything to do with his visit with the police chief the
day before?

He sat at a table toward the back of the bakery so the conversation
might not be heard. He saw Ellie walk through the door. He lifted one
hand and waved. She waved back, then got in line. Five minutes later,
she sat across from him, a cup of coffee steaming before her.

"Ellie," Jerry said. "I was a bit surprised by your call."

She ticced slightly, betraying her nervousness, though Jerry didn't
understand it as such. To him, ticcing was simply something Ellie did.
He did his best to ignore her tics, knowing the difficulty of having
something as publicly pronounced as physical movement announce
your neurological disorder to the world. He was quite good at looking
past them, his father having fought Parkinson's disease and seizures
for twenty years before passing away.

"Thanks for taking time out of your Saturday to meet me," Ellie
said.

"Certainly. What's the word on Reginald's death?" Jerry asked, knowing there were likely no developments overnight. Partially he wanted to see how much the police chief was sharing with her.

Nod-nod. Sniff. "The state is listing it as a heart attack. Natural causes."

"But you don't believe that?"

Ellie shrugged. "There's some unofficial evidence to suggest drug abuse. But that would seem so unlike him, especially on a performance night. I just couldn't see him losing control like that."

Jerry shrugged. "Everyone has a breaking point."

"I suppose. Also, I wanted to say that you were fantastic last night. An absolute trooper for going onstage with someone who isn't used to it."

"I have to say, Steve was excellent as a fill-in for Reginald," Jerry said. "You'd never know it was his first time onstage. He was a natural. I don't want to speak ill of the dead, but I thought Steve was even better than Reginald."

"He did well," Ellie said. "Surpassed my expectations. And I think he'll just get better as the run continues."

Ellie drank her coffee and took a big deep breath, like she was mustering courage. She said, "I also wanted to say I'm sorry about all this, how much Reginald upset everyone in the cast. In a way, it's my fault for letting it go so long. I knew there were problems, but when I talked to Merilyn, she said she had everything under control. Sounds like she didn't."

Jerry sighed the big sigh of someone who is lighter after getting something off their chest. "No, of course she didn't. She's too weak. I feel bad for her, especially because she's such a nice person and an excellent director. Actually, she got it all under control more than most people I think would have. But she could never fully exert authority because she doesn't have the strength."

A moment of silence hung between them as each considered their mortality, remembering Merilyn was quickly reaching the end of hers.

"How long does she have?" Jerry asked quietly.

"She won't tell me how bad it is," Ellie said, her tics reasserting themselves. "But anyone can see it's bad."

Jerry paused, his face pained as if he didn't want to bring something up.

"Reginald may have died of an overdose?" he said as if looking for confirmation.

"Possibly. Won't know officially for at least another week."

"Do you know what the drug was?"

"Again, not officially. If I were to guess, I'd say it was a benzo because we found a prescription for him. But something else could have been mixed in. Maybe an opioid, fentanyl or something."

"You know what fentanyl is used for?"

"Sure. It's a painkiller."

"Often used in surgical centers. But do you know what else it's used for?" Jerry's eyes flashed bright and fierce as if he had solved something in his head. Ellie worried about what would give him such a triumphant look and such a miserably sad one at the same time.

She shook her head, letting it bob on its own for a moment. "Post-op?"

He paused, his mouth a thin gray line. "It's used by late-stage cancer patients. To manage their pain."

Chapter Twenty-Nine

D arlene was less than enthused that Bill had chosen to go into work on a weekend morning. But she didn't gripe. She'd seen her mother called away from family events plenty of times because of police work.

Which didn't stop Bill from apologizing fifteen ways to Sunday. Finally, after hearing one too many *I'm sorry's,* she said, "Get out. Go do whatever it is you need to do and then leave it alone until Monday."

Bill promised he would, kissed her on the cheek, and left.

He sifted through the records and ran through the Triple I's again. There was Jerry's assault charge, and that was it. That was the extent of what he expected to find with this squeaky-clean cast and crew.

Which is why he was stunned when he got a hit for Merilyn Chambers. A fax had arrived from the Midtown South police precinct in Manhattan the night before, which surprised Bill. He assumed they would have digitized their records. But it was Manhattan, and they probably had more records than all of Massachusetts. Whenever the fax whine-buzzed, he shook his head.

He read through the old record, a bust on 42nd Street.

Soliciting.

He rubbed his eyes and reread the fax, thinking it had to be wrong. But there it was, in black and white: Merilyn Chambers, arrested for soliciting in New York City back in 1977. Before NYC began to move the hookers and the peepshows out of midtown.

Merilyn had once lived in New York.

Something stuck in Bill's mind. He pulled up Reginald's record, which was mostly clean. A bust for marijuana possession two decades ago, a bust for public drunkenness more recently, but that was about it. And those were in Massachusetts. No, something else nibbled at him.

He dug deeper, looking at old license records and voter registration information until he found it.

Reginald Thornton had lived in Manhattan in the seventies when he was in his earlier thirties. *Probably trying to become a Broadway actor,* Bill thought. One of the many who went off to seek fortune and fame in Hollywood or Broadway, only to fail.

Or did he? Maybe he didn't fail. Maybe he did have some success, only to see it fade. Fame was a fickle gal. *Luck be a lady.* Bill wondered if there was a quick way to check the decades-old Broadway theater history. A quick internet search confirmed that a website existed, but it was far less organized than its movie and TV rival, IMBD. He checked Reginald's name, and then Merilyn's, but came up empty on both.

But the important thing was that Reginald lived in New York.

And Merilyn lived in New York. At the same time.

His cell phone buzzed. Ellie.

"You'll never guess what I found," he said by way of a greeting.

"Did you know fentanyl is used by late-stage cancer patients to manage the pain?" Ellie said as if she hadn't heard him.

"Huh?"

"What?"

"All right, one at a time," he said. "You first."

"I was having breakfast with Jerry at a bakery in Worcester. We started talking about fentanyl." She sounded breathless. Winded. "It's used by late-stage cancer patients—"

"Okay . . ."

"Merilyn has cancer. Late-stage. Like, very late stage."

Bill fell silent. More pieces lay on the table, pieces to a puzzle he mentally moved around and tried to fit into a picture. They didn't quite lock together, but something was starting to emerge. An image of something—but what, he couldn't distinguish.

"You there?" Ellie said.

"Yeah, sorry. Thinking about something." He paused. "How bad is Merilyn?"

"Bad. She won't tell me, but one look and you can tell she's on borrowed time. Could be today, tomorrow, or next week the way she's going."

Bill considered this. Ellie said, "I'm sorry, I didn't mean to cut you off when you answered. What did you find?"

"Did you know Reginald had spent time in New York? Presumably trying to make it as an actor?"

"I did. He lists it on his résumé. Did some off-Broadway stuff, some off-off-Broadway stuff."

"Wait, you have a résumé for him?"

"Sure. Why?"

"Mind if I take a look at it?"

"It's at the theater. I'm headed there. There's a matinee today, so we're getting there early."

"I want to check some dates," Bill said. "Find out when he lived in Manhattan."

"If memory serves, sometime in the seventies," Ellie said.

Bill didn't blurt it right out, but there was no hiding it either and no soft way to say it. "I got something today from a precinct in Manhattan. Something about Merilyn."

"Something bad?"

"More like surprising. She was busted for soliciting back in the seventies."

Silence for a moment. "Our Merilyn?"

"Well, your Merilyn," Bill said.

It was Ellie's turn to be stunned. Bill could picture her, driving, staring out the windshield, turning this over in her head. He could hear the road noise through the phone.

"Ellie?" he finally said.

"You're thinking they knew each other back then, aren't you?"

"I am," Bill said. "I don't have all the dots to make the picture, but it feels like it's starting to be less blurry. To come into view."

"Up for some coffee?" Ellie said suddenly.

"Of course. I'm a cop."

*   *   *

Brewed Awakenings sat right off the center intersection of town, a few doors down. It was a favorite haunt of college kids from Worcester looking to get out of the city. It served soups, sandwiches, and smoothies, in addition to the many selections of coffee and the usual selection of pastries and baked goods. The proprietor, Elvis Quart, had veered dangerously close to Ned's Diner's territory with some of its breakfast selections. Chet, the owner of Ned's, and Elvis had maintained a rivalry most people in town still considered friendly, but only just.

Bill was already sitting sipping from a mug when Ellie came in. She waved to Elvis, who waved back. She ordered a coffee, took the mug handed to her, and brought it to the table where Bill sat.

"How does he do it, do you think?" Ellie asked.

"How does who do what?"

"How does Elvis manage to make the perfect cup of coffee?"

"I thought you were going to ask how he gets his hair to stay so high." Bill inclined his head toward the proprietor of Brewed

Awakenings. Elvis sported a jet-black pompadour. At first, Bill thought it was an effect for the shop, but when he saw Elvis outside his shop, he realized that was simply how he styled his hair—a throwback to a previous era. Bill wouldn't have been surprised to learn he had a leisure suit or two hanging in the back of his closet.

"That was my next question, but I thought the coffee one was more important."

"Honestly, I don't care, as long as he never stops making it."

They drank for a few minutes in silence, relishing the peacefulness of the space, Ellie charmed by the strings of white Christmas lights Elvis had run around the perimeter of the ceiling, and Bill admiring the heavy wooden tables, clearly not mass-produced crap.

After a moment, Ellie reached into her bag and pulled out the résumé she had fished out of her files at the theater. She slid it across the table to Bill. He picked up the paper and skimmed through it. Then he nodded.

"There it is. Theater work. Manhattan. Seventy-six through eighty-three. Then back up here."

"You think they knew each other?"

Bill nodded. "That's what my gut is telling me."

"Hard to believe about Merilyn. She seems so . . ." Ellie searched for the word but couldn't find it.

"Wholesome?"

"I think I was going for confident. Like, why would someone with such a strength of character work as a hooker?"

"I think it speaks to her character that she did it but then left that world behind her. Sometimes you gotta do what you gotta do to make it."

"Anything else in her record?"

Bill shook his head. "No, that's all. Just the one bust for solicitation, nothing since."

"Thank God," Ellie said, and Bill knew what she meant. Digging into people's records, people he knew, people he liked, and then finding something made you see them differently. It colored his relationships, which he hated. But it didn't stop him from digging when he had to. Sometimes history needed to be exhumed.

"You know one of us has to talk to her, right?"

Ellie sighed. *Nod-blink-blink. Sniff-sniff.* "I know."

"What else did Jerry say?" he asked.

"We talked about the show, and how it went last night. And I apologized for not being more on top of the theater. I feel so bad for not paying close enough attention during rehearsals. I thought Merilyn had it under control."

Bill pursed his lips. Ellie noticed and said, "What is it?"

"I think I need to fill you in on a conversation I had with Jerry yesterday." Bill told her about his discussion with Jerry and how it had been prompted by an assault charge Reginald had brought against the man.

Ellie sat and listened, stunned. Before she could answer, her phone dinged, and she set down her coffee and picked the phone up.

"Text from Dana. This afternoon's show is sold out. Cast and crew are starting to gather at the theater."

"Will Merilyn be there?" Bill asked. Ellie shook her head.

"She's too weak now. She's in her house, probably until the end."

"Do you have time to go with me to talk to Merilyn?"

"No, sorry, I have to get to the theater and help get the show ready, Especially since Merilyn can't be there."

Bill picked up his phone and began to text. "I'll take Turner with me."

"Please be nice to her," Ellie said. "She is the sweetest lady, and she's losing her fight. Please don't go all cop-y on her."

"I haven't gone all cop-y on anyone yet," Bill said. He smiled. "I don't plan to start now."

Ellie laid a hand on top of his. "Thank you."

He nodded, his mind on the interview ahead. "You betcha."

Chapter Thirty

S teve was standing outside the theater with a coffee in one hand and a cigarette in the other, alternating moving each to his mouth, when Ellie pulled up. He waved to her, which was primarily lifting his coffee cup in her direction.

"Ready for a repeat performance?" she asked.

Steve frowned and shrugged. "Do I have a choice?"

"No."

Steve took a drag and chased it with coffee. He dropped the cigarette and stepped on it, then picked up the butt to bring inside to throw out. Ellie had previously given Steve an earful over smoking, but at least he picked up after himself. He opened the door and said, "After you."

The familiar feeling that washed over Ellie when she stepped inside the lobby threatened to overwhelm her. *The feeling of a show day.* There was nothing like it. The air in the theater was different the day of a performance, humming with the nervous energy of actors and actresses, stagehands, and production crews. Everyone getting ready, volunteers putting out the usual assortment of theater junk food, the lobby noise growing as it filled with patrons waiting for the house to open. She carried these sights and sounds and smells with her everywhere, her love of theater nearly as old as she was. With every show, it came rushing up.

She stood in the lobby, her body still, her eyes becoming watery.

"You okay?" Steve asked.

"No, but I will be," she said as she crushed her nose with the flat of her palm. Twice. Three times. Then she was done. "Just a little overwhelmed by everything."

"I'll bet," he said.

"Should we start some coffee?"

"God, no." He held up his cup. "This is my third today. Any more and my heart might explode. I don't want to drop dead." They stared at each other a moment, and he grimaced and said, "Bad choice of words."

Ellie snorted and tried to suppress a chuckle, but couldn't. Before long, she was laughing so hard her sides hurt. Steve couldn't hold back, and soon he was laughing just as hard. When they finally got control of themselves, he looked at Ellie with more than a little embarrassment.

"Sorry," he said.

"I'm the one who should apologize. I started it," she said.

"Let's both agree we're going to hell, and we'll feel much better about ourselves."

"Done."

They started prepping for the afternoon performance, Steve doing double duty as the stage manager and as leading man, presetting the props and listening to a recording of his lines through his earbuds. Ellie started to feel better as she sprayed Windex on the glass doors and wiped them clean.

A little while later, Steve popped his head into the costume closest where Ellie had gone to look for a scarf Dana said she wanted to add to Kyra's costume.

"Headed up the ladder to adjust a couple of lights," he said.

"Now?"

"Don't like the way they shine down. Didn't realize it until I was under them last night. They can be adjusted."

"Do you want to wait for Tony?" Ellie asked. She didn't want her high school lighting guru to think they didn't need him anymore.

"Nah, I got this. You know I do."

"Right," she said. "I always forget you went to school for this."

"Yep," he said as they both climbed the stairs from the basement. "Fordham. There aren't too many other places where you can get a degree in lighting design. But it's what I love to do. Too bad lighting jobs are so damn hard to find in Manhattan. Gotta be union or have an in with the theater community."

Ellie nodded, knowing the rest of the story. When Steve couldn't find work on Broadway, he had come up to Massachusetts and started a lighting company. He eventually expanded to audiovisual work and now ran a thriving small business that catered mostly to local corporations putting on special presentations. It had led to teaching a couple of courses at the local community college: an entry-level lighting design course and an introduction to theatrical technology. But he couldn't stay away from theater and so did stage management work here. Ellie sometimes felt bad, like she was taking advantage of him. Like his loss was her gain.

Tony came in as Steve was climbing the ladder to the first light.

"Perfect timing," Steve said. "Get your ass up here and help me."

Tony put down his bag and joined Steve on the stage. Ellie smiled at her two-person stage crew. She knew that Tony had been involved in local theater programs since he was eight. He enjoyed being on the stage, but enjoyed being behind the scenes even more. Steve had trained him initially as a high school freshman, and in the last three years, Tony became one of the most confident lighting guys in the area.

Once Steve was back on the ground, Ellie asked him, "What did you think of Reginald?"

"The legend in his own mind?"

Ellie let out a snort, clapping her hand to her mouth in embarrassment. "Yeah, that one."

Steve shrugged and lifted a box of books that had filled up a bookshelf onstage and brought it to a shelf by the door. "I thought the same way everyone else did, I guess."

"You wanted him to drop dead?" *Grunt-grunt.*

Steve turned, startled. "No. I was going to say he was a dick."

Ellie put the tea set away. It had been thoroughly washed and dried, but she thought she might never be able to use that one again. She had brought a different one up from the basement. "Everyone thought that too."

Steve stared at Ellie as if she had said something extraordinary. "Are you saying someone in the cast killed him?"

"No, I'm not saying that, and I'm not implying they did." She felt bad about bringing this up, and her body betrayed her. *Blink-blink-blink-grunt-grunt.*

Steve fidgeted, disturbed by what she said.

"I mean," she continued, "it's not like anyone threatened to kill him, right?"

Steve thought for a moment. Ellie could see the troubled look on his face and said, "What?"

"Well. I mean . . . uh . . ." Steve stammered. "Jerry kinda did."

"You were there for that?"

"Yeah." His face scrunched. "Wait. You knew?"

Nod-nod. "I heard about it yesterday, but I was hoping there wasn't anything to it. Like, people say they're going to kill other people all the time. I remember my mom used to say stuff like that about my brother. He'd be in trouble for something or other, and she'd go, 'When he gets home, I'm gonna kill that kid.' But she didn't mean it."

"Right," Steve said, but Ellie could tell the conversation was making him uncomfortable. "I mean, yeah, people say it all the time."

Ellie came over to Steve and put her hands on his arms. She looked him in the face, but he averted his eyes.

"Steve, what is it?" *Blink.* "What are you not saying?"

He took a deep breath. "I like Jerry. I think he's a nice guy, and I don't want to get him in trouble. I think he got overheated."

"What happened?"

Steve sat down in a high-backed Victorian chair stored backstage. It was the perfect chair for a Sherlock Holmes–style mystery, which Kaleidoscope had yet to put on. But it was on Ellie's list.

"They were rehearsing, and Reginald was being Reginald. Total dick. Total douche. He and Jerry started to get into it, and Jerry couldn't hold his own. Never could, really. He's just not fast enough on his feet. Which is weird for an actor, I think. I mean, if you can't cover a scene when someone else blows a line, how can you do this?"

"Focus, Steve," Ellie said, trying to get Steve back on track.

"Right. Sorry. Anyway, there's a huge shouting match happening on stage, and Merilyn, you know, she's not strong enough to yell over people, especially the Dick." Ellie could hear the capital D when he said it. "So I peek out from backstage where I'm working on setting up the props table, ordering it so I know where everything is for all of the scenes. And I see Jerry throw a book at Reginald and storm off the stage and out of the theater. And he yells at the top of his lungs as he's walking away, 'I'm going to kill you!'"

Steve opened his mouth to say more, but he appeared to have run out of steam, and he closed it again. He said, "That's it."

Ellie sat down in a metal folding chair opposite Steve. So Jerry had threatened to kill Reginald—and not in an casual way, but with very deliberate words. But this was not what Jerry described to Bill, like he was defending Kyra's honor. Rather, it sounded like he was defending himself.

Things were increasingly muddier, and Ellie wasn't prepared for this. Had Jerry made up his story, or had he threatened Reginald more than once?

Nod-nod-nod.

"Did anybody not have a problem with the man?" Ellie asked, more to herself than to Steve.

Steve shook his head. "He was a dick to everybody. Kyra, Jerry, Merilyn. Hell, even Tony had a run-in with him over lighting."

"How about you?"

Steve shrugged. "Oh sure," he confessed. "He got on me about the props one night, saying I was handing him the wrong whatever—cane, book, teacup, hanky. Take your pick. He went at me."

"What did he say?"

Steve swallowed, as if embarrassed, or sad. "Said I was the worst at the job he's ever worked with, that my stage management skills were an abomination, and that my mother should have saved the world an embarrassment and aborted me when she had the chance."

"Holy cow."

"Yeah. Pretty specific. Probably why I remember it so clearly."

Ellie ticced ferociously for a moment. The embarrassment of not knowing how bad the situation had been between Reginald and the rest of the cast and crew was eating her from the inside out.

"Steve, I'm sorry. I was asleep at the wheel. I should have been paying attention more. I promise I'll never let anyone act that way in this theater again, be they actor, crew, or audience."

"Thanks." He stood. From onstage, there was more banging, then a crash. "We should probably get back out there and help out Tony before he hurts himself."

He crossed the room and slipped out between the curtains hanging in the wings. Ellie lingered behind, thinking about the crazy, hurtful things Reginald had said to Steve. She hated to think it, but it did seem like the world was better off without Reginald Thornton IV. Shaking her head, she followed Steve to the stage.

Chapter Thirty-One

When the doorbell rang late in the afternoon, it took Merilyn a full two minutes to get up from her chair in the living room and reach the door. When she opened it and saw Bill Starlin and Turner Milton standing on her front porch, her face lit up like she'd just been given the best surprise in the world.

"Chief, so nice to see you." She reached up and gave him a hug, surprising him. "And you too, Officer Milton." She hugged him as well. "Come in, come in." She stepped aside and let them enter.

Merilyn Chambers' house was like an advertisement for every piece of home medical apparatus anyone could think of. Bill and Turner wound their way around some of it to get to the living room.

"Would you like some tea?" she asked.

"No, thank you," Bill said.

"You sure? I was just about to make some for myself."

"I'm all set," he said.

"Let me make it for you, Ms. Chambers," Turner said, and started to thread his way through the equipment toward the kitchen.

Merilyn smiled and said, "A lovely offer, but I make my guests drinks in my home, not the other way around. I'm not dead yet."

"That's not—" Turner tried to say.

"Oh, yes, it is. Don't you lie to me, Turner Milton. Now you two go sit down in the living room while I make tea."

Merilyn started slowly toward the kitchen. Bill and Turner looked at each other, shrugged, and went into the living room. Bill sat while Turner wandered around the room, looking at photos.

Five minutes later, Merilyn came in bearing two mugs. She handed one to Turner, who was still standing.

"There you are, honey." She handed Bill a mug. He opened his mouth to remind her he had passed on the offer, then closed it again. *Oh, what the hell.* Merilyn settled into the chair opposite. On one side of her chair was a small table full of prescription bottles, and on the other side an IV pole.

"You're here to talk about the murder, I expect."

Turner started to sip the tea, trying not to make a face at its bitterness, but her words startled him, and he nearly choked. "What makes you call it a murder?" Bill asked while Turner coughed.

"Please. I've been a student of body language my whole life. Everything about you says you're investigating Reginald's death like it was a murder."

"It was ruled a heart attack."

"Why would you investigate a heart attack?"

Turner had recovered his voice enough to speak. "Ms. Chambers—"

"Merilyn, please," she said. "I hate being called Ms. Chambers."

Turner acknowledged her request with a nod. "Merilyn. We requested a tox screen. There is some indication drugs may have been a contributing factor."

"Contributing? Or the sole factor?."

"We're hoping the official tox screen will tell us," Bill said.

Merilyn sipped her tea. "And if it's drugs, you want to know who slipped them to him?"

"He could have been abusing them," Turner offered.

Merilyn waved her hand dismissively. "No chance. I've known Reginald for decades. He loved food and booze, but there is no way he would have allowed himself to become addicted to anything. Not if there was any danger it could impact his ability to perform onstage."

"The reason we ask," Bill said, "is because overdosing on a benzo alone is unusual. They're addictive, and the body tends to build up a tolerance, which means you need more and more. If Reginald wasn't showing the typical signs of benzo addiction, then it's possible something else was mixed in with it. Something strong."

"Like alcohol?"

"Or fentanyl," Bill said. He watched her face as he said it to gauge her reaction.

"Ah," she said slowly. "And you're here because late-stage cancer patients often take fentanyl."

"We're just checking things off the list. There's no evidence that fentanyl contributed to Reginald's death."

Merilyn sat silent for a moment. "Yet."

"Yet," Bill agreed.

"So, murder?"

Bill redirected the question back to her. "What do you think?"

Merilyn smiled but didn't answer. It struck Bill as a sad smile, something wistful and melancholy, like a sad memory.

Bill switched tracks. "What about Reginald's wife?"

"Valerie? What about her?"

"Do you know if maybe she has a drug problem?"

"Not that I know of, but you could certainly ask her."

Bill didn't need to. Having been out to see her, he'd already ruled it out. She might have her own prescription for Valium, but it would take a warrant to find out, and he wasn't likely to get one.

"Some people get addicted without trying," Turner said. "Not their fault. It just happens. He could have had a scrip for an anxiety attack or something, and then one pill becomes two, two becomes four, and soon it becomes a habit."

"Some people might get addicted, but not Reginald. Not unless I've wildly misjudged the man, which I doubt. I've known him too long."

"And how long is that?" Bill leaned forward.

Merilyn stared off into space, squinting her eyes as she concentrated. "Oh, let me see now. It has to be close to fifty years."

"Where did you guys meet?"

"I met Reginald in New York, if you can believe it."

"New York? Manhattan?"

"That's right."

"Were you doing theater together in Manhattan?"

"God, no. Theater was the furthest thing from my mind. Reginald was, though. That was his ambition. He was good. And very handsome."

"If you weren't doing theater, what were you doing?"

"Turning tricks," she said.

All motion stopped. Turner stared at Bill, Bill stared at Merilyn, and she stared back at him. It seemed to Bill that even the clocks in the house had stopped. Then she raised her teacup to her lips and took a sip like nothing had been said.

"I'm sorry," Turner said. "It sounded like you said—"

"I did say it." Her body may have been a diminished, shriveled husk of its former self, but her voice was as sharp as broken glass.

"That's what this is about, isn't it? Why you're asking about my past and about Reginald's past. Somehow you found out I was a hooker back then. Was it my arrest record?" Merilyn's steady voice had a cold edge. She readjusted the tails of the bright floral scarf wrapped around her hairless head.

"That's not why I'm here," Bill said. She gave him a look that told him what she thought of that. "That's not the only reason I'm here," he corrected.

"Then why are you here?"

Bill set his teacup down on the coffee table between them, folded his hands, leaned forward, his elbows on his knees, and stared at Merilyn.

"The state is not pursuing the case. We're still looking into it, and yes, fentanyl is sometimes given to cancer patients to help manage the pain."

"We?"

Bill waggled his thumb between himself and Turner. "We're chasing down leads, both of us. Trying to see the full picture."

Merilyn stared at Bill as he spoke, giving nothing away. He continued. "Are you taking fentanyl currently?"

She sat back in her chair and stared for a few seconds more. A grin sprouted on her face and grew. She chuckled. "I don't have to answer that question."

Bill sighed and hung his head, then looked up at her. "You're right, you don't. But it could be helpful if—"

Merilyn held up a hand to stop him. "I said I don't have to. I didn't say I won't."

Bill held his breath while she took a sip of tea. He sensed Turner behind him, as still as if he'd stared into the eyes of Medusa. A smile played about her face. Bill realized she was enjoying making them work for it.

"Of course I'm taking fentanyl," Merilyn finally said. "I'd get nothing done otherwise. And before you ask, I do have a prescription."

"Can you account for all your pills?"

"Not pills. Patches."

"Patches?" Turner said.

"Yep. The seventy-two-hour patch. Chock-a-block full of the good stuff. Lasts three days. And I keep an extra one or two with me in case I'm out somewhere when the three days are up."

"And do you have all your patches?" Bill asked.

"I haven't checked recently."

"Could you, please? While we're here?"

"Even if I didn't have them all, could you prove it was mine that killed him?"

Bill pursed his lips and shook his head. "Probably not."

"Then perhaps you shouldn't be in my home accusing me of murdering my lead actor."

"I'm not here to accuse you," Bill said, trying not to let his frustration show. "If I'm being frank, I don't think you have the strength to poison someone. Stop me if I'm wrong."

She shook her head, which he took as a sign to continue.

"Also, I don't think you have the temperament, and temperament goes for a lot in an investigation like this. I want to figure out if someone got hold of your pain med, cut into the patch, and stirred the contents into Reginald's drink. If so, then it could have accelerated whatever benzo he was on, which could have been obtained from anyone else in the theater who had them."

Merilyn held a tense pose for a few seconds longer, then her shoulders slumped and she nearly spilled her tea.

"I'm missing one patch," she admitted. "I thought maybe I was just careless and misplaced it." She indicated her living room. "It's not like I'm up on my housecleaning." She paused and seemed on the edge of tears. "I didn't want to think that someone could have taken it."

"Just one?"

She nodded. "From my purse."

Bill sat back, and Turner shuffled his feet. Where all motion seemed to stop before, now everything seemed to speed forward to catch up. Somewhere in the house, a clock began to croak out its cuckoo.

Turner said, "If you had to point the finger, who would you point at?"

Merilyn didn't answer right away, and Bill could see that she had someone in mind.

"You suspect someone, don't you?" he said.

Merilyn grimaced and closed her eyes, tears spilling out from the corners and running down the sides of her face. She shook her head.

"Merilyn, if you suspect someone, you need to tell me. Otherwise, if the state does open this case up again, you'll become a prime suspect."

"And what are the odds of that happening?" she said hoarsely.

Bill shrugged and thought about trying to bluff, knowing there was no way on this planet that Avery would let the state reopen this as a homicide. He made a noncommittal gesture with his hands. Merilyn laughed, a harsh wheezing sound. "You can't scare me, Chief. Not about this. Not after Reginald."

"Reginald scared you?" Bill asked.

"He had his moments, but not with physical intimidation. It was emotional manipulation in its most bravado form." She sighed, pulled a tissue from a box on the table next to her, wiped her eyes, and blew her nose. It was as if she were reapplying her game face, sealing the cracks in her facade—the easygoing, carefree face back in place. She sipped her tea as if she didn't have a care about anything. "My arrest record is how Reginald got the part in the play. How he got every part in all of my plays."

Bill blinked. "What do you mean?"

"In any play I directed, if there was the slightest chance that a part fit Reginald, he'd bring up the old arrest record and force me to let him have the part." Merilyn sighed a wet, post-weeping sigh. "I was always scared of him, of my past getting out, and everyone knowing the things I did in my youth."

"Everyone has a past. No one should judge," Turner said, thinking that it sounded stupid once the words were out of his mouth.

"But they do, don't they? And I would be shunned, ostracized from the community I love. I couldn't let that happen." She took another deep, rattling breath. With each breath, Bill worried fleetingly that it might be her last. "I'm fortunate he's good at what he does. Or, rather, what he did."

"Please clear something up for me," Bill said quietly. "How did Reginald know about the arrest record?"

Merilyn's eyes met Bill's. "Who do you think bailed me out?" Her voice was low.

"How did he know you needed bailing out?"

She set her teacup down. "Are you really that naive, Chief?"

"Humor me."

Merilyn pulled another tissue from the box resting on the side table. She dabbed her eyes and blew her nose. Bill and Turner waited until she had composed herself. Bill watched her with compassion, while Turner examined the room as if to avoid furthering her embarrassment.

"Reginald came to see me a few times." She used the word 'see,' but Bill understood. He tried to keep his face neutral but wasn't sure he succeeded.

"Remember," Merilyn said, "he was handsome back them. And single, newly divorced, alone in the big city, and lonely. Taking some comfort. Like Paul Simon sang in 'The Boxer.' He picked me up on the Deuce—they called 42nd Street the Deuce back then—and we got together a few times. After the first time, he came to find me specifically. He was actually kind of sweet back then. Not full of himself yet. Not like he is now."

"But once you both returned here and into the theater community, Reginald blackmailed you to get parts and threatened to expose your arrest record."

She blew her nose again. "Something like that."

"Who else do you think might have enough of a grudge to want to kill him?" Bill wasn't one hundred percent sure that Merilyn was innocent, but he was fairly certain it wasn't her.

"Everyone who ever met him," she said, but her eyes wandered off for a moment.

Bill waited for her to come back, which she did. "Merilyn, who were you thinking of just now?"

"Honey, I'm an old lady who's dying of cancer. Some things are probably better off going with me to the grave."

"But what about Reginald?" Bill said. "Doesn't he deserve some justice?"

She didn't answer for a moment. She looked at her hands with a sadness Bill could feel in his chest. "Perhaps justice was served," she said.

Bill and Turner looked at each other.

"His widow disagrees," Bill said.

"Valerie?" Merilyn chuckled, which turned into a cough, which turned into a coughing fit. Bill worried, not for the first time this visit, that this might be the end. He had his radio out and was about to call for an ambulance when she got it under control. The cough sputtered and fizzled out, and she took some deep breaths.

"Don't make me laugh," she panted. "You'll kill me."

"You don't think Valerie and Reginald were close?" Turner said.

"Not after the way he treated her."

Bill and Turner glanced at each other. "And how was that?" Bill asked, aware of what Ellie had told him about Reginald's wife.

"Like she was his property."

"That kind of treatment can breed a lot of anger and resentment over the years," Turner said. "Do you think it was enough to make her kill him?"

"I'm not sure Valerie has that level of violence in her," Merilyn said. "But she was royally pissed off the last time I saw her."

"Which was when?"

"At one of the rehearsals. She was not in a good mood."

"About anything in particular?"

"She was shouting something about some insurance policy. Saying something like, did he think she wouldn't find out?"

Bill rubbed his face with his hands. He knew from his conversation with Jerry that Valerie had confronted Kyra about her supposed seduction of Reginald. But no one had mentioned anything about Valerie confronting Reginald about something else.

"None of this makes sense," he said.

Merilyn gave a dry laugh. "Murder has to make sense?"

"There's always a reason," Bill said, "except for completely random killings, and this one wasn't. Most of the time it's love or money, sometimes fear. It's almost always something that makes sense, in a way at least."

Merilyn was quiet for a moment. She closed her eyes. After a minute, Bill thought she might have drifted off, but then she opened them. She was crying again when she spoke, and she spoke so softly Bill had to lean forward and ask her to repeat herself.

"You should speak to Alex Hillman."

"Who?" Bill said.

"Alex Hillman. He was the Thorntons' money manager. He was responsible for things like insurance policies. He might have more to tell you than I do."

"Would he know anything about the Thorntons beyond their money?"

"Ask him. He knows all kinds of things about his clients. All kinds of secrets."

"Secrets?"

"Everyone has secrets to keep. Some people pay to keep them."

Chapter
Thirty-Two

The next day Ellie went home after the last weekend matinee and slept like she hadn't slept in years. She was exhausted, physically and emotionally.

Bill, after a night of tossing and turning, puzzling over everything, called Ellie Monday morning and suggested going to talk to someone whose name had come up. By ten o'clock, they stood in front of the office of Alex Hillman.

"You don't mind me tagging along?" Ellie asked.

Bill shook his head. "You know the theater crowd more than I do. Your insight has been invaluable."

"Not sure Alex Hillman is part of the quote-unquote theater crowd."

"If Merilyn and Reginald both know him, then you never know."

Hillman's office was in a renovated Cape-style house just off Main Street. Bill took a moment to look around: slate-blue wooden siding with freshly painted white trim, lawn well maintained and free of leaves, thoughtfully landscaped front. By all outward appearances, the office of Alex Hillman looked affluent.

Ellie admired the front of the house, the yellow, orange, and purple mums exploding color in their beds. "Looks like he's doing okay," Ellie said.

"Looks can be deceiving," Bill countered, thinking of his discovery about Merilyn's past. He wasn't sure how to break that news to Ellie.

"Awfully cynical this early in the morning."

Bill ignored the jab. "Let's stay focused, talk to this guy, hopefully solve this thing quickly, and put it behind us."

"If there is anything to solve."

"You don't think it is murder anymore?"

Ellie shrugged, then ticced twice with her head, grunted once, squeezed her throat muscles together, and finished with a barrage of sniffs. "I don't know what to think. The deeper we dig, the uglier this gets. I'm almost scared about what we'll find out from this guy."

They went up the steps and into the front door. The inside of the house had been gutted at some point. Now the interior was largely an open floor plan, with a view straight to the back of the house, where a row of full-length glass sliders let in an enormous amount of sunlight. The sliders were cracked open, and the crisp air of October seeped in. The white walls gleamed like the exterior, and the hardwood floors shined with a high polish. To the left of the door was a desk, at an angle. A woman sat behind it, slim and attractive, blond hair perfectly done. Her navy suit was wrinkle-free and fit her like a glove.

"May I help you?" she asked.

Bill pulled out his badge and showed it to the woman.

"Bill Starlin, Chief of Police. We need a few moments of Mr. Hillman's time."

"Of course, Chief. If you stay here just one moment, I'll go get Mr. Hillman for you."

She rose and crossed the floor to a door on the far right side of the house. She knocked and entered. Ellie fidgeted, rubbing her right thumb on her thigh, then, because her body required things to be even, she rubbed the left one on her left thigh.

The woman returned momentarily, a man trailing her. He looked familiar to Ellie, but she couldn't place him.

The man introduced himself. "I'm Alex Hillman," he said, holding out his hand. Bill introduced Ellie as they shook hands. "What can I do for you?"

"Mr. Hillman, do you mind if we talk in your office?"

"Not at all." He turned to the woman in the navy suit. "Debby, hold all calls until we're done, please."

"Of course, Mr. Hillman."

He led them back across the floor, his stylish leather shoes clicking on the hardwood.

They went inside the office, and he closed the door behind them. The office was like the rest of the house—white paint, austere, with a few pictures on the walls for color. The entire back of the office was a floor-to-ceiling window. Two large skylights above them flooded the office with light.

Hillman gestured to the chairs opposite his desk. Modern and minimalist like everything else, they had a shiny aluminum frame with black leather wrapped around it, crisscrossing in a latticework to make a seat. Ellie sat and found the chair surprisingly comfortable. Bill sat tentatively, worried it wouldn't hold him.

"So," Hillman said, sitting down. "You must be here regarding Reginald's death."

At Bill's quizzical look, he added, "What else could bring the town police chief and the owner of the Kaleidoscope Theater to my door?"

"You know who I am?" Ellie asked, surprised.

"I do indeed. You're unaware of this, of course, because I prefer to be anonymous, but I'm a large underwriter of Kaleidoscope Productions. The donation for seal-coating the parking lot? That came from me." He said it matter-of-factly.

Ellie stammered for a moment, lost for words, her head bobbing at the surprise before she could contain it. She had not expected to be face to face with someone who had contributed such a large amount. Hillman frowned while watching Ellie tic, but said nothing.

Bill said, "That was very generous of you, Mr. Hillman. But we still have some questions, if you don't mind."

"Might I ask why? Do heart attacks usually warrant a police chief showing up and questioning someone?"

"Not usually. Unless the heart attack was not natural."

Hillman phrased his next question carefully. "Are you saying someone deliberately induced some type of cardiac event in Reginald?"

"That's what we're trying to put to bed. We want to rule it out. Hence the questions," Bill said.

"Very well. What can I help with?"

"We understand you are the Thorntons' money manager?"

Hillman blinked. "Ah. You're here because you want to know about the state of Reginald Thornton's finances before he perished?"

"Correct," Bill said.

"I spoke with Valerie Thornton a few days ago," Ellie said. *Nod-nod-nod.* "She indicated there was no life insurance policy." *Sniff-sniff-sniff. Grunt.*

Hillman's smile faltered slightly. "Has this become a homicide investigation, Chief?"

For Bill, the mood in the room shifted. He spoke carefully. "Reginald Thornton's death was ruled a medical event by the state police. Heart attack."

"Which is why you are here instead of them."

The man's calmness somehow made Bill think that Hillman had expected them. Again, he spoke carefully. "We're simply following up on some things to close out our investigation."

"Because you don't believe Reginald's death was natural."

Ellie sat up straighter, head bobbing, eyes blinking, thumbs rubbing her thighs in an alternating rhythm. Bill leaned forward.

"Naturally, we want to eliminate all doubt, and naturally Mrs. Marlowe feels the same, considering the death occurred in her theater," Bill said slowly.

Hillman returned the smile, sharp and adversarial. "Very good, Chief. I spoke with Valerie Thornton this morning, and she indicated you"—he gestured toward Ellie—"spoke with her three days ago, and that you"—he gestured toward Bill—"wanted to perform an autopsy because the state police would not."

"Mr. Hillman—" Ellie started to say.

"Please call me Alex," he said with a smile.

"Okay. Alex, if you talked with Valerie Thornton, then you must have figured we were going to come see you at some point." *Blink-blink-grunt-grunt. Nod.*

The man didn't answer, but focused on Ellie to the point of her discomfort. She opened her mouth to say something when he spoke.

"Tourette syndrome?"

She blinked in surprise.

"Excuse me?"

"You have Tourette syndrome?"

To date, she had never encountered someone who asked her this so bluntly. Most often, people she knew eventually asked—as if embarrassed, couching their questions in exploratory phrases like "Can I ask you something personal?" Often, she could predict the next question, sometimes with the exact words.

But this man had brushed all that aside and just asked. In a way, she found it refreshing.

"Yes," she answered. "I do."

Alex nodded, as if confirming it for himself. "I thought so. I have a cousin who has it. Not quite as prominent as yours, but it's there if you know what to look for."

"Mine is a case of highs and lows," Ellie said simply. "Some days, it almost disappears, some days I can barely stop moving. Stress has a lot to do with it."

Bill observed this exchange and fought his urge to shut it down and plow forward. Sometimes listening was more important than trying to steer a conversation toward a desired outcome, however difficult it was for him to stay patient and to not, well, interfere because he felt protective toward Ellie, his younger sister's best friend with a condition that often caused snickering reactions from people. Ellie and this very direct man, however, somehow had established a rapport.

"I can only imagine the stress that Reginald's death and the unknowns around it must be causing," Alex said.

"You have no idea," Ellie muttered.

Bill finally broke in. "Mr. Hillman, Valerie indicated to Ellie that there was no life insurance policy. Is that correct?"

"No."

Bill and Ellie sat forward together, and together said, "No?"

Alex shook his head. "No, I'm afraid that's not correct. Reginald Thornton did have an insurance policy on his life."

"She said it had been canceled," Ellie said.

"Quite the contrary. Reginald renewed the policy last autumn."

"Would his wife have known that?" Bill asked.

"I didn't tell her, mind you, not my place. In matters of money, I dealt strictly with Reginald. Valerie's signature was not required. I'm assuming he told her, but it's only that: an assumption. She could have known that he let it lapse—but there's a grace period for payments."

"She was the sole beneficiary?" Bill asked.

He paused for a moment, then nodded. "Correct. She and Reginald never had children."

"Would she have lost her beneficiary status if she had divorced him?"

"No, not unless Reginald changed the beneficiary on the policy."

Bill took notes as they talked. "You said you talked to her this morning?"

"I have certain fiduciary obligations to her now that her husband is deceased." He paused, then added, "If I were to offer an opinion, though I should keep my opinions to myself, I would say she is better off without Reginald."

Bill cocked an eyebrow. "Money could help soften the blow of a loss," he observed.

Alex shrugged. "I was thinking more emotionally, but you are correct. In the event of his death, the policy offered a fairly nice payout."

"How much?" Ellie asked. Her head stayed relatively still, behaving itself, but she was in danger of wearing blisters into her thumbs from her jeans.

"If memory serves," Alex said, "it's in the neighborhood of quite a lot of money. Of course, I'm not at liberty to reveal that to you."

Bill rubbed his chin. "Could we see a copy of the policy?" Bill asked.

Alex sat back in his chair, reclining slightly, his hands laced across his stomach. He smiled at them, closed mouth. He gazed at the ceiling for a moment, then returned his stare to the two people in the guest chairs in front of him.

"I'm afraid, for that, I will require a warrant."

Bill knew he lacked the authority to compel Alex to cooperate, but it was frustrating to be so close to something tangible.

Ellie leaned forward. "Mr. Hillman—Alex," she said. "We're trying to help. We think someone may have deliberately killed Reginald, and we want to find out if that's true, and who could have killed him." *Blink-grunt-blink.* "We're not trying to dig up secrets or pry into people's personal lives." *Blink-grunt-blink. Sniff.* "And I'm sure you, as Reginald's money manager, are as interested in learning the truth as anyone."

"That's flattering," Alex said. "But the truth of the matter is that Reginald Thornton was an awful human, and, quite frankly, I'm glad I no longer have to deal with him."

Bill leaned forward. "Why?"

Alex shrugged, as if caught in a slight transgression but not really caring. When he spoke, his voice was clear and direct. "Reginald was a bastard. Anyone who dealt with him knew this. You, Mrs. Marlowe, must surely have realized this, given he was in one of your shows."

Ellie didn't react. Forced herself not to tic. Not to give anything away.

Alex continued. "Reginald was repugnant, and I don't use that word lightly. I managed money for him for many years. At least a decade. And in that time, I rarely saw him treat another person with any measure of decency."

"Including yourself?" Bill asked.

"Especially myself. Anyone who was in his service or employment was treated like an untouchable member of the lowest caste. If I'm being truthful, I was on the verge of dropping the Thorntons as clients."

"Because of his attitude?" Ellie said.

"In part. But also because he was broke."

"Broke?"

"Yes. He was heavily leveraged and struggling, I think, to meet basic bills. I'm talking about things like cable, cell phone, electricity."

Bill was surprised. "Then how did he afford a life insurance policy?" he asked.

Alex spread his hands before him in a type of shrug. "I don't know. He had not paid for my services in over six months, yet somehow paid on the policy."

"Do you usually let clients float for that long?" Bill asked.

"No. I did it for Valerie's sake. I didn't want to leave her in the cold."

"You sound as if you're fond of her."

"I have become so, yes."

"In a romantic way?" Bill asked.

Alex smiled and looked amused, which made Bill think he was the butt of a joke. Ellie, seeing the smile, understood immediately.

"You're gay," Ellie said, as if it were a major revelation.

"Thank you," Alex said, "but I was already aware of that."

Ellie reddened and ticced in embarrassment. "I'm sorry. I didn't mean it like that. It was more like an *aha* moment for me. It takes the possibility of you being Valerie's jealous lover off the table."

Alex laughed, and the mood in the room shifted again. "Most decidedly."

Bill nodded as if he was finally getting it. "Merilyn mentioned you might know about more than just money?"

"Merilyn?"

"Merilyn Chambers," Ellie said. "The director of the show."

"Ah, yes. Well."

"Do you know her?"

"Not really, no."

For the first time since the beginning of their conversation, Bill thought the man across the desk from him was out-and-out lying. He rubbed his chin with his hand, wondering what that meant and whether now was the time to pursue it. He asked, "Then why might she imply you have—or know—secrets?"

"Secrets?" Alex smiled his amusement, and Bill saw the mocking in his eyes.

"So there's nothing else you can tell us about the Thorntons?"

"Nothing that comes to mind without the benefit of a warrant."

Bill nodded. He understood. The interview was over. Still, it was worth one last shot. "Mr. Hillman, is there anything you can share with us about Reginald's death?"

Alex leaned forward, hands clasped together, arms on his desk.

"I'm afraid what I have shared is everything I can share at this time, and perhaps something I shouldn't have."

Bill stood.

"Thanks for your time today, Mr. Hillman," he said. Alex remained seated.

Ellie stood and then Alex stood, as if bound by some type of male chivalry. He stretched out his hand toward Ellie. She reached out and grasped it.

"Thank you for your time, Alex." She forced her body to stillness so that shaking her hand wouldn't be like shaking the hand of someone holding a joy buzzer.

"A pleasure," he said. "I do want to say I think the work you do at the theater is wonderful. I've been happy to be a patron, and will continue to be one."

Ellie opened her mouth to respond, but nothing came out, caught off guard once more. She wasn't sure how to respond. Her tics betrayed her embarrassment.

"Thank you so much for your generosity," she finally managed. "I'm sorry we couldn't have met under different circumstances."

"Me as well. Perhaps sometime in the future, circumstances will allow us to converse without the difficulty of a non-homicide investigation in between."

"I'd like that," Ellie said, but she wasn't sure whether she would or wouldn't.

"We'll see ourselves out," Bill said.

*   *   *

Alex crossed the floor with them and saw them out. When they had left the house, he continued to watch them until their car pulled away, and then headed back to his office.

"Hold my calls, Debby."

"Certainly," the receptionist said.

He closed the door of his office and picked up the phone. He dialed the number, one he knew by heart. He waited. On the fifth ring, the call was answered.

"We need to talk," he said.

Chapter
Thirty-Three

Bill drove Ellie back to her car, silent the whole time. Each new revelation left them with more questions. They both dwelt in their thoughts, turning the puzzle over and over in their head, trying to make sense of it.

Ellie didn't want to think any of the people involved in her theater could be capable of something like this. *Murder.* Her mind would not keep quiet, not until she analyzed each one, a mental evaluation of what she knew of their personalities, their motives, and their opportunity. She sorted the group into those who could—Valerie, Jerry, Kyra, Steve, even Dana—and those who couldn't—Merilyn, in this case, the only person in that group. And there were those she didn't know until today, namely Alex Hillman. How many others might be out there waiting to be uncovered?

She thought of it like a bread trail, with herself and Bill as Hansel and Gretel. They found a crumb and chewed on it for a bit, wondering if there was more, then suddenly spied another crumb off in the distance. All the while, they went deeper into the forest and got more lost while each crumb tasted the same—bitter.

Bill, for his part, was trying to bring his anger to heel. Nothing about this case sat right with him. Murders happen all the time, in cities and suburbs, small towns and horse country. One minute someone was alive, then was dead at the hands of someone else. The means were different, the tools varied, and the motives might be polar opposites, but one thing could be counted on in a murder: dead was dead. There was only one other common element of murder besides death.

Trying to hide it.

Everyone they talked to was holding back or outright lying. Everyone was hiding something. And pointing fingers. Valerie pointed at Kyra, Kyra at Jerry, Jerry at Merilyn, Merilyn at Alex, Alex at . . .

Who was Alex Hillman pointing at? No one. Perhaps Valerie. She had to have known about the insurance policy, right? Perhaps not. Reginald had held her back, kept her down. Effectively quashed her music career. And what was in the insurance policy? To find out, Bill would need a warrant. And with idiots like Avery deliberately trying to hold back everything, help from the MSP seemed unlikely. He wondered if there was a way to force the state to open the case up as a homicide. Probably not unless some evidence was found.

He pulled into the Avalon police station parking lot, and Ellie got out.

"So where to now?" she asked through the passenger window.

He shrugged. "I'm going to dig deeper into backgrounds. See what else I can dig up."

"And if that gets you nothing?"

Bill sighed. "Then it might be over."

Ellie looked stricken. Her tics confirmed her displeasure. "Bill, no. You can't."

"Can't what? Can't stop investigating something I have no authority to investigate in the first place?" He lifted his eyes to the police station, an old brick building on a street off the center of town that had started life as an inn two hundred years earlier. The inn had traded hands a dozen or so times over its first hundred years and was then bought by the town, which sat on it for the next fifty. Only in the last forty-five to fifty years had the town finally decided to make use of it by turning it into the police station.

"There has to be something else we can look into," Ellie said.

Bill shrugged again. "Like I said, I'm going to poke around the records some more, see if any of them lead anywhere. In this Information Age, we've got lots of records online. Social media stalking, deep dives with Google, that sort of thing. But as far as interviews, I think we're done."

Ellie turned her back to him, breathing deeply through her nose. She closed her eyes, trying to will away the tears. It felt like her whole body was convulsing. When she had better control, she turned around.

"Okay," she smiled, trying to hide how upset she was. "Let me know if you find anything."

"Of course," Bill said grimly.

She could see his sadness in the straight, bloodless line of his mouth and the furrow between his brows. "I'm going to swing by home first, then head to the theater. I have some post-weekend cleanup to do before our shows this coming weekend."

She walked across the parking lot to her car. Just before she climbed into it, Bill called out to her.

"You know what Friday is, right?"

Ellie nodded. As if she could ever forget—Ava's birthday.

"I'm headed to the cemetery on Friday. You . . ." he paused as if hesitant to ask, then finished. "You wanna go with me?"

Ellie couldn't hold back the tears and wiped her face with the flat of her hand. She nodded. "I wouldn't miss it."

Chapter
Thirty-Four

After leaving Bill behind at the station, Ellie went home. Plenty of work waited for her at the theater, but she couldn't bring herself to go there yet. The past weekend had overwhelmed her, and the conversation with Alex Hillman had not helped clarify anything. On the way back to the station, Bill had filled her in on his conversation with Merilyn, and the thought of losing Merilyn swamped her. It wasn't that Ellie had taken a myopic view of Merilyn's condition. Anyone could see how bad it was. But to hear about it from Bill's perspective made it seem that much more real.

And the anniversary of Ava's death was coming up this Friday. It was too much. She just wanted to go home where she could wrap herself in a blanket and curl under the covers of her bed. She wanted to sleep and wake up when this was all over.

But it was over, wasn't it? That was the problem. There was nothing else to do. Reginald had been murdered, she was sure of that, yet no formal investigation existed on which to hang her hope.

She pulled into her driveway, and her heart sank. On the other side of the yard, raking leaves, thankfully fully dressed, was Judy. Ellie sighed, knowing she would never be able to get into her house without having to talk to the old woman. A line from an old movie popped into Ellie's head—like the character Glenn Close played in

Fatal Attraction, she would not be ignored. Although Judy wasn't a complete psycho, and maybe just somewhat lonely.

Might as well get this over with, Ellie thought. She climbed out of the car. Judy greeted her, then waved her over. Ellie slowly went over to Judy's side of the yard. She hoped her eyes had lost some of their redness, but she had cried on the way home.

Judy wasn't fooled a bit. "Why you been crying, honey?"

Ellie sighed and shrugged. *Nod-nod.* "Been a tough week so far." She paused, then added, "Plus, this Friday would have been Ava's thirty-second birthday."

Judy nodded as if she understood and kept raking leaves into piles. "That was a tragedy. A goddamn tragedy. I'll never forget it." She stopped raking. "I was the first one down there. Did you know that?"

Ellie looked at Judy like she was seeing her for the first time. *Blink-blink-blink.* The old woman had dropped all traces of her trademark sarcasm. She stared at the lawn as if lost in a memory.

"I was walking Bjorn, my dog, at the time. We were down by the reservoir, his favorite place to walk. We heard the yelling for help and hurried over."

Ellie felt herself falling backward through her memories. She and Ava, both twelve that summer before seventh grade, had been playing in the reservoir, even though they weren't supposed to be. No one was allowed in the water. But of course the town children would sneak down there, mainly early in the morning or late in the evening, especially in the stifling dog days of August. The police knew. How could they not? It was one of the worst-kept secrets in town. But most kids were strong swimmers, and most went with a group. If one got in trouble, the others would pull them out.

The state water officials hated it, of course. This was drinking water for Boston and its surrounding neighborhoods. They didn't mind people fishing in the reservoir, with the DRC going out of its way to stock it with trout every year. But they drew the line at swimming. They left standing instructions with the town police department to ensure no swimming, with fines and jail terms specified. But if someone went for a dip, the town, tasked with policing a reservoir of other people's drinking water, mostly looked the other way.

Until Ava.

Ellie tried to remember Judy being there and couldn't. It didn't surprise her. The scene, once the shout went up, had been chaotic with police and rescue personnel, and well-intentioned citizens who dove in to help but had to be rescued themselves. After Ava went under and didn't come back up, the crazy panicked dives to the bottom started. Divers used their hands to feel along the bottom, searching through the weeds and silt, with their eyes closed and the breath bursting in their lungs, hoping and praying to lay a hand on something that was human and alive.

"Are you okay, honey?" Judy asked. She reached out a hand to steady Ellie.

"I had no idea," Ellie tried to say but only managed to whisper.

Judy leaned the rake against the picket fence, took off her yard gloves, and guided Ellie toward her house. Ellie let herself be led.

"Come inside," Judy said. "I'm going to make you some tea. And you're going to sit and drink it."

Halfway across the lawn, Ellie's head bobbed and her fist mashed against her nose, accompanied by grunts and sniffs. She pulled free of the old woman's grasp and said, "Thank you, Judy. But I need to get home."

"You're going to come inside and have tea with me."

"I really can't."

"You gonna say no to an old woman? This could be my dying request, and you're saying no?"

Ellie looked sharply at Judy, but Judy's face dared her to say something, and surprising herself, Ellie smiled. Sadly.

"Okay," she conceded. "Okay."

*   *   *

Judy put the mug in front of Ellie, who wrapped her hands around the ceramic. It nearly scalded her, and on a crisp autumn day it was perfect. Better than a campfire on a chilly night. The tea smelled strongly of chamomile and less strongly of mint, and Judy had put at least three spoonfuls of honey into it. Ellie brought it to her lips and grimaced at the overwhelming sweetness. Yet she sipped more. It tasted like a warm honey candy melting in her mouth, reminding her of something from her childhood that she couldn't quite pinpoint.

They sat in silence, Ellie enjoying the heat of the tea through the mug on her hands. Her tics settled into a manageable few, an occasional head bob, a sniff here and there, but that was it. She felt mentally and emotionally exhausted, and her body felt the same.

Judy watched with compassionate eyes. "Been looking into the big guy's death?"

"Yes," Ellie nodded.

"You got some mess on your hands, honey," Judy said. "Some mess."

Ellie shrugged. The statement spoke for itself.

"What're you gonna do about it?"

"I don't know." Ellie sighed and took another sip of the honey candy tea. "I'd like to get some answers, but, then again, maybe I already have them."

"What answers would those be?"

"That Reginald was a closet drug addict who needed to be high to get through his performances, and that he took one hit that was too strong."

"How's that sound to you?" Judy asked.

Ellie shrugged and said, "Reasonable, maybe. I'm a former non-profit person, not a philosopher, but that whole Occam's razor thing is starting to sound pretty good."

"The simplest solution is often the correct one," Judy summarized. Her tea sat in front of her, untouched. It seemed as if she had made tea because she thought it was something people did to help with sadness, but she appeared to have no intention of drinking it.

"That's the one, and it makes sense," Ellie said. "Except my gut doesn't agree."

"What's your gut telling you?"

Ellie stared at Judy for a moment. Judy's concentration was intense. Ellie blinked and looked around the spotless kitchen. The counter and appliances practically gleamed. It struck Ellie that there were no fingerprints on the appliances, even the stainless-steel refrigerator. It looked like Judy cleaned every day, possibly every hour.

"Judy, your kitchen is lovely," Ellie said, changing the subject. *Nod-nod.* "Not at all what I expected."

"You expected some kind of country colonial kitchen, I'm guessing? 'Cause I'm an old lady?"

"No," Ellie said, "that's not why."

"But that's what you expected."

"Well, yes, I guess."

"Nope," Judy said, breaking her gaze away from Ellie for the first time. Ellie sighed with relief. "I'm a gal who likes to mix modern with Art Deco."

Ellie could see what she meant. The rounded counter corners were rimmed with a gleaming lip in two parallel lines that shined like chrome. There was a black corded phone on the wall with a rotary dial, and in one corner sat a Bakelite clock. Yet the appliances were stainless steel and the coffeemaker was a Bunn Speed-Brew with a glass pot. Ellie found it incongruous but mesmerizing.

"What is your gut telling you?" Judy said, returning to her original question.

Ellie clenched the mug tighter. It hurt her hands, too hot to handle, but that odd, homespun comfort in the hot mug of tea remained.

"My gut is telling me that Reginald was murdered."

Judy nodded. "Now what's your gut telling you about the who?"

"I probably shouldn't say."

"Why not? There's no investigation, there's no murder according to the staties. Don't get me started on those idiots. You got no professional need to protect somebody's privacy. This is just two ladies talkin'."

Ellie laughed, a small, little sound, but genuine. She glanced at Judy, who wasn't laughing or smiling, but Ellie thought she spied a glint of amusement in the corners of the old woman's eyes.

"Judy," Ellie said, "I can't. It wouldn't be fair to the people we've talked to."

"We, huh?"

Ellie shook her head, slow and deliberate. "You are one hundred percent wrong on this one. I've known Bill for almost thirty years. If anything, he's more like a brother."

"Mm-hmm."

Judy's gaze was intense and embarrassing, and it made Ellie start to blush and tic. Ellie sipped some of her tea, the mug hiding her face slightly. The heat from the drink provided an excuse as to why her face was slightly flushed. The fact is that she had thought about it, occasionally, over the years—her and Bill. And if she thought about it at all now, it made her squirm slightly, awkwardly, because she had known Bill for nearly three decades.

And then her mind would drift to Ava.

"We're going to the cemetery together on Friday," Ellie said. "Ava's birthday. I don't expect a lot of people will be there other than us. There's no ceremony or anything like that. Bill's mom is dead, and his dad is in Whisper Springs. But we'll be together because we both loved Ava. So please don't start any rumors if you see us."

Judy made another "mm-hmm" sound and finally brought her mug to her lips. Ellie saw it was nothing but an act, a pantomime.

Judy's lips never parted, and the liquid in the mug never decreased. Judy set her mug back on the table.

How much of the town is an act? Ellie asked herself. *How much of it is a pantomime?*

Ellie wondered what she could be thinking when she asked, "Would you like to join us?"

"At a graveyard?" Judy barked with laughter. "Thanks, no. I expect I'll be seeing one sometime in the near future anyway."

"Judy," Ellie admonished.

"Oh, I know I'm an old biddy. But"—her tone softened—"I do appreciate the invitation."

"Does Bill know you were the first person on the scene?"

"I don't know if he remembers any more about that day than you do. He never made it to the scene. He only heard about it later, after work. He was working at a pizza joint on Route 70 close to the Worcester line, if I recall. I think he didn't hear about it until after his shift."

"I can't imagine what it was like for him," Ellie said.

"Didn't you all ever talk about it?"

"No. I saw him just after the funeral, we hugged and cried for a bit, and he left."

"The Army."

Ellie nodded. "Yes. He left. Broke his mother's heart, I think, but it was the only thing he knew to do. Put as much distance between himself and here as he could."

"Must have surprised you when he came back."

Ellie laughed. "It surprised me when *I* came back. But yes, I was a little shocked."

"There's that twinkle again. That one there in the corner of your eye."

"Oh, stop it, you old tease. I think the whole town was shocked, not just me."

"What's Bill think about this murder business?" Judy asked.

"He agrees with me." Ellie went on. "He was a state cop before taking the police chief job. Nothing about this sits right with him."

"Who does he think did it?"

"Judy," Ellie said, making the word long and tired, "I can't talk about it. And I have to get going. Thank you for the tea. This was lovely."

Ellie smiled, rose to go, and unexpectedly for both of them, bent down and hugged the old woman. Judy stiffened at first, then relaxed and returned the hug.

"If you change your mind," Ellie said, "we'll be at the cemetery Friday morning."

"Thank you," Judy said. Ellie turned to go, and Judy added, "I think you're right, by the way."

"About what?" Ellie asked, turning back.

"That it was murder."

Ellie stared at her neighbor.

Chapter
Thirty-Five

B ill spent the rest of the day digging deeper into public records, but that got him no closer to understanding who killed Reginald. He would find something online, print it, spend a bit of time reading it, then set it aside. He found a lot of backstory for the primary suspects, but nothing he read was a silver bullet.

Toward the end of the day, his eyes felt like they might fall out of his head. He made a list on a yellow legal pad with the names of everyone who had been interviewed and a few who hadn't been, including Valerie, Jerry, Kyra, people from the theater—Steve, even Dana—and the rest.

He turned the legal pad sideways and wrote their names along the long side of the pad. Below their names he listed motives. Then he drew a line across the page and listed their whereabouts at the time of Reginald's death, or rather, the moment he suspected Reginald had been poisoned. Below that, he drew another line and wrote what he knew about the relationship between each suspect and the deceased.

When he finished, he laid the pages, which numbered three in total, across his desk. He looked for a pattern or some other distinguishing feature that popped out. Something that would reveal itself, like a picture when enough pieces of a puzzle are snapped into place. But that didn't happen. Too many of the names had more than enough motivation, or a close relationship with Reginald, good or bad. There was no discernible pattern that Bill could coalesce a theory around.

In the end, one person's list was the longest.

One person had plenty of motivation, about as close a relationship as it got, and the opportunity to poison Reginald. One person with whom he needed to have a conversation, a deeper conversation, if she'd let him.

He stood up from his desk, picked up his keys, and walked out of the police station.

Chapter
Thirty-Six

Ellie came home from Judy's house weary and disoriented. She entered her home and listened to the noises of the house: Mike upstairs on the phone, the hum of the refrigerator in the kitchen, the hiss of steam through the radiators, and the German cuckoo clock that had been her grandmother's.

She stood, taking in the sounds and trying to control her breathing and her body. Her body was alarmingly quiet, still in a way it rarely achieved. Ellie had made a conscious choice not to dwell on Ava's death, especially after moving back to town. Now, with Ava's birthday looming on the calendar, the death of an actor in her theater, and the realization that someone may have gotten away with murder, she was almost too exhausted to think.

The talking stopped, and a door opened.

"Hello?" came a voice down the stairs.

"Hi, hon," she said, trying to keep her voice level. "I'm home."

Mike came into view at the top of the stairs and descended two steps at a time. He stopped short of his wife, concern on his face.

"What's wrong?" he asked.

Ellie opened her mouth to speak, but no words came. She thought she made a sound, something like a creaky door, as if the words had lodged in her throat and needed oiling to get loose. But in the end, they did not come, and Ellie started crying.

Mike looked at Ellie, concern blooming to full-fledged alarm. He didn't know what was wrong, didn't know what had started this, but he knew to take her into his arms. He held her, silent and strong, as she wept, his arms holding her and his hands gently rubbing her back.

When her crying began to slow, she apologized between hitched breaths. He led her to the couch, and they sat.

"What's happened?" he asked.

"Nothing. It's nothing."

"An awful lot of tears for nothing."

"Okay," she admitted, using part of her sleeve to wipe her eyes. "It's not nothing. It's just . . . I don't know. Stuff I haven't dealt with in a while."

She told him about the morning interviewing Alex and about her plans to go to the graveyard on Friday with Bill. She told him about her conversation with Judy and ended with a sigh.

"I guess I feel like I'm back in time, twenty years ago, going through Ava's death all over again. Reginald's death has hit me, and between that and Ava's birthday on Friday, I feel like life is caving in on me."

Mike held Ellie's hand while she talked, not saying anything, just listening and watching her. She rambled a bit more before barking out a laugh while wiping tears. "You can say something. It's okay."

"Seems like what you wanted was to talk it through. That you needed somebody to listen."

She smiled. "Ten years together and you're still surprising me."

"I listened in therapy," Mike said with mock indignation.

"I know you did." Her voice was soft now, gentle.

"Want my opinion?" Mike asked.

She said nothing, and he went on. "You need to put this behind you. You need to let it go. Reginald's death was tragic, and it's crazy that it happened in your theater during one of your productions. Like, what are the odds? Maybe he was using drugs, maybe not. But the state police don't think it's a murder. You need to accept that and move on."

"I think I liked it better when you were listening."

"I know your gut is telling you it was murder. But there's no hard evidence to back that up, and what would it accomplish if there were?"

Someone I know could have murdered someone—a man who was deeply disliked.

Ellie thought about it. Would it be terrible to let it go, even if someone *did* kill Reginald? So what if it happened in her theater, on her watch, practically in her presence?

He took her hand in both of his and kissed it and held it to his face. "What I don't want is for you to get so wound up in this that you can't let it go."

"You mean like my old job?"

"I didn't say that."

Ellie looked at him.

"Okay, fine. Maybe I thought it. I don't want a repeat of what brought us back to Avalon in the first place. Leaving your old job. Involuntarily. The inability to let things go. You're obsessed with this, whatever it is. It's not a murder because the state police have already said it's not. But that's not good enough for you, is it? You have to find the pea under the pile of mattresses."

Ellie's face had become stone. For a brief moment, she hated Mike for pointing out her perseverations, bringing up her past, and questioning her now; the hate was intense, burning hot, a nuclear brightness.

She stood and pulled her hand away. She walked away from the couch, into the kitchen. Mike stayed on the couch, knowing he'd gone too far, kicking himself for having less restraint but secretly fearing they were on the downside of their rollercoaster.

The Last Line

The phone rang in the kitchen. In the quiet stillness of the house, it sounded as loud as an air horn, and it made Ellie jump. She took the cordless phone off the cradle and looked at the caller ID. *Bill*. She answered.

"What's up?" she said as she answered the phone. Mike came to the kitchen doorway, leaned against the frame, and stared at her.

From over the phone, Mike could hear Bill's answer.

"I think we can cross Valerie off the list of suspects," Bill said.

"Why?" Ellie said, not caring that Mike could hear. "She's the best fit. Lots of motive, lots of opportunity."

"What now?" Mike said, interrupting. Ellie glanced at him and turned her back on him. *He didn't get to be a part of this. Not if he didn't believe her. He didn't get to participate if he failed to support her, if he could only criticize.*

"Both true," Bill replied. "Which is why I went to see her. I was going to talk it over with her again and see if I could catch her in a lie or something."

"What happened?"

"Someone got there first."

Ellie felt her heart flutter. She turned back around. He saw her look, her face white. Her hand cradling the phone started to tremble. His brow furrowed deep with concern, and he mouthed, "What?" She shook her head at him and put a hand to her face.

"Someone hurt her? Is she—" Ellie started to ask.

"Dead?" Bill finished. "No, but not for lack of trying. She's in a coma."

ACT 3

"It is a wise father that knows his own child."

Chapter Thirty-Seven

Detective Chuck Phelps walked around the scene. Several people from the Crime Scene Unit were taking pictures, dusting for prints, and cataloging everything in the living room. Phelps took out his phone and took a few pictures. He knelt on one knee next to the blood spill and examined it. He wore blue latex gloves but didn't touch anything.

"So," he said, "is it safe to say the blow to the head was caused by the candlestick?"

The crime lab guy with the camera took another picture, the flash popping and leaving little black dots dancing in front of Phelps's eyes. Phelps blinked hard twice to try and clear them.

"Need to get it back to the lab first, officially," the crime lab guy said. "But yeah, that'd be my guess based on the wound and the blood on the candlestick."

"Professor Plum, in the conservatory?"

The crime lab guy forced a brief smile.

"Any prints on the candlestick?" Phelps asked.

"Didn't appear to be."

Phelps nodded. "The perp either wiped them clean or wore gloves. If he wore gloves, he came here with a purpose."

The crime lab guy nodded. Phelps peeled off his gloves and tossed them into a makeshift trash bag. He walked over to the foyer, where Bill Starlin stood with Davis Whitney.

"Well, Bill," Phelps said. "Looks like this time you actually got a crime. Not a murder, but definitely an attempted one."

Jim Avery, who had come to the scene with Phelps, guffawed. Bill took a step forward, prompting Davis to put a hand gently on his arm.

"Actually, I'm the police chief for Clifton," Davis said. Stocky and potbellied, Davis Whitney had a full head of snow-white hair so fine the faintest breeze would make it unruly, which was why he wore his police hat nearly everywhere. His officers, who respected him tremendously, ribbed him that he probably wore it in the shower. Davis would merely smile and wink. Now, he said, "So give me the update, please."

Phelps looked at Davis with a sour expression.

"Looks like the victim got brained with a crystal candlestick," Phelps said. "No sign of forced entry, so odds are she knew the person. Other than that, I don't have much else to tell you. We're still processing the scene."

Bill wanted to say more, but didn't. He stood there a moment, taking in the scene, making a mental list of what he saw. The piano stood open, as if she had been playing the piano when she had been hit. In front of the piano lay the candlestick, which one of the crime scene guys now picked up and bagged. The crystal base was smeared with blood as well as black powder from the fingerprinting. A bloodstain was evident on the carpet. As a crime scene went, that was it. The rest of the room seemed exactly as it was when he visited her earlier. Nothing had been disturbed. The desk in the corner did not appear to be rifled. The only evidence of anything wrong was the blood. He knew that the crime scene boys would continue to dust for prints, vacuum for fibers, take pictures, all the usual stuff. But nothing looked out of place. She apparently had opened the door to the attacker and let the person in. She had known whoever it was.

"You guys actually going to do your job this time?" Bill said.

Before Phelps or Avery could respond, Davis took Bill by the arm and led him out the front door.

To his surprise, he found Ellie sitting on the front stoop, face propped up by her fists.

"All right." Bill tugged himself free of Davis's grip.

Davis let him go and pushed his cap back a little on his head.

"I know you don't like these guys, Bill, but I have to work with them to figure out what happened here. So I need you to play nice, okay?"

Bill took a deep breath and let it out slowly. It took a moment before he nodded.

"Good," Davis said. "Listen, I get it. They dropped the ball on Valerie's husband. From what you described to me, it sounds fishy to me too. But I need their cooperation here. I don't want them to box me out of this, or I'll lose visibility as to what's going on. So, I ask you, one chief to another, stay out here and let me deal with them."

Bill frowned, his face a study in deep frustration, but he nodded and said, "Okay."

Davis squeezed Bill's shoulder, pulled his cap back down, and went into the house. Bill watched him go, then looked down at Ellie. She sat on the top step looking up at him. He sat down next to her.

"What are you doing here?" he asked.

"I drove over the moment I hung up with you. I would have come in, but the uniformed officer at the door stopped me."

"Yeah, well, it is a crime scene."

"I thought it was her," she said. "I thought that was why she had come to the theater that night. I really did."

"Still could have been," Bill answered. "She could have killed Reginald, and someone else came after her for some other reason or for something linked to her husband's death."

"I suppose," she said, but didn't sound convinced.

Bill looked at her. "Yeah, I don't buy that either," he said with a grimace.

"Do you think whoever killed Reginald tried to kill Valerie?"

He shrugged. "I want to think that so I can sleep at night. If I thought we had two killers in this tiny area, operating independently of each other, I'm not sure I'd ever let the kids out of the house again."

"I never thought of you as a helicopter parent," Ellie said.

He stared straight ahead. "If Ava hadn't died, I might not be. But her death scared me bad. When Aiden was born, I had a panic attack, right there in the hospital."

Ellie shook her head, her eyes wide at the revelation. She held her body still.

"I haven't told many people," he said. "As the chief of police it's a bad idea to advertise you're prone to panic attacks."

"Your secret is safe with me."

He took her hand in his and squeezed briefly. Then he stood, brushed off the seat of his trousers, and said, "Why don't you go home? I'll stay till they're done and call you tomorrow."

Ellie nodded.

Chapter
Thirty-Eight

Ellie got home to a quiet house. She didn't hear Mike upstairs. He hadn't mentioned anything about going out. Had he left because of their disagreement? Was he out on an errand? Had he grown hungry and then gone out to grab something to eat? Or was he out at a bar, knocking back one or two to unwind, hanging out with a few townies, talking local politics? Hopefully not eying an attractive woman or two in the bar, wishing he had married someone less complicated, less driven. Someone without Tourette syndrome.

She shook her head hard to clear it. Her brain was going to places it had not traveled to for nearly five years, since they had fled New York and moved here to her hometown. These thoughts used to torment her, and not just about Mike. She had these thoughts about everyone at some point. *Perseveration.* She learned the term in a therapist's office. Thoughts of doom and gloom, thoughts of bad things happening, or spirals of shame as she became certain everyone was mad at her and she didn't understand why. It came with the territory. It came with her case of Tourette's.

She knew that not everyone with TS experienced the things she experienced. Everyone's head was different, billions of unique brain chemistries wandering throughout the world. Who could say what made one person perfectly sane, and the next person a cannibalistic psychopath? Nature versus nurture, subtle but alarming distinctions in brain chemistry, maybe? It was all anyone's guess.

Not that an anxiety disorder was unique to people with TS. But it wasn't uncommon for people with TS to own a group of disorders. She had the misfortune of having TS in combination with generalized anxiety disorder.

That's what this is, she told herself. Her head working against her. Her brain chemistry struggling for control.

She had handled these better back when she worked full time or more. A vice president in an educational consulting nonprofit, she worked sixty hours per week easily. These things were easier to manage when she didn't slow down enough to feel them. But overworking came with its own host of issues, the strain on her marriage being the prime one. When her normally patient software developer husband complained about how much she worked, a problem clearly existed. One only counseling and constant effort could untangle.

But that had been five years ago. Her marriage had survived and even blossomed once she walked away from the nine-to-five world— although it was really seven thirty to ten at night most days—but her brain chemistry seemed to crave the constant busy-ness. She found it ironic that leaving her stressful job was the catalyst for her going onto a suite of anti-anxiety medications.

She sat down in the living room, unsure what to do next. It wasn't like her to sit around and mope, but she couldn't find the motivation to do anything other than sit in the chair and feel sorry for herself.

The front door opened. The sound made her nearly jump out of her skin. She hadn't realized how tightly she had been coiled, ready to snap at the littlest thing. As Mike came in from the foyer, she tried to make her voice sound calm when she asked, "Where did you go?"

He held up a white paper bag, folded closed at the top.

The Last Line

"Went to Scoops," he said. "After everything that's happened, and this attack on Reginald's widow, I thought ice cream might be in order."

She went to him and put her arms around his neck and kissed him. Then she put her head on his shoulder and cried.

Chapter Thirty-Nine

B ill Starlin woke up late, having hit the snooze button on his alarm three times before shutting the damn thing off. Finally, Darlene shook him awake at quarter to nine. His eyes fluttered open and rolled around for a bit before focusing on his wife.

"Mmph," he managed.

"Babe, it's nearly nine. Are you going in today?"

"Mmph."

"Yeah, well, okay. I'm about to head to work."

"Okay," he mumbled.

Darlene paused by the door of their bedroom and said, "You should at least tell somebody you're running late."

"Mm-hmm."

"And your phone has been going crazy this morning."

Bill came a little more awake. Normally the town didn't wake up early enough to wander into serious trouble until at least one or two in the afternoon. But Avalon wasn't anything close to normal right now.

"Phone?"

"Yeah," Darlene said. "Buzzing every other minute, I swear."

Bill managed to drag himself to a sitting position. He was not awake enough yet to hold himself fully upright. He had a fleeting memory of his Army days, where when the sergeant woke you, didn't matter the time, you damn well better wake up and hit the floor, fully upright, fully at attention. Those days were gone. He was an older man now, and waking up took some time.

His wife eyed him from the doorway. "What time did you come to bed last night?"

Bill sniffed and rubbed his face, still trying to wake up. "Late. After midnight."

Darlene stepped into the bedroom a little ways. "Did you hit a bar last night?"

He looked up at her and shook his head. "Why would you think that?"

"You look hungover."

"I'm not. I just couldn't turn my head off."

"The crime scene?"

"Avery caught it," Bill said.

"At least now the overtime he logs might be real," she said. Bill managed a half-amused grunt.

She sat on the bed next to him. He raised his eyes to meet hers. Darlene put a hand on his face, his scruff short and scratchy. "You wanna talk about it? Grab some lunch?"

Bill shrugged. "Maybe some coffee."

"Sure. Brewed Awakenings? Eleven thirty, twelve?"

He nodded. "Sounds good," he said. "I'll text you."

She stood and bent down and kissed his forehead. "In the meantime, go take a shower. You look terrible."

He made a face, but she grinned at him and left. He stayed in bed as she went down the stairs. Eventually, he heard the front door close, the car turn over, and the engine noise as she pulled into the street.

He had no thoughts in his head, just a blur of light through his half-drooped eyes. He might have sat in bed all day if it weren't for the sudden buzz of his phone.

He took a deep breath and swung his legs over the side of the bed, bare feet on the hardwood floor. He stood, grabbing the dresser for support.

He went to the short table in the little nook at the top of the stairs in the hallway, where everyone kept their phones overnight. House rule by Darlene: no cell phones in bedrooms. He and Darlene left their phones there, plugged in for the night—a good habit for when the kids would have phones of their own. He picked up his phone.

After flipping through texts, he called up Margot, who answered on the first ring.

"Morning, Chief."

"Margot."

"We've been wondering where you are. Are you coming in today?"

"Yes."

"Okay, good." She sounded relieved. "We have lots of people looking for you. We've had all kinds of press here, and they're looking for a statement about the actor. The dead one. Not his wife, of course, but the actor. Isn't that the craziest? Someone makes an attempt on the wife and suddenly everybody's interested in her dead husband, the actor. Also, the DA called. My goodness, such a sharp-tongued woman. I felt like a little girl being scolded when I told her—"

"Margot," Bill said. He was trying hard to be patient and not tell her to hurry up. "What about the DA?"

"She called once, and her assistant called a couple of times. She wants you to call her as soon as possible. That's a direct quote, 'as soon as possible.' She might have even used the word 'humanly,' like, 'as soon as humanly possible.'"

Bill took a deep breath. "She texted me. I'll respond. Did she say anything else?"

"No, just to call her," Margot said. "Sounded impatient and annoyed."

"I bet I know why."

"When should we expect you? We've gotten a lot of other calls this morning."

"I'm going to shower and then I'll be in."

He hung up and dialed the Worcester DA's office on Main Street. The receptionist put him on hold before a stern female voice came on the line.

"Starlin?"

"Chief of Police Bill Starlin," Bill agreed.

"You screwed up my crime scene, Chief." She said his title as if it was something she wiped off the bottom of her shoe.

"Nice to hear from you, Alice," Bill said in the sweetest voice he could muster. He had known Alice Keaton for a long time, having worked MSP crime scenes on more than one occasion. They were never close, but Bill had always thought of Alice as a levelheaded professional. They had never had a run-in until he quit. This "Angry Alice" side of her might be held over from the circumstances of his departure. But the crime scene comment didn't make sense.

"That's District Attorney Keaton to you, Chief."

"Whatever you say, Alice."

Silence on the other end of the line. Then he heard her sigh.

"Goddamn it, Bill," Alice said, her tone switching from anger to exasperation. "Why did you have to go and trample my crime scene? How am I supposed to present evidence in court and not have it tossed?"

Bill sighed. "Alice, we've known each other how long? Have you ever known me to be that stupid?"

"The boys in the lab tell me you contaminated the scene."

"The lab boys told you that? Or is that what Phelps and Avery told you the lab boys said?"

A moment's hesitation. "Phelps told me. But he wasn't mixed up in any of that shit from years ago."

"He works for Avery, doesn't he?"

"With, not for," she corrected. "And I do know that Avery was mixed up in it."

Bill laughed mirthlessly. "Oh, yes, he just wasn't caught. It sounds like you've been fed a line, Alice."

"Why would Phelps lie about this? What's in it for him?"

"For him? Probably nothing. For Avery? Lots."

"Such as?"

"Such as covering the fact they might have misclassified a death, right here in town."

"Are you talking about the dead actor?"

"Yes."

"I reviewed that report, Bill. There wasn't enough evidence to investigate."

"There was plenty to investigate," Bill said, his voice growing sharp and pointy, like his anger. "Avery had Phelps slap the heart attack label on it because Avery is a lousy detective, plain and simple."

"Last I checked, it's still a heart attack."

"Give the lab a call. Bet you a hundred-dollar bill they've moved the sample to liquid chromatography."

There was a pause at the other end of the line, then Alice said, "You've already talked to the lab, haven't you?"

Bill didn't answer. Another pause at the other end of the line. Bill imagined Alice rolling this information around in her head. "You think by claiming you contaminated the scene of the wife's attack, Avery can cover for him and Phelps?"

"You've known Avery for a while, Alice. Would it surprise you?"

After another moment of silence, Alice said, "Why don't you come down to Main Street? Fill me in on what you have."

For a reason he couldn't pinpoint, something in the way Alice said this sounded like a setup to Bill. He wanted to believe Alice Keaton had more integrity than that, but service in the Middle East had made him wary of walking into situations without knowing the lay of the land. This didn't feel right to him. There was no way he was heading into Worcester today. He wanted them on his turf.

"Tell you what," he countered. "Why don't you come out to me? It's been a while since we've done lunch. Come on down, and we'll grab some food and talk."

"Okay, fine. Where should we meet?"

"A place called Ned's Diner," Bill said.

Chapter Forty

At eleven thirty, Bill entered Ned's Diner. He had been planning to meet Darlene at that time for coffee and hated having to call her and break their date.

"Ugh," Darlene had said. "You really need to close this thing out."

"I know," Bill responded, feeling more guilty with each passing minute. "I'm trying."

"Try harder," she said, and ended the call. Bill sighed.

He saw Ellie in a booth. She had chosen one relatively close to the front door. He came up to the booth and said, "Thanks for agreeing to come. Now, switch."

"What?"

"Switch. I need to be able to watch the door."

"Why?"

"Because you won't recognize Alice Keaton when she walks in."

Ellie nodded. She slid out of the booth and into the other seat. Bill slid into the spot Ellie had occupied, noticing the warmth of the seat.

"Do you think it will be a problem if I'm here?" Ellie asked.

"You know as much, if not more, about all these characters than I do. It will be good for her to get your perspective."

Cheryl came over and Bill ordered coffee. When she asked if he wanted anything to eat, he said no, thank you. Cheryl had started in on one of her rambles when Bill put up his hand. Cheryl made a crack about him raising his hand to ask to speak, but followed his gaze toward the door.

A woman, attractive but severe-looking, with the sharp angles of her face accentuated by her bob haircut and straight bangs, had entered the restaurant. Two men in sports jackets flanked her. Bill thanked Cheryl again and waved the new arrivals over to the table.

Alice Keaton looked at the table, Bill on one side and Ellie on the other.

"And where am I supposed to sit?"

"Either side. Plenty of space. We'll scooch over for you," Bill said.

"What about them?" Alice asked.

"Do you always travel with bodyguards these days?" Bill said.

"I believe you've met Detectives Phelps and Avery."

Bill nodded. "They can sit at the counter if they like."

"They need to be part of this conversation."

"No dice."

Alice Keaton frowned and put her hands on her hips. She said over her shoulder to Avery, "Why don't you sit at the counter? I'll motion if I need you."

Avery shrugged like he didn't care, while Phelps glowered at Bill. He and Avery took stools directly across from the booth. Ellie switched sides, sitting next to Bill, and Alice took the seat across from them. Cheryl approached to take Alice's order, but the DA waved her off without looking at her. Cheryl *hmfphed* and stalked away.

"And you are?" Alice said to Ellie.

"Ellie Marlowe. I own Kaleidoscope Theater."

"And that makes you qualified to be involved in this investigation because . . . ?" At the counter, Jim Avery chuckled at the barb.

Ellie's head bobbed, and she blinked before saying, "It doesn't. Owning a theater makes me qualified to choose which play or musical we'll produce next."

Alice Keaton stared at her for a moment, eyebrows raised, then said to Bill, "You brought a civilian?"

"Seemed only fair, since it was her theater where Reginald dropped dead."

"And the crime scene?"

"Which one?" Bill asked. The jab wasn't lost on Alice.

"The only one which had a demonstrable crime."

"The front door was open. I went in, calling Valerie Thornton's name. She never answered. I went farther into the house and found her beside the piano, wound exposed. I checked for a pulse, found one, and called it in. The Clifton EMTs rushed her to Memorial where, as I understand it, she has been put in a medically induced coma. You guys were the first call after the EMTs."

"I'm told your boot prints were all over the scene before the MSP got there."

Bill reddened but kept his voice moderate. "I wasn't wearing boots. But I seem to recall Jim was."

Avery spun on his stool, stood up, leaned over the table, and said, "You're a liar, you piece of—"

Alice put up a hand and said sharply, "Sit down, and shut your mouth."

Avery looked like Alice had slapped him. He started to sit back down on the stool when Alice stopped him. She pointed to a set of stools at the other end of the counter. "Sit down there."

"But we won't be able to hear anything."

She made a waving motion with her hand, like shooing a small child. "Go."

In a huff, Avery, joined by Phelps, went to the other end of the counter and sat. Ellie watched this with a stillness in her body, a watchful anxiousness that superseded her need to move. The reprieve ended, her body twitched, and she grunted.

Alice observed her for a moment and chose to ignore it. She spread her hands before her in an inviting gesture. "Okay," she said. "Explain it to me."

Bill laid the situation out for her, from the moment Reginald collapsed to what they found in his personal items, to the people they had spoken with. He explained that he had thought Valerie the most likely suspect, and had gone to her house to have another talk with her.

"What exactly was your plan when you went in there? Slap on the cuffs and haul her down to the station?"

"I'm not new at this job, Alice. I've investigated a crime or two in my career, even arrested the odd suspect or three."

Alice mulled this over. Softer, she asked, "How sure are you Reginald was murdered?"

Bill and Ellie traded looks, and Ellie shrugged. "We can't be one hundred percent positive," she said. "Especially since no real forensic work happened at the scene, and the scene is long gone." *Grunt-grunt-blink-blink-blink. Nod-nod.*

"I had my department detective dust for prints," Bill said. "You can imagine how many prints we found in a theater."

Alice nodded, displeased.

"But if we go by what we've learned already," he continued, "coupled with the fact that someone brutally attacked his wife, then yeah, I think it's ninety, maybe ninety-five percent sure."

Alice sat back. She was quiet for a moment, thoughtful, then addressed Bill.

"I don't like that you worked on this on your own."

"That was from Phelps."

Alice frowned, looked past Bill to where Phelps and Jim Avery sat at the counter and watched. "What do you mean?"

"He told me I should feel free to take statements."

She gave him a look that seemed to ask if he thought she was stupid. "Him telling you to take statements is not an invitation to run your own investigation."

"Someone needed to—"

She held up her hand. "However, I also don't like that these guys chose to ignore your input. Holdover issues from days gone by."

"You put that more kindly than I would have."

Alice folded her hands together as Cheryl came over to the table with a carafe of coffee.

"Want some coffee, hon?" she asked Alice, emphasizing the word "hon" in an nonpleasant way.

"Any good?" Alice asked. Bill couldn't tell if she was asking Cheryl or him.

"Yeah," he said. "Diner coffee, but good diner coffee."

"Fine," Alice said. Cheryl smiled sweet as pie as she flipped over the mug in front of the district attorney and filled it nearly to the top.

"Anything to eat?"

"No, thank you. Coffee will be fine."

Cheryl left, and Alice lifted the mug to her lips. She took a sip and pursed her lips. "Pretty good for diner coffee."

She set the mug down again and stared into it for a moment. Bill waited, knowing not to say anything, willing Ellie to remain silent as well. They were about to come down to brass tacks, and Bill liked the odds. Ellie sat, hands in her lap, willing her head not to move, her throat not to clench, her voice not to betray her. She rubbed her thumbs furiously along her thighs in an alternating pattern.

"The assault obviously needs to be investigated as an attempted homicide," Alice finally said. "Straightforward enough, we just need to land on a suspect. But all the shit with the husband is a complicating factor. And you guys are in it deep."

Bill opened his mouth to speak, but Alice kept talking.

"I don't mean that in a bad way. I'm saying you guys have done some digging, a lot of digging, actually, and are closer to this than we are. Fair statement?"

Bill nodded. He didn't trust his voice.

"I don't want these guys involved in this," Alice said with a sigh. Ellie took it as a sigh of resignation, or perhaps recognition that the DA had two cops who didn't exactly appear on the straight and narrow. "They'll hate me for this, and as much as I don't like you going rogue on this, I like their conduct less. I have my own concerns about dealing with this barracks. If these guys mess it up to screw you, assuming we find the culprit and make an arrest, my life will be very hard as a prosecutor. But obviously, we need to drive this investigation."

Bill held his breath.

"So I'm going to sign paperwork putting you formally in charge of the case."

The breath he had been holding escaped, Bill's mouth a thin, bloodless line.

Ellie's mouth dropped open. "I didn't realize that was an option," she said.

"Not unless a DA delegates that responsibility, which, technically, is an option," Alice said.

"A highly unusual one," Bill said. "And not one that goes over well with the staties."

"I'll deal with them. You'll report to me. I'll expect regular updates. You're lead on the investigation now." She turned to Ellie. "And he can deputize you if he wants to. Up to him."

Ellie couldn't help herself, unable to hold back any longer. *Blink-blink-blink-nod-nod. Grunt-grunt.*

Alice said nothing, and when Ellie appeared to be finished, the DA stood and looked down at them. "We all clear?"

Bill nodded, and Ellie said, "Yes."

"Good. I want a report in my inbox tomorrow morning, first thing."

"Done," Bill said.

Alice motioned to the other two detectives still sitting at the end of the counter. Without another word, all three left the diner. Once they left, Ellie, a smile on her face, after a few nods, said, "Now we can get to the bottom of this thing."

Bill stared out the window, watching the DA and the two detectives pull out of the lot.

Chapter
Forty-One

B ill finished the report for Alice Keaton around two. She had said noon the following day, but Bill didn't want to wait. Paperwork was a necessity, no getting around it. Especially since now he was essentially reporting directly to the Worcester County district attorney. But he didn't want paperwork to sideline him and prevent him from investigating.

He took his time, wrote clearly and cleanly, organized in a way that only a former Army vet would appreciate. If there was one thing the Army had drilled into him, it was organization. He wrote up the circumstances of both incidents, the list of suspects, the past records he had found, and the rundown of the interviews he and Ellie had conducted. It took time to write it the way he wanted, to tell the story he wanted to tell. When satisfied, he fired the report off in an email and pushed back from his desk.

He stood, grabbed his keys, and left the office, telling Margot he was done for the day. Margot raised an eyebrow but replied, "Okay, see you tomorrow."

Out the door and down the steps, he keyed his car remote as he called Ellie on his cell phone.

"Report's on its way."

"Okay," Ellie said with a deep breath. "What's next?"

"I want to go through the Thornton place. I don't trust the state guys to not screw it up, or to not sit on anything they found just to spite us."

"I wish I could have seen their faces when Alice gave them the news." Bill thought he detected the sound of her smile through his phone. Truthfully, it made him smile a little bit too. Until he remembered he was now on the hook for closing the investigation, not MSP.

"Want me to pick you up on the way?"

"Sure. I'm at the theater doing some cleaning."

"See you in ten."

* * *

Ellie hung up the phone and turned to Steve and Dana, both of whom had come in to keep working on Steve's new role. He had told them he really wanted to be more comfortable in the role for the following weekend, so Ellie and Dana agreed to come in and help him with lines and blocking.

Steve wore a wry smile. "Leaving again?"

She nodded and explained the situation, with Bill now actively investigating Reginald's death. Steve whistled low, and Dana managed a "Good luck" that didn't sound like she meant it.

Bill arrived, and Ellie climbed into his car. Twenty minutes later, they were back in the big, beautiful home, looking around the living room, wondering where to start.

"Do we need gloves?" Ellie asked.

"Nah. The Crime Scene Services Section has finished processing this place. They would have taken anything they thought they could lift prints from that might be evidence," Bill said. "I don't think we'll find any smoking guns. Plus, if we were worried about evidence and chain of custody, you wouldn't be here."

"Valid point," Ellie said. "Whatever we find will be indirectly related at best."

The Last Line

They spent the next hour and a half going through the house slowly and meticulously, but found nothing new. They went through drawers and rummaged through the refrigerator and the freezer. Bill lifted the lid of the toilet tanks, and Ellie checked behind all of the pictures on the walls. They didn't know what they were looking for. They hoped something would pop out at them, but after ninety minutes, they had nothing.

Ellie took a break, wandering alone into a small room off of the living room. She sat down on a couch and took in the room. The room was very masculine, wood-paneled, with a large flat-screen TV on one wall and an entertainment center with shelving built into the wall below it. An assortment of DVDs and Blu-rays lined one side, and a selection of CDs lined the other. It had already been a long ninety minutes, and this room remained unsearched. All of these discs would each have to be opened and reviewed. On a whim, she went to the DVDs and started opening the cases. Each of them had a matching disc inside.

Until the last one.

The case was for a basic rom-com movie, nothing special. But the disc inside did not match. Ellie pulled the disc out. The top side of the disc was imprinted with the label DVD-R. A writable video disc. She flipped it over. On the bottom, she saw discoloration starting at the rim and moving partway toward the center, the hallmark of a burning. This disc was not empty.

She turned on the entertainment system, which was fairly complicated and took some time to start. But she finally got it powered up, opened the DVD player, and popped in the disc. The start-up menu came up on the screen. She pressed Play and began to watch.

* * *

Bill wanted a smoke. Badly. He hadn't smoked regularly since the service, only having a cigarette or two when he felt stressed or under pressure. He felt quite a bit of both at the moment. He also hadn't had the chance to work out in a few days, and the tension in his body was straining him.

He had hated this part of the job when he was with the state police. The slow picking-through of someone else's home, the turning-over of each and every item of someone else's life—it was akin to an invasion. Never mind that the occasion of the search was usually a violent crime.

An hour and a half in, Bill finally paused. He hoped to find something, anything, but so far he found only disappointment. He stretched his back and wondered if some spot in the kitchen might hold a hidden pack of cigarettes. Which would've been a horrible breach of crime scene protocol, but considering that the crime scene had already been processed, that he and Ellie were going over old ground, and that it had technically already been contaminated by Avery or Phelps or someone tromping around in boots, he didn't care.

He leaned against the counter. The kitchen was beautiful, immaculate, and organized. The counter was black quartz, and the cabinets were white. The counter was empty except for a coffee maker, a plug-in percolator, something he hadn't seen in years. He wasn't sure he could figure out how to use one. He reached over and took the lid off the percolator. He didn't expect to find anything related to Valerie's attack, but he hoped maybe a stash of smokes might be hidden inside. He wouldn't even care if they were menthol.

He put the lid back on the percolator, disappointed, and sighed and shook his head. This was a waste of time. There was nothing here. Avery and Phelps had already done this, probably messed up anything left that would have been useful. And though their shenanigans had been found out by Keaton, they didn't seem to be holding back anything else.

There was still more house to go through, but he had lost his resolve. It was probably time to call it a day. He could always come back tomorrow. Nothing was going anywhere soon.

"Bill!"

The cry, surprising in the quiet, deathly still space, made Bill jump away from the kitchen counter. He bolted from the kitchen into the TV room, looking around wildly, expecting trouble, and wondering what had happened to Ellie. It took him a moment to realize Ellie was perfectly fine, sitting still, and staring straight ahead.

"Ellie?"

"Sit down," she said quietly, blinking furiously. "I found something."

She stared at the large flat-screen TV with something paused on the screen. Bill joined her stare, trying to decipher the image through the paused motion blur, but if he had to guess, it looked like—

"Is that a porno movie?" he asked.

"Yes."

He wasn't sure what to make of that.

"Ellie, are you—"

"I found something," she said, her voice soft. Her eyes still locked on the flat-screen.

"In a porno?"

"Yes."

"Ellie—"

"Just sit down, Bill," she said, her voice strained, her left thumb rubbing furiously against her jeans, and he got the impression she held back tears. He sat next to her on the wide leather ottoman. He prepared himself for anything.

Ellie pressed Play, and the video resumed. Bill watched as the woman on the screen was taken roughly by the man she was paired with. His sense of discomfort grew as he stole glances at Ellie to try and understand her thinking. He would have been lying if he said he had never gotten off to a porn flick. But sitting and watching one with Ellie made him realize how skeevy the whole business was. He started to say something.

"Keep watching."

"Ellie—"

"Recognize her?"

Bill turned back, realizing now that Ellie was seeing something in the mess on the screen. Bill tried to focus on the faces of the actors. He focused on the woman, a young woman, attractive but too heavily made up, with large breasts and permed-out hair. This was something from the seventies or early eighties. It had that grainy quality he remembered from watching pirated flicks in the basement of one of his school friends back when they were teenagers.

He tried to push the nudity out of his vision. The face was where he needed to concentrate.

The face reminded him of someone. He couldn't quite grab hold. It was at the edge of his mind. There was something about the eyes, and the smile, strangely genuine for this type of movie, a warmth that—

"Holy shit!" Bill whispered. "Is that who I think it is?"

Ellie nodded.

"I think so." She paused at the moment where the camera focused on a close-up of her face and nothing else. Bill stared, shocked, a little aghast, and thoroughly disgusted with himself. He felt dirty and had an overwhelming desire to wash his hands. And possibly his eyeballs.

"What the hell is she doing in a skin flick?"

"Remember her bust for solicitation?"

"A bust for hooking is a long way off from starring in a porno. How does that even happen?"

"The question isn't how she ended up in a porno. The question is, why did Reginald—or Valerie—have a copy?"

Bill agreed. Another missing piece that, when fitted into the puzzle, started to show the picture. But a very confusing picture.

"Is this what got Reginald killed?" Ellie wondered. It was a reasonable question, except for one problem.

"Merilyn couldn't have killed Reginald and made an attempt on Valerie," Bill said. "Even if she did somehow manage to poison Reginald, she would never have had the strength to make the trip here, much less bludgeon Valerie with a candlestick."

Ellie stared at the frozen screen, jaw set, nose flaring. "Then we are looking for two attackers?"

Bill rubbed his eyes and shook his head. "No," he said. "I think there's only one culprit. But this fits in somehow. It's too much of a coincidence linking them together, so it must connect in some way. We just need to figure out how it does."

Ellie nodded. "We need to go back and visit her again."

Chapter Forty-Two

They headed straight to Merilyn's house. The calendar was not on their side, or hers. The fading director had joked about borrowed time, and Ellie knew she wasn't being hyperbolic.

They pulled into the driveway of Merilyn's house and stopped. Ellie's heart started racing. Bill's face prickled as it lost color.

An ambulance sat in the driveway, lights strobing. A pair of EMTs was wheeling a gurney into the front door. Next to the ambulance sat a police cruiser, lights flashing but no siren.

Ellie was out of the car first and running toward the house. Dennis Hassert, one of Bill's officers, stood by the door. He stepped in front of Ellie to block her path.

"You can't go in there, ma'am," he said. He acted as if they had never met.

Bill came up after her, his face hard. Hassert mistook the look on Bill's face for a reprimand and stepped aside.

"I'm just doing my job, Chief."

"What happened here?" Bill asked.

"We got a call for a wellness check for the woman in the house. I rolled up first, knocked on the door, but no one answered. I peered in through the windows and saw her slumped on the couch. I immediately radioed the EMTs. We jimmied the door and went in."

"Is she still alive?" Ellie asked.

"She was when I left her."

At that moment, the EMTs wheeled the gurney out of the house. Merilyn was strapped in, and they had started an IV. Ellie raced to her side and saw Merilyn was unconscious.

"Will she regain consciousness?" Ellie asked.

"Can't say," answered one of the EMTs. "The doctor will have to tell you when he gets a look at her."

"Who called it in?" Bill asked.

"Don't know," answered the other EMT.

A crowd of neighbors had gathered, straining necks and eyes to gawk.

"Get everyone back," Bill told Hassert. "Let's give her some privacy if we can." The EMTs wheeled the unconscious woman outside and into the back of the ambulance. They closed the back doors, and one of them climbed into the driver's seat of the truck. Bill motioned Ellie into his car, cranked the engine, and hit the lights. The emergency truck rolled out first, and Bill followed close behind.

*   *   *

They arrived at St. Vincent's Hospital, where they were instructed by one of the nursing staff to wait in the ER. Bill showed the nurse his badge and told her as soon as the doctor was free, he needed to talk to him.

"Her," corrected the nurse.

"Whatever," Bill said testily. "I need to talk to the doctor whenever they're finished. The woman they just brought in is a witness in a murder investigation."

The nurse cocked an eyebrow as if to say, *This woman won't live to see the trial.* She nodded. "I'll inform the doctor."

"Witness?" Ellie said when they sat down in the waiting room.

"Nobody would believe she's strong enough to be a suspect." He sighed and shook his head. "She might be more of a victim than anything else."

They sat together in silence for nearly thirty minutes before Ellie jolted upright in her chair, briefly ticcing madly.

"Oh my God. I forgot to call Mike."

Bill, his head back against the wall, his eyes closed, muttered, "Well, you better do that."

"Don't you need to call Darlene?"

"I texted her that I'm stuck at the hospital with a suspect."

Ellie didn't say anything, knowing how Darlene felt about her. Bill's wife didn't hate Ellie or even have a strong dislike of her, but Ellie sensed a certain level of jealousy because of the past Ellie and Bill shared.

Ellie stood, pulled out her phone, and walked to the hallway leading to the waiting room. Mike answered on the fifth ring.

"Where are you?"

"I'm at the hospital."

"What? Are you okay?"

"I'm fine, it's not me."

"Then why—?"

Ellie told him about Merilyn, and how she and Bill had gone to see Merilyn after searching through Valerie's house.

"You found something at the Thornton house that sent you to see Merilyn?" Mike asked.

"We did. I can't go into it now, but I'll tell you when I come home. But it was bad. We found the EMTs at her house hauling her out."

"Jesus. What happened?"

"Not sure. She may just be very ill. Somebody phoned in a wellness check."

"Who?"

"Don't know that either."

Mike paused on the other end of the line, then said, "Not a lot about this case is certain, is it?"

Ellie sighed. "Not yet."

"How long will you be?"

"I'm not sure. Bill drove us, and he's waiting for the doctor to come out and talk to us. Between you and me, I think Merilyn doesn't have long left."

"God, Ellie, I'm sorry. Do you want me to come down, or . . . ?"

She knew she had been trying his patience recently. The strain was becoming more evident. Like the early days. For now, though, she decided to embrace his sweetness.

"No, honey, but thank you. You'd just be sitting around with us, and when we do get to see her, I'm fairly sure you wouldn't be allowed to go with us."

"Okay."

"I'm sorry about this, Mike. This is not where I want to be right now."

Another pause. "I'm worried about you, Ellie. This case is eating you alive," he said.

"You're not wrong."

"If I ask you to let it go, would you?"

Ellie considered the question. A valid one, one she asked herself from time to time. But she didn't need to consider it long.

"I can't. Especially not now."

Mike was silent on the line. She could guess what he was thinking. She figured he was asking himself if he was losing her to her old self, the self that pushed too hard and became obsessive. He was probably wondering if he would have to go through all the old pain again.

"I know you have no control over when the doctor will come out, but try not to be too late. I'm driving down to Manhattan in the morning."

She winced, blinked, and grunted. She had completely forgotten tomorrow was one of Mike's monthly trips into the city for work.

"I'll get home as fast as I can." *Grunt.*

"If I'm asleep, wake me up so I know you got in okay."

"I will."

She hung up the phone. Overwhelmed by worry, the death of Reginald, the attack on Valerie, and now Merilyn in the final stages of her life, she wrapped her arms around her body and cried.

*　*　*

Forty minutes later, Dr. Nirmala Singh came into the waiting room. A tall, elegant woman with dark hair piled under a scrubs cap, she led Bill and Ellie back into an unused exam room.

"How is she?" Ellie blurted out, unable to contain her emotions any longer.

Dr. Singh's face bore a troubled sadness, a look Bill had seen on the "devil doc" surgeons in the desert.

"She's fading quickly, I'm afraid. She's been getting treatments for stage four breast cancer."

"I know. She told me it spread just about everywhere."

Dr. Singh nodded. "I spoke with her oncologist, who told me he was honestly amazed Ms. Chambers has lasted this long."

"She's a fighter," Ellie said.

Dr. Singh's sad look deepened. "I'm afraid she's nearing the end of her fight. She's weak, her pulse is fluttery, and she's rejecting most of what we've been trying to give her. I don't expect her to make it through the night."

Tears welled in Ellie's eyes and spilled down her cheeks. Dr. Singh put a hand on Ellie's arm in comfort.

"Doctor," Bill said. "I hate to be the jerk here, but we do need to talk to her. I have just a few questions I need to ask her about a murder and an attempted murder."

"Murder?"

"And an attempted murder. Long story, but the short version is that Mrs. Chambers is a witness, and I need to ask her a few things."

Dr. Singh shrugged. "It's not like Mrs. Chambers is going to improve if we leave her alone. But understand, she is on morphine for the pain, to keep her comfortable. You may not get any answers."

The doctor led them farther into the ICU, stopping at a nurse's station first to provide each of them a mask. She led them into a room where Merilyn was the sole occupant. Hoses of all sorts ran in and out of her. The machines made beeping and whirring noises, and the acrid smell of antiseptic stung their nostrils.

"I'll give you some privacy," Dr. Singh said. She drew the curtain around them and left.

Ellie leaned down and picked up Merilyn's hand. It was cold and bony and frail, and Ellie feared she could break it if she did more than lightly touch it. She called gently, "Merilyn. Merilyn."

The old woman did not wake up. Ellie said her name a little louder, and Merilyn's eyes fluttered for a moment, then opened, rolling up and down as consciousness returned to her slowly. Finally, she looked at Ellie, and a small smile spread across her face.

"Ellie," she whispered. "What are you doing here?"

"We came to see you at your house, but they were taking you out. How are you feeling?"

"Tired. Ready to be done with all of this."

"Oh, honey," Ellie said, and despite her best effort, began to cry, her head down against the edge of Merilyn's bed.

Bill stepped forward. He realized Merilyn's counter ticked down minutes, not hours left in her life.

"Merilyn?" he said, a little louder than Ellie but trying not to startle her. "It's Bill Starlin."

"Nice of you to visit an old lady, Bill."

229

He smiled sadly. Such courage. Rarely had he seen such courage, except in the service. "Merilyn, I need to ask you a question or two."

"About Reginald?"

"And Valerie."

"What's wrong with . . ." she sighed, as if out of breath. Her words were becoming harder and harder to get out, her breath struggling. "With Valerie?" she finished.

"Someone tried to kill her."

Merilyn said nothing for a moment but closed her eyes. A single tear ran from the corner of her eye down the side of her face, burying itself in the hair at her temple.

"I'm sorry to bring you such bad news," Bill continued. "We were going through the house, processing the crime scene, and we found something we need to ask you about. Uh . . ." He stopped. How could he say it without sounding like a total asshole to a dying woman, or embarrassing himself? Ellie stepped in for him.

"Honey," she said. "We found a video, an old one. Of you." Ellie swallowed and took a breath. "Having sex."

Merilyn opened her eyes and rolled her head slightly toward Ellie. Something flashed in her eye. She said, "He . . . kept it . . . I . . . can't believe . . . he kept it."

"He who?" Bill asked. "Reginald?"

Merilyn nodded slightly, a single nod.

"How'd he get it?"

Her breath rattled in her lungs. "He . . . filmed it."

Bill leaned forward. "Merilyn, I'm going to ask once. Understand this can be considered a deathbed confession, and that I don't plan to harass you either way. Did you kill Reginald Thornton? Did you poison him with a benzo and your fentanyl?"

A struggling breath, then, "No."

"Do you know who did?"

"His wife."

The Last Line

Bill straightened up. The look on his face told Ellie everything she needed to know. Merilyn had no idea who the killer was. Ellie looked from him back to Merilyn.

"Merilyn, honey," she said, "is there anything we can do for you?"

The old woman closed her eyes, and her breathing grew rhythmic, weaker, and Ellie figured she'd fallen asleep.

Merilyn's eyes opened and appeared to be looking into the distance, seeing nothing, or perhaps everything, in her final moments. Then she closed her eyes, for what they knew was the final time.

Ellie, sobbing, brought the frail hand to her lips for a gentle kiss.

Chapter
Forty-Three

B ill made every attempt to be quiet as he entered his house. It was late, and he didn't want to wake anyone. But after accidentally letting the screen door bang behind him, then tripping over Aiden's shoes in the middle of the floor and catching himself loudly, his hands banging against the wall, he cursed and gave up.

He went to the kitchen, opened a cabinet, and pulled down a bowl. He had been at the hospital so long, he never had a chance to eat, and now he was ravenous. He poured a bowl of Frosted Flakes and topped it nearly to the rim with milk. He sat at the kitchen island, spooning the sugar-encrusted cereal into his mouth like a steam shovel. When he finished, he poured himself a second bowl.

The light popped on, and he yelped, spilling a generous portion of the cereal on himself and the floor, and let out a string of expletives.

"You're in fine humor," Darlene said, standing by the light switch. He had been so tired and lost in his thoughts that he didn't hear his wife come downstairs.

Bill set his bowl down and began to clean up his mess. "Long, long, long-ass day," he said. "And not a good one."

"You were at the hospital this whole time?"

"Yeah."

"And?"

"And what?"

"And did you learn anything?"

"No. Yes. Hell, I don't know." She gave him a confused look, and he sighed. "I learned stuff I didn't know before with no idea what it means. This whole thing is a gigantic puzzle. We shake out a new piece, I think I can figure out where it fits, and the picture starts to make sense, but then another new piece pops up, and the picture turns back into a jumble." He let out an exhausted breath. "I think I'm just tired."

Darlene sat down next to him at the kitchen island and handed him a fistful of paper towels.

"What are the pieces?"

Bill told her what they found at the Thornton house while he cleaned up the milk, scooped the spilled cereal into his hand, and dumped it into the sink. He told her Merilyn had confirmed her part in the video, and that Reginald was responsible for filming it.

"Jeez, you never can tell what lurks in a person's past, can you?" She sat next to her husband as he shoveled what remained in his bowl into his mouth. "How is Merilyn?"

Bill put down his spoon and stared across the kitchen, out the window to the dark shadows of the trees beyond. His eyes refused to focus on anything in particular, but just beyond his sight swirled the emergency room and the sight of an emaciated Merilyn.

He sighed. "She's dead. She died about an hour and a half ago."

Darlene put a hand on Bill's back and rubbed up and down. "Oh, baby, I'm so sorry."

"Me too."

"So what's next?"

Bill shrugged. "I need to talk with the DA and get permission to go through Merilyn's house to see if I can find anything related to this case."

"Any chance there might be?"

"Who knows? Did I mention Merilyn was busted for prostitution in the late seventies, and Reginald bailed her out? I'm not sure how that fits in, and I'm certain it does, but it paints a pretty seedy picture of a dead woman's life."

"You think she attacked the Thorntons?"

"She could have poisoned Reginald, maybe. But everything we have is circumstantial. I need to go through the house and see if I can find anything linking back to his death or to the attempt on Valerie. I don't believe she was strong enough to go after Valerie herself, but in theory she could have hired someone."

"Do you think that's likely?"

"If I'm being honest, no, I don't. Just before she passed, I asked her if she knew who killed Reginald. She said Valerie did. How she would know that I have no idea. But if it's true, then who hurt Valerie? I just want this thing over with."

Darlene took his hand and pulled him gently to his feet.

"Come upstairs. Shower. Crawl into bed."

"I think I'll just crawl into bed."

"Oh no you won't," she said, suddenly stern. "God knows what you brought back with you from the hospital. Plus, you're still wearing some cereal. You'll shower first, then bed. Otherwise, sleep down here."

He put his hands up in surrender. "Okay, okay. I'll shower."

The shower felt good. It was just the thing he needed to shed the rotten day and leave the stress behind him. He came out of the shower, dried off, and wrapped the towel around his waist. He was brushing his teeth when a soft knock at the door made him look up. In the mirror he watched Darlene slip into the bathroom.

"I'll be out in a sec," he said around his toothbrush. He rinsed and spit and put his toothbrush back, glancing in the mirror. Darlene was still standing in the doorway.

The Last Line

"What's wrong?" he asked. She smiled, her green eyes flashing with mischief. She tugged at his towel, drawing him closer.

"Follow me," she whispered. She led him to the bedroom and locked the door behind her. She took a firm grip on the tuck of the towel and pulled it loose, letting it fall to the floor. She pushed him down onto the bed, backward.

"You've had an awful day. An awful week. With an awful day coming up on Friday."

"If this is meant to be sexy talk," he whispered hoarsely, "you need to up your game."

She smiled and climbed on top of him. She kissed him long and deep, and he wrapped his arms around her. He didn't realize how much he needed her until just that moment, needed to be with her, in her, next to her. He sighed as they swayed with the movement.

Chapter
Forty-Four

The next day, Bill had the type of headache that only came from lack of sleep, but he was content. He chased three Tylenol with a cup of coffee and rubbed his eyes. Darlene was still buried under the covers upstairs. He herded his kids out the door and waved to the bus driver as they pulled away before he picked up the phone and dialed Alice Keaton.

"I want to go into Merilyn Chambers' place and look around," he said.

"What links her to the murder and the assault?" Alice asked.

"Nothing solid. Only circumstantial. All in the report I sent you."

"I haven't read it yet. Did I hear correctly that she died last night?"

"Yeah. We were there when she passed. I managed to ask her if she knew who killed Reginald."

"What'd she say?"

"She said his wife."

"Well, that's tidy."

"Sounds like you have some doubts," Bill said.

"I can't close this out with just the word of a dying woman. Some actual hard evidence would be nice."

"Agreed. There's a porno angle Reginald was involved in back in his days in Manhattan. We have a video from his house of Merilyn performing. Last night, she told us Reginald was the one behind the camera."

"Like a porn ring?"

"I'm wondering if that was enough to drive her to murder. Or murder for hire."

"After, what, nearly fifty years?"

"Yeah, I don't buy it either."

Alice said, "Okay, I can make the case for a warrant. Go in, give her place a look, but if you find anything . . ."

"Strict chain of evidence," Bill said. "Check."

"Come by my office in a few hours and pick it up."

Later that morning, armed with the warrant with signature ink practically still drying, he let himself into Merilyn's house. He pulled on a pair of blue latex gloves and started going through the house. It was slow work, made slower by the disorder inevitable from the last days of her sickness. A proud woman, Merilyn had declined any invitation for someone to help her clean. The resulting chaos made the search hard.

An hour in, his pocket buzzed. He pulled out his phone and answered.

"What's the plan for today?" Ellie asked.

"Going through Merilyn's place, looking for . . . well, I don't know. Anything, I guess."

"Don't you need a warrant for that?"

"Already got one."

"Find anything?"

"I found her fentanyl and bagged it to send to the crime lab. Not sure if the lab can verify it's the same stuff used to kill Reginald, but never hurts to ask. Other than that, and a lot of garbage everywhere, nothing to find in here. I suspect she lost the ability to take care of herself, much less the house."

"I wonder if she called the wellness check-in on herself," Ellie said.

"I'll have Turner look into that, though I'm not sure it matters now. I've already got him pulling Valerie's phone records, so adding Merilyn's shouldn't be a big deal. Where are you today?"

"Headed back into Worcester. Going to talk to a friend who might be able to shine some more light into Merilyn's past."

"If you hear anything good, call me."

"You know I will."

He hung up, pocketed the phone, and sighed. He was never going to make it through all this stuff. This should have been a multi-man crew kind of operation, a team that wouldn't need to spend a full week going through everything. He thought about calling Alice again, asking for a team to be sent out, but in his heart, he balked. Especially after seeing the video. He didn't want anyone else to stumble upon a violation of Merilyn's memory.

He looked around.

The bedroom was next.

Chapter
Forty-Five

Ellie took the elevator up to the *Telegram & Gazette* offices, the elevator dinging as each floor passed, her heart rate ratcheting up a little bit the higher she went. At the fifth floor, the doors slid open, and she stepped out. Paul Koehler sat at his desk typing furiously, doubtlessly trying to get a review of something out before a deadline. She strode over to his desk and rapped on it with her knuckles, startling him.

"Ellie! I didn't know you were coming. Janice never rang me," he said.

"I told her not to. I was in a hurry. I didn't want to go through the tollgate." She ticced a fury of movement, revealing her agitation.

"Well," he said, folding his hands over his little potbelly, leaning back in his chair, and looking at her, his work on the computer all but forgotten. "What can I do for you?"

"When I visited the other day, I told you that whenever you felt like telling me what you claimed not to know, give me a call. Well, I'm out of time. I need you to tell me everything. Now."

"Has something happened?"

Ellie, quiet for a moment, said, "Merilyn died last night."

The news hit Paul between the eyes, stunning him into tears. He blinked a few times, trying to muster the strength to keep from crying in front of Ellie and in front of his colleagues. Failing, he wept into a tissue he took from his desk.

"Paul?" asked a woman to his left. She eyed Ellie with suspicion. "Everything okay?"

"It will be," he snuffled. "Just learned someone I knew a long time ago has passed away."

"Oh." The woman's face became sympathetic. "I'm so sorry."

"Thank you."

"Paul," Ellie said, grunting and blinking. "Is there somewhere we can go and talk?"

"Yes, of course."

They went down the elevator and out to Main Street which, to Ellie, was a poorly named road for the amount of activity and commerce it supported. "Main Street," to Ellie, conjured up images of small towns and brick buildings with banners between them congratulating the hometown baseball team on their state championship. Main Street in Worcester was a cramped, noisy, exhaust-ridden thoroughfare that stretched from the north to the south. It had a variety of areas, not least of which was the "bad" section of town, Main South. They were in the heart of Main Street Worcester, which comprised mostly business or government.

They ducked into a Subway and sat down in one of the booths. The two clerks behind the counter glanced over, but if they harbored any disapproval at Ellie and Paul not ordering anything, they didn't show it.

"Cancer?" Paul asked after they had settled. He had some napkins with him from the counter in case he started crying again.

"Yes. It was overdue, honestly," Ellie said. "She never said how long the doctors had given her, but she outlived their predictions by a lot."

"Quite a brave move you made, hiring her as a director, knowing she was outliving her prognosis."

"She came to me. Begged me to let her direct the show."

"What was the plan if—?"

"My stage manager, Steve, was ready to take over if need be. But she got stronger and stronger as the rehearsals progressed, so I never worried. I think she lived off shows. I think they kept her alive. When this one ended, especially the way it ended, she knew there would be no more. That was her final bow."

"And now . . ." he didn't finish, his voice unsteady.

Ellie put her hand over his and squeezed gently. She felt a tic emerging that would cause her to squeeze Paul's hand until it felt right. That was one of the hardest things to make people understand about Tourette syndrome. She had to tic until it "felt right." She couldn't describe it any clearer than that. She pulled her hand away quickly.

"And now . . ." Her voice, soft and compassionate, informed him he wasn't alone in his grief.

But she couldn't soften. Not now. Not so close to the full truth. "Paul, I need to know about Reginald's time in New York."

"I already told you, I didn't really know him. I knew of him, but that's not the same thing."

"How about Merilyn?"

His eyes flicked left to right quickly. Ellie recognized him searching for a better lie.

"Ellie, I—"

"Paul, I'm going to share something with you. The DA for Worcester County has given Bill Starlin, the police chief in my town, the authority to investigate this whole mess, and for me to help. I could make life difficult for you. I could ask Bill to come down here and arrest you."

"For what?"

"How about obstruction of justice? I don't want to because I consider you a friend. But if push comes to shove, I will, because I need to solve Reginald's murder and the attempt on his wife's life."

Paul's mouth dropped open, and he mouthed more than said, "What?"

Ellie told him about Valerie's coma and the circumstances surrounding it.

"I probably shouldn't say anything, considering this is an active investigation. But we found evidence yesterday connecting Merilyn to Reginald back in their days in New York City. I think it's all connected, but I can't figure out how. So I'm trying to put it all together. Who would kill Reginald, then try to kill Valerie, and how are they connected to Merilyn?" She looked at him with pleading eyes. "Paul, I need information about their time in New York."

Paul got up from his seat. He walked over to the counter and muttered something to the clerk. The clerk walked him down to the register, where Paul paid and the clerk handed him a cup. He added ice to the cup at the soda machine, then soda. Ellie watched from where she sat.

He came back to the booth and sat down. His hands shook badly. *Something has him spooked,* she thought. *And it's not just Reginald's death.*

"What is it?" she asked.

"You said you found evidence Merilyn knew Reginald in New York City."

"Yes."

"In the seventies, I'm assuming."

"Yes."

"I think I know what you found."

Chapter
Forty-Six

I n an old shoebox, under Merilyn's bed, Bill found them. He pulled
out the shoebox, covered in dust so thick he couldn't tell what the
original color of the top of the box had been. He opened it. Inside were
Polaroids. Dozens. Maybe a hundred. Maybe more.

He took a stack and turned over the first one in the bunch. A
candid picture of a naked woman. She wasn't in a compromising position. It was more like a pose for reference: fully nude, facing the camera, hands by her sides. At the bottom was a handwritten notation:
"Stacey 1978." He flipped over the next picture. Same woman, still
nude, except this time in a side profile. "Stacey 1978." Next one, same
woman, nude, back profile. "Stacey 1978." Bill flipped over the next
one. This time, it was a different woman, frontal nude, with the handwritten caption "Barbara 1978." He flipped over the next two Polaroids. Same woman, side profile, then back profile. In the next photo,
the sequence started again with a new woman.

He took out another stack and flipped through them, then
another, and another. They were all the same setup: three Polaroids
per woman, showing their bodies in various reference poses. Dozens
of them. Front, side, back, front, side, back, until . . . He picked up a
new stack, and the content changed. Now the women were in various
sexual situations, their partner's face obscured but theirs prominent.

At the bottom of each photo were more handwritten notations of who and what year.

Bill realized he was looking at a shoebox full of tryout photos for women for porn. He was a little sick to his stomach. He could imagine himself as a fourteen-year-old boy finding this box and valuing it as a treasure beyond measure. Now it just made him nauseous.

He put the photos back in the box and put the lid on. He brushed the dust off the lid, trying to clear as much as possible. He stood, the box under his arm, feeling as if he was somehow naughty by taking the box with him. Protocol stated he should bag it as evidence. But evidence of what, exactly? Was the contents of this box related to the attacks on the Thorntons? Probably too soon to tell, but he didn't want this to come out in the investigation. Merilyn had suffered enough. Why drag her name through the mud with a box of homemade girly photos under her bed?

The room was quiet, almost eerily so to Bill, and the silence started to crawl under his skin like a horror movie. He needed to get out of this house, strewn with clutter and old medical equipment. The sooner the better. He found the whole thing unnerving, and he jumped when his phone rang. He pulled it out of his back pocket.

"What do you have for me, Turner?"

"I have the results of the phone records, Chief."

"And?"

"Not much phone activity on Valerie's end. She didn't call a lot of people, and a lot of people didn't call her. There was a brief spike around the time of Reginald's death, but I'm making the assumption those were well-wishers and sympathizers."

"Probably," Bill said, finally outside the house, closing it up, happy to put the gloomy interior behind him.

"But a few calls, three from a single number, came just before she was attacked."

Down the steps and into his car, Bill pulled the door shut, feeling safer already to be in the space of his police vehicle. "What's the number?"

"It's for a local business registered to an Alex Hillman."

Hillman. This thing is going in circles, Bill thought. No, not circles. Loops. Twisty loops that folded back in on themselves with every new revelation.

"Turner," Bill said. "Meet me at the station. I've got something really unpleasant to do, and I think I'll need your help."

Chapter
Forty-Seven

"Was it the video, or the stills?"

Ellie cocked her head. Did she hear that right? *Stills? Did he say stills?* Paul took her silence to mean Ellie had found both.

"I felt so bad for her," he continued, rubbing his face with his hands. "She was so young, and he was such a prick. Handsome, but a prick. I mean, you should have seen him in his day. He was what the kids used to call a stud muffin. Is that something kids still say?"

"I don't think so."

"Well, whatever they say these days, he was it. Which is why he thought he had such a good shot at being a star. He thought he was hot shit. And he was trained. Not Juilliard, of course. A toll collector's son from Worcester could never afford something like that. But he did study, and studying made a difference. Christ, was he good. But . . ." He drew out the next sentence like he found something distasteful in his mouth. "I don't want to speak ill of the dead, mind you—"

"You called him a prick a moment ago. Twice." *Nod-nod.*

An embarrassed smile crept across his face. "Oh yeah. I guess I did. And he was. But what I was going to say was that, as good as he was, he wasn't as good as he thought he was. Certainly not Broadway material, but he could never accept that. His ego got him in trouble, not his talent. He got a lot of doors slammed in his face because of his attitude. But, like I said, he had the looks."

"You mentioned that, like, five times already. What does handsome have to do with anything?" *Blink-blink-blink. Grunt.*

Paul stared over his glasses at her. With the glasses, his white mustache, and the tufts of white hair along the rim of his gleaming brown head, he reminded Ellie of the orphanage cat from the movie *The Rescuers.* Talking about Reginald's Manhattan past made Paul uncomfortable. That, plus his knowledge of the video, presuming he was talking about the same video she found, and if there were also still photographs, presumably of the same subject matter, she had a good idea why Paul seemed so squirmy.

Paul took a long sip of soda through the straw. Ellie thought he grew a little green around the gills. Truth be told, she felt a little bit the same.

"Merilyn," Ellie said, "before she died, told me Reginald shot the movies."

"She said that?"

"Yes."

Paul shook his head from side to side as if to say, not quite. "Well, directed them, maybe, but he didn't shoot them. Hard to film from his position."

"What do you mean?" Then Ellie processed what he'd said and connected it to the video. She realized she had seen more of Reginald than she ever wanted to. She nearly retched, but ticced fiercely instead.

"Oh my God," she said, putting her hand over her mouth.

"It was a whole racket. He and some other guy had a deal going where they would bail out girls busted for prostitution, or possession, or even public drunkenness, but only if they agreed to 'perform' for them. They took pictures, a lot of Polaroids for reference for the future, plus a lot of videos and thirty-five–millimeter photographs, and they would sell them on the Deuce. Right there on the street.

Remember, these were the days before the internet, before a laptop became a twenty-four-hour adult bookstore in your living room. You could find a lot of that sort of stuff on 42nd Street in those days, the days before they started to clean up that part of the city. That was some time. The city, in the seventies. The Bronx is Burning, Son of Sam, all that shit. God, it was awful."

"Were you involved in any of it?"

He threw his hands up in surrender. "No. No no no no no."

"How about Valerie?"

"Not that I know of. I don't think they met until he moved back up here."

Something occurred to Ellie. "You sure? Maybe they met before that, maybe she had been part of Reginald's unwilling harem? Under a different name?"

"Not that I can remember."

"Paul," Ellie said, a warning in her voice. *Nod.*

"Christ, Ellie, we're talking so long ago. I don't remember my roommate's name back then, much less any of the girls Reginald forced to perform."

"Don't lie to me, Paul." Her voice was hard. "I'm going to call Bill the moment we're done here and have him run your record, so I mean it when I say this, Paul: Don't. Effing. Lie to me."

Paul's face grew hurt, and Ellie regretted going at him so hard. This case was making her do and say things she hated.

"I'm sorry, Paul," she said, her voice softer. "I'm not trying to be a bitch. I'm—" she didn't finish. Everything jumbled around in her head, and she didn't know how to make it into a picture. "I guess I'm just lost in all this. I'm trying to solve a murder that no one wanted to believe was a murder. Except his wife is in a coma now, definitely from an attack, and I think they're related, and now Merilyn is gone too, and I feel like she deserves some kind of justice, except maybe justice was served when Reginald died, except . . ." Ellie ran out of words. A nonstop stream of consciousness had poured out of her mouth, only to peter out. Once she'd started, she couldn't stop, and now that she had, she felt spent.

This time, Paul put his hand over hers. She blinked back the tears.

"I know, Ellie. I'm not saying Reginald deserved to die," Paul said, "but he kind of did. I moved back here before he did, and when he finally did, I looked him up. He was still making videos and taking pictures. Not for money anymore, but leverage. Did a lot of recruiting of his girls in the shows he did, and would use that leverage to get roles or girls he wanted whenever he wanted."

Ellie turned that over in her head, and a face blinked to life in front of her eyes. A young woman who had a nasty fight with Reginald. A fight that drew blood. She stood suddenly, the connection making her hands shake.

"Everything okay?" Paul asked.

"I need to go talk to someone else. Someone in the show with Reginald."

"Is it a woman?"

"Yes."

"A younger woman? In her twenties, maybe?"

"Yes."

Paul nodded. "Might be what you're looking for."

Grunt. "Thank you, Paul. This has helped." *Grunt.*

He stood and leaned in to give her a hug. The gesture surprised her, and she hugged him back.

"If I think of anything else, I'll call you," he said.

Chapter
Forty-Eight

"Whatch'ya got there, Chief?" Margot asked.

"Nothing," he said brusquely. He hurried past her, box of Polaroids under one arm, ignoring the surprise on her face.

"Turner's in your office waiting for you," she called to him. He closed the office door without answering. Margot shook her head. *He is being so strange these days,* she thought.

Inside his office, Bill considered whether he should lock it, wondering how that would look to his officers and staff.

"You okay, Chief?" Turner asked. He'd been sitting in a chair waiting and rose quickly when Bill entered.

"Not really." Bill locked the door, then placed the shoebox on his desk as gently as he would a bomb. "Turner, what I've got in here is going to be icky and unpleasant. And you need to avoid talking about it to anybody but me when we're done. Is that clear?"

"Absolutely," Turner said, though he couldn't suppress the confused look on his face.

Bill took a deep breath, removed the lid, and started sorting the Polaroids by subject.

* * *

Kyra Bennett looked at her phone. Again. Watches weren't her thing, and she was using her phone to check the time. Normally, sitting at the reception desk, she relied on a laptop to tell the time, but the computer system was down, and the techs could not provide an ETA for when it would be back up. Right now, only the phone system was functional, and those calls were quick. Anyone calling to book an appointment was met with the most courteous "I'm sorry, our system is down, please try again later" she could muster. Muttering from the other end of the line often followed, and sometimes annoyed follow-up questions like, "How could you let this happen?" to which she offered her best, "Our technical department is working to resolve it." In the meantime, she played games on her phone.

Which is why she saw Ellie's text immediately. She made a face, shook her head, and tried to ignore it. But then Ellie sent a second, then a third, then called. On a normal day, Kyra would have ignored her completely. But with systems down and nothing to do, she decided to answer.

"Ellie."

"Kyra? Do you have some time to talk?"

"Pretty sure you said everything you needed to last time we talked."

"I'm really sorry about that," Ellie said, and Kyra thought Ellie sounded like she meant it. "We've learned some new things, and I need to ask you about them."

"Oh, goodie, more ways you can insult me by asking me if I'm a murderer."

"Kyra, I really need to talk to you. Do you want to meet me after work, or do you want me to send Chief Starlin down to pick you up?" So much for a polite Ellie.

Kyra shook her head, biting back her anger, wanting to unload on Ellie. But she knew she couldn't and wasn't sure she wanted to.

251

The theater community in central Massachusetts was a small one, and once word got out you were mouthy or hard to work with, people stopped casting you. And this whole thing was a crazy situation. She said, "There's not much more to say, Ellie. I didn't kill Reginald, but I'm not sorry he's dead. Go look into his wife."

"Valerie's in a coma," Ellie said.

A prickly sensation spread all over Kyra's face. "Sorry, what did you say?"

"She was attacked and left for dead. In her house."

Kyra's hands started to shake as she held the phone.

"There's more," Ellie said, taking a big breath. "The saddest part."

Kyra held her breath. "Oh no. Merilyn?"

"Yes. Last night."

That was the breaking point, the one that hurt. Reginald's death was fine, good even, and the attack on Valerie was, well, not great. But Merilyn, the woman who Kyra had so admired during the show—her death was more than Kyra could bear, though it had been coming for a while. Kyra put her hand to her mouth, tried to stifle a sob, and failed. She burst into tears, groping blindly for a tissue in the box on the desk.

Ellie heard the sobbing through the phone, and her eyes teared up. She sniffled and sniffed and grunted and said, "I know, Kyra. Drive up to the theater and meet me after work, okay? Let's just talk, and I can grab us some dinner."

"Okay," Kyra said, her voice wet and muffled and hard to understand. "Okay, I'll be there."

*   *   *

There were more girls than Bill could keep in his head, so he started writing down the information on a pad of paper. He wrote their names; the year scribbled on the pictures; the type of film, whether Polaroid or regular still; and the type of shot—reference, posing, or sex act. He would get his chicken scratch into a spreadsheet when he was finished so he could sort and filter the list. Two hours later, he and Turner finished.

"I feel like I need to shower," Turner said.

"Yeah," was all Bill could manage.

He scanned through the list, looking for the later years. He wished he had started out entering them in a spreadsheet. He had the front and back of two legal-sized sheets of paper filled with notes. One thing he didn't have was location. He figured many of these girls were from New York City, but knowing Reginald had moved back to Massachusetts at some point, he couldn't guarantee they all were. Plus, some pictures showed beaches, with palm trees in the background. Florida or California, he figured.

Or not. Someplace that had nude beaches. He had no idea where that might be. Did nude beaches exist in the United States?

The last date he found was 1990, with the next closest year being 1985. He scanned his notes one more time, this time looking for a name. Merilyn. There was a Mary, a couple of Marias, but no Merilyn. Not even the normal spelling of Marilyn. She probably went by an alias, but he had scrutinized the faces of the women in all the pictures. None looked like the Merilyn from the video Ellie had found.

"So now we have a list of all the girls we found, but what does it tell us?"

"As far as I can see, not much," Turner said. "We have first names and the dates, and if we had to, we could write up physical descriptions. But that's it. No location, no last names, no other identifying data points. I'm not sure what our next steps are."

Bill sat back in his chair and rubbed his face with his hands. He put all the pictures back inside the box, and put the lid back on it. He folded his pages of notes and gave them to Turner.

"Take this list and get it into a spreadsheet. And then call up the Midtown precinct in Manhattan and see if they will send you a list of all the girls busted for prostitution between, let's say, 1978 and 1980.

Let's try to match those first names and arrest dates with what we have in our list."

"You're thinking it was a whole racket? Beyond just Reginald?"

"Had to be. This many girls? No way our old buddy Reggie was the only player involved."

"Then what?"

"If we can make some connections, then I think we hand it over to Alice Keaton, and let her liaise with the DA for the Southern District of New York. I think we've stumbled on something bigger than just one guy."

Turner nodded. "Could be somebody from Thornton's old life is cleaning up loose ends."

Bill shook his head. "If that were the case, they would have just shot Reginald in his house. Valerie too, I imagine. No, I still think this is more personal. But I think what we have here"—he pointed at the list in Turner's hand— "is the start of something bigger."

He stood and handed the box to Turner, who took it as if it were a porcupine. "Get that thing into the evidence locker and start the chain of custody paperwork."

"Will do."

Bill picked up his keys and left.

Chapter
Forty-Nine

The clock on his dashboard read four o'clock when he pulled into the driveway in front of the little house Alex Hillman had converted into his office. Bill entered. A different woman sat at the receptionist desk.

"May I help you?"

Bill showed her his badge and didn't bother asking her name. "Is he free?"

"I can check for you." She picked up a phone to dial.

"If he's not free, he needs to become free," Bill said. The receptionist looked at him for a long moment, found no humor in Bill's face, and nodded. She spoke into the phone for a moment before saying, "He can see you immediately," as she hung up the phone.

Bill crossed the open floor to the white door of Alex's office and entered without knocking.

Alex Hillman sat behind his desk, fingers tented in front of him, watching as Bill came in and closed the door.

"Chief Starlin. I'm surprised to see you back here. Won't you please sit?"

"No thanks. I don't think I'll be here that long." Hillman raised his eyebrows. "I want to see the life insurance policy."

Alex smiled and said, "As I explained last time, Chief, for that you will need a warrant."

"Let's cut the crap, shall we?" Bill snapped. "The Worcester DA has formally turned the investigation over to me. And if I want a warrant, I can probably obtain one in three minutes. But the beneficiary of the life insurance policy is now in a coma. Doubtlessly you've heard."

Alex's face stayed impassive. "Yes, I have. It is incredibly sad, tragic really. But my confidentiality agreement still stands, even so."

"Why? There's no kids or family to protect."

Alex raised a single eyebrow, a Mr. Spock–like move Bill used to want to be able to do. He had practiced for hours as a kid in front of a mirror, holding one eyebrow down while raising the other, like a strength training exercise for his eyebrows. He ultimately failed miserably. Bill was destined to be a two-eyebrow kind of guy.

"The matter has to make its way through probate," Alex said, "then my agreement with the estate may be revisited. Until that time, as I said before, it will take a warrant."

Bill came close to the desk and leaned down, fists on the flat surface.

"Who are you protecting?"

"I'm not protecting anyone but myself."

"Yourself?"

"My reputation. If word gets out that I hand over my clients' information to the police simply because they lean threateningly on my desk, I will quickly lose those clients, and my business will be ruined."

Bill stood. Something about this man made Bill want to hit him. Except Alex was right, and if Bill was honest with himself, he admired the man—at least somewhat—for his willingness to stick to his guns in the face of a threat. Bill nodded and said, "Fine. I'll be back with the warrant."

"If it takes you longer than three minutes, you'll need to return tomorrow. I'll soon be closing up for the day." Alex smiled.

"By the way," Bill said as he opened the door. "You remember Merilyn Chambers, right? The woman you only met once or twice?"

"Yes."

"She died yesterday. Cancer finally got her. Thought maybe you'd want to know that."

Bill waited for Alex's reaction. The man's smile had vanished. He showed almost no reaction except in his voice, thin and strained, when he said, "Thank you for letting me know."

Bill waited a moment longer, and when no further reaction was forthcoming, he left, pulling the door shut hard behind him. Alex listened as Bill crossed the converted house and heard the front door open and slam. Alex sat forward in his chair, his arms resting limply on the arms of the chair. He breathed through his nose, trying to compose himself for a moment. He pressed the intercom button on his phone and said, his voice growing hoarser by the second, "Hold all calls, Denise."

He didn't hear her response before folding his arms on the desk, face down in them, sobbing.

*   *   *

Bill called Ellie but got her voicemail. He didn't like mentioning the treasure trove of smut on her voicemail, but he didn't want to hold anything back. He explained what he found at Merilyn's house and that he spent the afternoon cataloging the pictures. He told her about the calls to Valerie from Hillman, and how he struck out when he visited the money manager. When he finished, he dialed Alice Keaton's number. Time to get that warrant for Alex Hillman.

Chapter Fifty

Ellie checked her voicemail on her way out of Panera, picking up dinner for her and Kyra. She listened to Bill's description of the photos in the shoebox. Her heart raced and her hands shook, nearly causing her to drop the bag of food as she listened. It sounded like the exact situation Paul had described. And she hated that she still didn't quite believe Paul when he said he had nothing to do with it. She wanted to believe him so badly, but a little doubt tugged at her in the back of her mind. Pornographers back then were a secretive lot, their merchandise being highly illegal at the time. *How could he have known about it if he wasn't involved?*

She pulled into the theater parking lot next to a car already parked in a space. But the car was not Kyra's, who wouldn't be there for another fifteen minutes.

She went into the building, calling out, "Steve?"

"In the theater," he called back.

She placed the food on the ticket counter and walked into the theater itself. "Hey, Steve," Ellie said. "I didn't realize you were coming in today."

"Walking through the blocking and reciting my lines. The blocking makes memorizing lines so much easier."

"You knew most of these lines cold during the rehearsals. What happened?"

Steve blushed. "Knowing the lines and reciting them is a lot easier when you're not the actor and not the one onstage that everyone is looking at."

"Steve," Ellie said with surprise, "do you have stage fright?"

He didn't answer but just looked at his book and moved to the next place his character was supposed to be. Ellie joined Steve on the stage and put a hand on his shoulder.

"Thank you," she said. "You have probably saved this theater. You kept going the last few days while I've been . . ." She waved her hand in the air like she didn't have the words to finish.

"Tilting at windmills?" Steve smiled. "I only work here. I don't run the place. I can't imagine how hard it's been to try and corral this thing."

She sighed, then sniffed, then blinked, then nodded her head. "Yeah. It has definitely not been fun, that's for sure."

She looked around, wondering how to politely kick Steve out. She wanted her conversation with Kyra to be private, away from restaurant tables or diner booths or coffee shop patios. She didn't think Kyra would come out to Ellie's house. The theater felt like the perfect place for neutral, quiet territory. Except Steve was here. She had to hand it to the guy—he was conscientious.

"What brings you in?" Steve asked.

"I'm meeting Kyra here for dinner."

"Kyra? For dinner? Here?" She heard the questions in his voice, the ones he asked and the ones he didn't.

"I wanted someplace where she and I could talk. In private."

Steve nodded. "Yeah, that's cool. I understand. I can pack it in for the day anyway. I'm more or less done for now."

"You're sure you don't mind?"

"Nope. I'm getting hungry anyway. I hear Five Guys calling my name."

He shrugged into a jacket, which looked comical with his cargo shorts. He was ready to head out when he paused, as if he didn't want to ask the next question. "How's the investigation going?"

"Slow. Fast. Weird. I dunno. We keep finding new things we can't plug into anything else. Every time I think I'm close, I'm lost again."

"You and Bill still plugging away?"

"Yeah. The Worcester county DA authorized us to investigate, mainly because the state police don't want to. There's some kind of weird history between them and Bill that makes it hard for them to take anything he says seriously. So we're doing our own thing. I'm here to talk to Kyra, and he's talking to some finance guy about the Thornton estate."

"Reginald had a finance guy? That sounds about right for him."

"He's a nice enough guy," Ellie said. "Name of Hillman. He's actually a pretty big donor to the theater. Which makes this whole thing awkward. Which is why Bill is tackling it and I'm staying back."

Steve's eyes narrowed. "A donor to the theater. And the guy who does—or rather, *did*—Reginald's finances. That's a weird circle."

Ellie nodded. "No argument from me. I don't know what to think anymore. All I know is that it may involve a life insurance policy that may or may not exist, and that nothing is what it seems. I imagine a forensic accountant would have a field day with it."

Steve rolled his eyes. "God, that sounds boring."

"Yes, but it's Bill's problem, not ours." Ellie smiled. "He should have the warrant by tomorrow."

"A warrant for finances?"

"Yeah, the guy won't give them up without a warrant."

Steve thought about that. "A finance guy isn't a lawyer. Is there a confidentiality law between finance guys and their clients?"

"No clue. But he's being stubborn, so Bill's off to get the warrant. And then he'll spend hours up to his elbows in numbers. I don't envy him."

"Yeah, I prefer having to build a set overnight for a show opening tomorrow over doing that."

Ellie nudged him in the ribs. "I gave you a week."

Steve smiled. "And I didn't complain then either."

He and Ellie went back into the lobby, and Steve grabbed a cup of water from the sink behind the concessions counter. Down at the end of the counter sat the short stack of programs for *Murder in a Teacup*, and the sadness of Merilyn's death hit Ellie hard. Her face fell. Steve's brows knit, and he asked, "Everything all right?"

Tears welled up in her eyes, and she pulled a tissue out of a box on the counter.

"Merilyn passed away last night."

Steve took a big breath and let out a long sigh, muttering, "Damn."

They stood in silence for a minute, neither apparently knowing what to say to the other. Steve broke the silence.

"Was it at least, I dunno, peaceful?"

"As peaceful as it can be, I guess, when wires and tubes are running in and out of you." She opened her mouth to speak again, but nothing came out, and suddenly she was sobbing like her heart was breaking.

Steve, wide-eyed with panic, came around the counter and bent down, his arms halfway to her but holding back. Sobbing women weren't exactly his specialty. He had thought to hug Ellie, but he didn't think they had a close enough relationship for hugs. But she clearly needed comfort. He looked around the lobby, hoping and praying for something, anything, that would give him a clue.

At that moment, Kyra walked in. She saw Steve standing next to Ellie and Ellie sobbing hysterically and rushed over and punched Steve on the shoulder.

"Ow!"

"What did you do?"

"Nothing!" he barked. "She was talking about Merilyn, then collapsed into a puddle of mush."

Kyra went to Ellie and put her arms around her. Ellie leaned in and sobbed more heavily onto Kyra's shoulder. Tears began to run down Kyra's cheeks. Steve continued to stand next to them, arms halfway out.

Eventually, the sobbing began to let up, and Kyra, her eyes and face wet, looked at Steve and said, "How about you find us some tissues?"

"That I can do," he said in relief and stood quickly. He got a box from the concession area and handed it to Kyra. She took several and offered some to Ellie.

"Sorry," she said. "I didn't mean to lose it like that."

"It's okay, Ellie," Kyra said. "We all miss her."

"It's not that. I mean, it is, but that's not why. I was thinking about why I had gone to see her. To get answers. Answers to more questions that have come up. Instead of asking how she was, if she needed anything, or just to tell her how much I loved having her at the theater, I went there to grill her."

"You can't beat yourself up over that," Kyra said.

"Why not? I've been so focused on getting answers I didn't ask how she felt. She was probably in terrible pain. And there we were grilling her . . ."

"About what?"

Ellie threw up her hands. "So stupid! So selfish!"

"What?" Kyra said, almost pleadingly.

"We were asking her about this stupid case. When we should have been a source of comfort, we were pestering her about who could have killed Reginald and attacked Valerie."

"Did she know who did it?" Steve asked, wide-eyed.

"I think she was hallucinating," Ellie said. "She said Valerie killed Reginald. But now Valerie is in a coma, so we'll never really know."

Kyra looked at Steve, who looked back. "So that's it, then? As far as Reginald is concerned?" Kyra asked.

Ellie shrugged. "It's probably up to the DA to decide."

"Wow," Steve said. "I knew Valerie could let fly with some serious rage. I mean, we all saw it that one rehearsal. But I never thought she could kill."

"You sure she said Valerie?" Kyra said. "Words get jumbled all the time, especially when someone is very sick and at their last moments." She looked suddenly very sad. "Trust me, I know."

"Bill asked her if she killed Reginald. I think we both agreed there is no way she could have attacked Valerie. But poisoning Reginald? Sure. She said she didn't. Then Bill asked if she knew who had, and she said his wife."

The three of them were silent for a moment, then Steve said, "I guess that's pretty definitive."

"I pushed too hard," Ellie said. "I pushed, and Merilyn slipped away before I could tell her how much she meant to me."

"I'm sure she knew how much she meant to you," Kyra said.

"Yeah," Steve added. "The shows she did here were amazing. And no one was more appreciative than you. She knew what she meant to you."

Ellie sighed, a big, wet, rattling sigh. "I hope you're right."

Chapter
Fifty-One

"I won't be able to put it in front of a judge until tomorrow morning," Alice Keaton said over the phone. "You think there's something in the policy?"

"Would it be wrong to say I hope so?" Bill said.

On the other end of the line, Alice made a noise as if she didn't like what she heard. "You're gonna need to do better than hope, Bill."

"I know, I know. I don't have any evidence tying anything back to anything else. At least not where Hillman is concerned. But I think something is in that policy he doesn't want anyone to see, and he's forcing the issue by making me get a warrant."

"Just for the policy?"

"Yes, for the moment. I never asked about any other financial records."

"If we go for one, we might as well go for them all."

Bill liked the way Alice thought and said as much.

"I'll have someone start writing the warrant. I think, since the husband is dead and somebody tried to do the same to the wife, we should have no problem opening those records up to peek inside. It should fall under the umbrella of our investigation."

The Last Line

"Okay. In the meantime, I found something else today I'm not sure what to do with."

"What is it?"

Bill took a deep breath and said, "You better sit down. There's nothing you're going to like about this one." And he started telling her about the photos in the shoebox.

Chapter Fifty-Two

S teve had left as soon as humanly possible, leaving the two women to sit on the floor of the lobby and eat their food.

"Are you sure you wouldn't rather stay?" Kyra teased him, smiling. "Share your feelings, get in touch with your emotions, have a cry with us?"

Steve shifted his feet with discomfort. "Uh, no. I'm good. See you around," he said, looking worried, and quickly exited. They watched him go and, eyes still wet with tears, burst into giggles.

When the giggles subsided, the two women were left with a great sadness they were unable to bridge. So they did what Ellie did best in times of deep grief: they ate.

She pulled the bag to the floor and gave Kyra her Cobb salad and bread, then withdrew her own salad. They sat on the ground, ate, and drank a couple of Pellegrinos Ellie had picked up at Panera.

In between mouthfuls, they spoke. Ellie explained what they found at Merilyn's, and what Paul had told her about Reginald's past.

"He never asked you to pose for nude pictures?" Ellie asked.

"No," Kyra said, trying not to spill food as she talked and ate, something that would have mortified her late mother. "He never did that. That's, just, ew."

"Ew is right," Ellie said, taking a swallow of the carbonated water. She talked while she ate, with a healthy dose of ticcing mixed in. In truth, she didn't care for eating. It's not that she didn't like food, but the act of eating was often too much like a skirmish between mastication and uncontrollable movement, especially in her jaw and throat. She loved the taste of food. She loathed the battle of eating.

"It looks like most of that behavior took place in New York City. But that doesn't mean he stopped when he left."

Kyra shook her head. "No, he never asked me to pose naked. Only to sleep with him. Honestly, I would've posed naked first before doing the other."

"He didn't just film the videos. He was in them."

Kyra put down her fork and pushed her salad away. "I'm not hungry anymore."

"He looked different back then. Not like how he looked when we knew him."

"Still, good God, yuck."

Ellie set down her fork and leaned back, her arms behind her, propping her up. "Kyra, I hate to ask this, but so we can clear you and get you out of the picture, do you have an alibi for the other night when Valerie was attacked?"

"I do. I was at a bar with friends."

"Until when?"

"Probably ten thirty or eleven."

Scratch-sniff-sniff. "Okay."

Ellie stood, gathered the trash, shoved it back in the Panera bag, and put the bag by the door to take to the dumpster when she left. Kyra stood and grabbed her phone and her keys.

"Any idea when the funeral is?"

"No," Ellie said. "But as soon as I hear, I'll pass it on."

"Okay."

"Bill will probably call you to ask for the names of your friends to confirm the alibi. I don't want you thinking we're trying to pester you."

"I don't. I was angry before, but I'm not anymore. Now I'm sad."

"Me too." Ellie opened her arms to hug the younger woman. Kyra hugged her back, and the two enjoyed a warm moment—two sad souls able to grieve in each other's arms. Kyra could feel the little movements of Ellie's tics as she tried to stifle them. Ellie felt the stillness of Kyra's body, wondering what it must be like to always be still, not constantly in motion, drawing strength from the younger woman's stillness to quiet her tics as much as possible. Then the hug ended, and they went outside.

"Don't let this craziness keep you from auditioning here again. Or anywhere," Ellie said. "You're very, very good. Kaleidoscope would be lucky to have you back."

Kyra smiled at her.

Chapter
Fifty-Three

The next morning found Bill waiting impatiently in the office of the District Attorney for Worcester Country. He sat, leaning forward, elbows on knees, hands folded together between his legs. If he wore a brimmed hat like some of the local town cops did, he would have been spinning it in his restless hands. Instead, he folded them together to keep them from driving anyone else nuts.

When the door finally opened, Alice Keaton stuck her head out, and beckoned him into her office with a crooked finger.

Bill entered and shut the door behind him. Alice went behind her desk but didn't sit down.

"The judge didn't give me a lot of trouble, but the state DA did."

"Really? I'm surprised she got involved at this level. This is pretty basic stuff for her to be watching."

"She's been watching ever since I turned the investigation over to you. You're kind of a litmus test for us. If this goes well, we could look into turning some investigations over to the local jurisdictions. It would save the state money, and the locals have their ear closer to the ground than the MSP would. But—"

"But for every town police force that can do it, another is such a Rosco P. Coltrane they couldn't find their nose with GPS coordinates and Google Maps?"

Alice smiled wryly. "That might be the first *Dukes of Hazzard* reference this office has ever heard." She handed a folded set of papers over to Bill and said, "Call me if you find anything. Call me first. Don't go sifting through boxes you find under a bed in a house you should have tagged as evidence."

"I promise," he said with the most innocent smile he could muster.

* * *

Ellie woke up early, tied her running shoes on, and hit the pavement. Mike was in Manhattan overnight. Sometimes he made the trip in a day, but lately, more and more, after driving down early in the morning and spending all day in the actual office, he usually spent the night in a room the company paid for. She had talked to him last night, a phone conversation that consisted of her doing most of the talking and him doing most of the listening.

She unloaded everything she'd learned and everything that had happened so far, and after twenty minutes of stream of consciousness, she apologized to him and asked him about his day. He laughed and said his meetings weren't nearly as interesting as her day had been. He promised to be home as early as possible and said he loved her. She told him she loved him too, very much. They both hung up gently.

The morning dawned bright and cloudless, a sunny but brisk day. She could tell already it would be a cold one. The wind was up, the leaves on the trees holding on for dear life.

She chose to leave her phone at home. She wasn't in the mood to listen to music. She just wanted to hear the sound of her shoes on the pavement and the breath going into and out of her lungs. One less thing to carry.

After five miles and long, satisfying leg stretches on the front lawn, she went first to the kitchen sink and grabbed a big glass of water. She leaned forward and ducked her head under the faucet. She dripped on the floor when she stood up, decided she didn't care, and stripped out of her wet clothing, leaving it on the kitchen floor. She marched upstairs and straight into the shower, which she set as hot as she could stand, then cranked it down to as cold as she could.

Thirty minutes later, clean, dressed, and running gear scooped from the kitchen floor and taken to the basement laundry, she sat down with a yogurt and a half a grapefruit. She felt spartan this morning, not wanting anything more after her run. That, and a cup of coffee, and she was good.

Finally, after settling at the kitchen island with her breakfast, she picked up her phone.

The caller ID read "Worcester Telegram."

Paul Koehler had called.

Four times.

Chapter
Fifty-Four

B ill entered Alex Hillman's office and didn't bother with the receptionist, the third in as many days. She tried to stop him, but he
flashed his badge wordlessly and kept on walking. She picked up the
phone and dialed. By the time he reached the office door, Alex had
opened it and stepped out.

"All right, this is quite enough. Chief, I'm rather busy this morning, so if you would please—"

Bill handed him the papers without a word. Alex took them and
read through them.

"Better have her clear your schedule," Bill said. Alex looked up,
and Bill realized for the first time the man was scared. He said with a
shaky voice, "Betty, please clear my schedule today. I'm afraid I will be
occupied most of the day."

The receptionist nodded and clicked back to her desk by the door
in four-inch heels. Bill watched her go. Her hips swayed as they moved
her butt, which waggled cute, high, and tight. He turned back to Alex.

"How many of them do you have?"

"Pardon?"

"Your receptionists. She's the third one. Do you have one for every
day of the week? Do you grow them in flowerpots somewhere?"

Alex wore his distaste for Bill's comments openly, but he did not rise to the bait. Instead, he made an inviting gesture with his arm into his office.

"Shall we, Chief?"

*   *   *

"Paul, what's going on?" Ellie asked.

At the other end of the line, Paul sounded excited, his breath short, his voice eager, which came through clearly over the cell phone towers.

"I just remembered something else."

"What is it?"

"Keep in mind I have no hard evidence, only what I had been told by people who knew him, but, the rumor at the time, when Reginald was down here—"

"Paul, skip to the end."

Not even Ellie's curtness dampened Paul's excitement. "The last time we spoke, you asked if Valerie was involved in his little side industry."

"I remember."

"And I said she wasn't."

"I remember that too." She wondered where he was going.

"But back then the rumor was that Reginald was married."

Ellie shook her head, failing to understand the point. "Well, sure. His wife's attack is one of the things we're trying to solve."

"Ellie," Paul said softly, "do the math."

Ellie heard what Paul said, and math started up in her head, almost of its own accord.

"Wait a second. He was only married to Valerie for something like fifteen or twenty years."

"Correct."

"Which means . . ." Ellie felt slow, like a dunce needing to be put in the corner of the classroom and made to wear the conical dunce cap. "Which means Valerie is his second wife."

"At least," Paul said. "Could be his third for all I know. Again, this is all gossip, but the rumor back then was he was finalizing his divorce and had left the girl back home, here in Worcester."

Ellie closed her eyes, trying to figure out what that meant. How could this be connected to the murder? Was this what Merilyn meant when she said Reginald's wife killed him? Maybe she was talking about his ex-wife. If she and Reginald were roughly the same age when they married, she could still be alive. Seventy-five wasn't knocking on death's door, as it had been a century or so earlier. Was this whole thing some kind of weird blast from the past that finally caught up with Reginald, and Valerie just got in the way?

Her eyes popped open with an idea. *A records search.* Why hadn't she thought of it before?

"What was the ex-wife's name?"

Paul stumbled around for a moment. "Honestly, Ellie, I have no idea. Could have been Sophia Loren for all I know. All I can tell you is the rumor at the time."

"Paul, this has been very helpful. Thank you."

She didn't catch his response before she hung up and opened her laptop.

Chapter
Fifty-Five

B ill had skimmed through the insurance policy once and, having not found anything useful, read through it again, slower and more cautiously. He tossed it back on the desk in frustration. Alex, sitting still and quiet in his chair, said, "Find what you were looking for?"

"There's nothing here," Bill admitted.

"I certainly hope the time you spent reading through the policy was worth the time you spent getting the warrant."

"Don't worry. I have all day, and the warrant allows me to dig into all the financial information related to the Thorntons."

Alex sighed and leaned forward. "Chief Starlin, perhaps we can cut through the crap, as they say, and move directly to what you're looking for."

Bill paused before speaking. "The truth is, I'm not sure what I'm looking for. There are a lot of moving parts to this case—revenge, jealousy, you name it—and it's probably in there. But law enforcement investigations have an old adage. Know what it is?"

Alex shook his head.

"*Follow the money,*" Bill said. "This case seemed personal to me. Someone poisoning Reginald during a theater performance?

Hitting him where it hurts the most? Very personal. Except there's a strange little voice in the back of my head saying that maybe this is about money. Money Reginald supposedly didn't have. Except I've seen his house. For someone on the verge of being broke, he lived very well."

"He would not be the first person to live beyond their means."

"True. And if this whole case does have something to do with money, I can't figure out how. I thought maybe it was Valerie. Maybe she killed him for money, for something in the policy. First, the policy is gone, then we find out a new policy exists and she would receive a pretty big payout. Except as far as she knew, no money existed. Then she's attacked. So it's clearly not her."

Bill paused and looked Alex squarely in the eye. "And then there's you."

Alex's face became a study in indignation.

"Don't give me that look. You tell us Valerie had a payday coming, but before that, the Thorntons were essentially broke and not paying bills." He paused. "I want to see the books."

"You want the details of all their finances?"

"The warrant gives me access. I just hoped to avoid spending my day looking at numbers."

"Are you more of a hands-on kind of fellow?"

Bill detected the snark in Alex's voice and gave him a sour look. "I'm not an idiot, thank you very much. But I'm also not a forensic accountant."

Alex put his hands up as if in surrender. "My apologies."

Bill sat back, and he and Alex looked at each other. A kind of understanding blossomed between them. Something akin to mutual respect developed as they sat there in silence.

"Chief," Alex finally said. "If I help you navigate the Thorntons' finances, can we agree that you will leave my name out of the investigation if at all possible?"

Bill was greatly tempted by the offer. He didn't relish the idea of digging into ledger books alone. It would take him all day, and maybe into tomorrow. Help would be most welcome.

Except . . .

"Alex," Bill said. "I'd like nothing more than to have help going through this stuff. But, in all honesty, you're still a suspect."

"Me?"

"Yes, you. Do you have an alibi for the night of Valerie Thornton's attack?"

Alex's gaze dropped to his hands, folded neatly in front of him. Without looking up, he said, "I do not."

"You see my problem? I need to clear you before I can accept your help. Unless, of course, you want to guide me through your finances as well. To help clear yourself of suspicion."

Alex became quiet, clearly struggling to decide what to do. Bill watched and waited. People often became so worked up that they eventually broke down and gave you what you needed, if only to make the uncomfortable silence go away.

The strained silence broke Alex's resolve. "I do not have an alibi for that night. But I had no reason to want to kill Valerie. She is a lovely woman. Perhaps a little cold, but we have a good relationship, since both of us had to put up with her prick of a husband."

"You said the first time we were here that you barely knew her."

"I lied. I know her very well. I called her the moment I learned Reginald had died. We arranged to meet to discuss options."

Something that had been nagging at the back of Bill's mind broke free, and he could finally see it clearly.

"You were the one at her house when I went to visit her."

Alex nodded. "I was. She didn't want our association to be known, so I stayed out of sight while you tried to badger her into a private autopsy."

Bill ignored the dig. "Why were you there?"

"To determine if she wanted to cooperate with any investigation."

"Based on her unwillingness to have the private autopsy done, I'm guessing her answer was no."

"You guess correctly. Valerie Thornton wanted her private life to remain just that. If she let the authorities start digging into that life, all the dirty secrets would come out."

"We've found a lot of dirty secrets so far," Bill said. "What's a few more?"

Alex's eyebrows went up, and his face flushed. A bead of sweat formed at his temple, something not lost on Bill. "What kind of secrets have you found?" he asked.

Bill considered how much to tell Alex. He didn't want to show his whole hand yet. Maybe leading Alex down a path and letting him fill in the details was the answer.

"How well did you know Merilyn Chambers?" Bill asked. "And remember, you're trying to be honest here, and clear your name."

Alex's face grew sad. "Very well. She and I had met many years before. She was one of the few people that knew I am gay."

"Are you still in the closet, so to speak?"

"I keep my private life private, including my sexual orientation. My clients tend to be conservative. Don't look so surprised, Chief. Wealth tends to be conservative, and the wealthy contribute to conservative candidates, as they are the politicians most likely to give them a tax break." He put up a hand as Bill was about to speak. "We can argue the point all day, Chief, but our opinions here do not matter. The fact is, my client list is very conservative, and some of them would not be overly fond to learn their money was being managed by a gay man."

"Who cares as long as you're making them money?"

"And I am," Alex said, a measure of pride in his voice. "But there are lots of money managers out there, and if the one they have doesn't match with their values, they won't hesitate to make a change."

"Did Reginald know you're gay?"

Alex nodded. "As does Valerie."

"And he was blackmailing you?"

Again, Alex nodded. Bill sighed. "This isn't helping you. You just gave me a motive as to why you might want to kill him."

"Reginald, yes, but not Valerie."

"She doesn't care about your sexual orientation?"

"If she does, she's never said anything to me. And whenever we meet, she is always sweet, kind, and polite to me. I am accustomed to sensing when someone doesn't like me because of my sexuality. I feel no such animosity from Valerie."

Bill rubbed his chin with his hand. "And the reason you're telling me this now is because, when I start to dig into the Thornton finances, I'll see payments from you."

Alex lowered his eyes and nodded. "Cash deposits, mostly, except for two times when I did not have the requisite cash on hand to meet his demands. For those, I cut checks from the business."

"How'd Reginald find out?"

"I believe Merilyn told him."

Bill nodded. "He used the video against her," he said.

Alex's eyes widened, and he leaned forward, his voice low. "You know about the video?"

"We found it—"

"We?"

"Ellie Marlowe and me. It took a bit to realize what we were watching, but then we recognized Merilyn. Once we realized who she was, it was impossible not to see her."

Alex stood, then sat, then stood again, like he had a wellspring of nervous energy for which he had no outlet. A mask of anger flashed across his face. Bill realized the man was fighting back rage.

"How did he . . . ? Where . . . ?" Alex was having trouble forming complete sentences.

Bill waited for Alex's paroxysm to run its course.

"He told me I had the only copy," Alex said. "He said he'd given it to me for safekeeping. That it was the only one."

"You're saying a blackmailer lied to you?"

Managing to recompose himself slightly, Alex sat back down and said, "Your sarcasm is not appreciated, Chief."

"Reginald got information from Merilyn," Bill said, trying to get the conversation back on track, "and he used that to get money from other people. Sound about right?"

"Yes."

"What do you know about his past in New York City?"

"Almost nothing."

"Did you know he was a pornographer?"

"He was an actor, I thought."

"Both. He was a struggling actor trying to break into Broadway, and a porn pusher. Have you seen Merilyn's video?"

A look of abject disgust passed over Alex's face. "Yes."

"Did you recognize Reginald in the video with her?"

Disgust transformed into horror. Alex managed to shake his head.

"He'd been coercing hookers who had been picked up for solicitation by paying their bail if they performed for him," Bill continued. "Hundreds of photos of dozens of girls. Was he blackmailing any of them?"

The disgust on Alex's face was palpable. "This is the first I've ever heard of this."

"You have no knowledge about an old shoebox full of these photos in Merilyn's possession?"

"Merilyn? How would she get her hands on that kind of material?"

Bill shrugged. "I was hoping you might tell me."

Alex shook his head. "I'm afraid I don't know anything about it."

"None of these women were being blackmailed by Reginald?"

"If they were, he did not set up the payments through me."

Bill considered that for a moment and asked, "How about the other way around. Any chance any of the women were blackmailing him?"

Alex shook his head again. "There is only one person I would say had any sway over Reginald Thornton. Only one person I dealt with that Reginald told me to pay to make him go away."

"Who?"

Alex raised his eyes in surprise. "His son, of course."

Chapter
Fifty-Six

Ellie pulled up the Worcester City Clerk's website. She had a vague idea of how to begin. Start with marriage certificates. She didn't need specific details, just the names.

Worcester had digitized their marriage certificate records all the way back to 1686, which made her search simple. No going down to City Hall, no begging or cajoling someone to give her moldy, dusty ledger books full of records. A quick internet search and she was there. She had a moment of doubt before she launched into her search. What if Reginald had not gotten married in Worcester? Then it would be like looking for the proverbial needle in the digital haystack.

She pushed the doubt aside and began her search.

She typed THORNTON in the Last Name field and REGI-NALD in the First Name field.

Two records popped up, listed in ascending order by date. The second one was for Reginald's marriage to Valerie. The first one was for his marriage to his first wife.

Annie.

She read the listing twice, worried she perhaps had performed the search incorrectly. But it was correct. The name of the first wife was right there on the computer screen.

Annie.

But it was Annie's maiden name that made Ellie's blood run cold.

Chapter
Fifty-Seven

"Son?" Bill's mouth hung open, then snapped shut. "You said he didn't have kids."

"No, you inferred that from your reading of the insurance policy."

Bill's face flushed hot, and he took a deep breath to avoid losing his temper at the man across the desk from him.

"When we were here the first time, you said Valerie was the sole beneficiary, and that she and Reginald never had children."

Alex nodded. "All true."

"Then what the hell . . . ?"

"Reginald had a child, singular. Not with Valerie but with his first wife, Annie."

"Did Merilyn know about his first wife?"

"Possibly. Though I doubt she'd remember her."

"So it was just dumb luck," Bill said to himself.

"What was?"

"We asked Merilyn if she knew who killed Reginald. She said his wife. I think she meant Valerie. But she might have stumbled into a version of the truth, even if she didn't realize it."

"Or even realize that he had a first wife?" Alex added, to which Bill nodded in agreement. "He did indeed. His first wife bore him a son."

"Whom Reginald paid to go away."

283

"Well, he certainly tried."

Bill cocked an eyebrow. "What do you mean?"

Alex sighed. "The boy—well, hardly a boy. A man now, but I tend to think of everyone male younger than myself as a boy, I suppose. He came to me a year ago. He claimed to be Reginald's son and said he had documents to prove that claim. Of course, documents can be forged, though I'm no expert on identifying them. But I keep a private investigator on retainer for these kinds of things."

Bill looked surprised.

"When you're dealing with people's money, it becomes an absolute necessity to have someone you can use to verify information. Such was the case with this boy. He presented documents, and I contacted my man and had him begin the search. Interesting results, I must say. The boy's mother died of cancer after the divorce. The boy ended up in foster care as a result. No other relatives to take him in. Meanwhile, I reached out to Reginald and informed him of the situation. He insisted I halt the investigation immediately and simply pay the boy off."

"Why?" Bill said. "He could have proven yes or no by a basic paternity test. And even if he was Reginald's son, who cares? There's no way to sue for child support once you're no longer a child, unless it had been court ordered in the past."

"You bring up all the same points I brought up. But Reginald was stubborn. He often wanted my advice and then completely ignored it. So his response did not surprise me at all. In my opinion, I think Reginald was ashamed of this child and wanted the matter to simply go away. He worried that it might ruin his reputation, that he had a child he abandoned. Cancel culture, and all that. I made one more argument, but to no avail. And the client gets what the client wants. So I paid the boy to go away."

"Did it work?"

"Initially, yes, for a while. I had not seen or heard from this gentleman, and I use the term loosely, in about a year. Then he contacted me again, demanding more of Reginald's money. This time, Reginald refused. He said he was broke, and quite frankly, he was. Reginald threatened to turn the boy in if he ever contacted him again."

"And then Reginald turns up dead."

"Quite a response to being told no."

Bill scratched his chin. "But why attack Valerie? Unless . . ."

"I suspect the boy was worried Reginald had told his wife and was therefore worried that charges might still be pressed despite Reginald being out of the picture."

Bill imagined a boy, abandoned by his father, his mother dying from a disease for lack of money, and growing up full of rage as he bounced around the foster system—a bad system for children to grow up in now, and likely ten times worse forty or fifty years ago.

"It wasn't about the money," Bill muttered.

"Pardon?" Alex leaned forward.

"It wasn't about money," Bill repeated, louder. "It was never about money. It was about revenge. About screwing the man who screwed his mother."

Alex nodded. "Literally and figuratively. Until Valerie."

"He went to the Thornton house that night because he was worried Valerie might turn him in," Bill said. "And tried to kill her."

Alex nodded. "That is my assumption. Valerie was a loose end he needed to tie up."

"He must have been in a panic, because he didn't finish the job," Bill said. He stared at Alex, sweating now and looking pale. Bill realized Alex had played an enormous role in this drama, possibly letting a murderer slip through without calling the police. And he himself, as someone with knowledge of the whole situation, was a loose end.

"Aren't you worried you are in danger because he used you as a go-between?"

"I'm in danger from far more than the son. My business is built on reputation. If word gets out that I aided and abetted a blackmailer, I will be finished. Not just with this company that I built from scratch. All credibility will be lost. Everywhere. No one will ever hire me, and no one will ever allow me near their money again. The best job I'd find would be a bank teller. Maybe."

Alex pulled a key from his shirt pocket and unlocked the top right drawer of his desk.

"The search warrant gives you access to all of the financial records surrounding the Thorntons, Chief. And though you wouldn't be looking at my finances directly, there are tendrils that snake out, that will come back to hurt me. Tendrils that would lead to an investigation of my finances. A scrutiny that could end badly for me."

He opened the drawer.

"But I already have a plan for that contingency. You see, I understood any dealings with Reginald Thornton could potentially end badly. Not just for him, but for all involved. I wished I could have said no to the man. My client list back then was thin. I needed the business. And back then, Reginald was paying me. Paying me, even as he blackmailed me. Such irony."

He reached his hand into the desk. Red flags went off in Bill's head. He started to rise from his feet. But he was too late.

Alex pulled out a small handgun. "Am I worried? Of course I am." He smiled weakly, then cocked the gun.

Chapter
Fifty-Eight

*N*o, Ellie told herself. *It had to be a coincidence. They couldn't be related. Could they?*

Check first if the woman was still alive. That was what she needed to do.

A quick search of the death records ruled that out. Annie Thornton had died in 1983. She couldn't have killed anyone unless she had reached from beyond the grave.

Which meant . . . She didn't want to believe it.

Ellie filled in the Last Name field on the Birth Certificate page. She tried THORNTON first, knowing it wouldn't be there. There were plenty of Thorntons but no first names she recognized. No surprise. She was just ruling it out, and maybe postponing finding out a truth she didn't want to find.

Then she tried Annie's maiden name and again got several hits. But only one stood out. One with the right first name and a birth year near enough to be what she assumed was Reginald's child. A son.

Her hand trembled. Her tics had virtually vanished as her body replaced the involuntary motor movements with the quivering that comes from being scared.

All these months. Throughout the show.

He had been there all along.

Her phone rang next to her, and she yelped and clapped her hands to her mouth to keep from screaming. She looked at the number. With a shaking hand, she sent the call to voicemail and dashed out of the house.

Chapter
Fifty-Nine

"A lex," Bill said slowly. "Hand me the gun, please. Slowly."
"I never meant to hurt anyone," Alex said. "All I wanted to do was help make things go away. And now, I'm likely a target for this man."

"We can protect you."

Alex laughed, a mirthless sound that grated in Bill's ears. "You don't understand, Chief. Everything we've discussed would all come out when you find him. Everything will be examined, every paper, document, Post-It note—they will all be turned over."

Bill breathed heavily through his nose. Alex had caught him flat-footed. Of course he had his own weapon, but Alex could fire as soon as Bill made a move for it.

"When all of this comes out in the papers, I will be ruined," Alex continued. "My business, my reputation. Nothing will be left."

"Alex. Please. The gun."

"But worse, there's a chance I could go to prison." Alex pointed the gun. "Do you know what happens to men like me in prison?"

He moved it slowly toward his head.

"Alex, we can make a deal," Bill pleaded. "I can work with the DA. I'm already working with her, for her. We can get you some kind of immunity."

"I've been involved with a blackmailer, Chief. You don't get immunity from that, at least not from the public."

"It's not too late," Bill said. "Especially if you help me."

"Help you?" Alex looked up.

"The name of the son," Bill said. "Tell me."

Alex smiled a sad, nervous smile that reminded Bill of a lost little child, some poor little boy abandoned on the midway of a carnival and lost in the glamour of the lights and spinning rides.

"You haven't figured it out? You already know him, Chief."

"Who is it?"

"He is part of the theater."

"Kaleidoscope?"

"Yes. I didn't realize at the time, not when I went to see it. I went for Merilyn, to support her. Imagine my surprise when I ran into him. The look on his face. Oh, it was simply too good." He laughed, the gun wavering. "I can only imagine the look on mine."

Bill racked his head and came up with only two men in their forties who were currently attached to the theater in some way.

In the lag, Alex brought the gun to his temple. Bill half-stood from his chair.

"Wait!" he said. "The name!"

Alex didn't lower the gun, but he didn't pull the trigger. "That's what's important to you, isn't it? Not whether I kill myself, but whether you figure out who the killer is."

Bill sat slowly.

"I'm sorry. It's all important to me, Alex. But you're the one holding the gun. You're in control here. I can try to stop you from pulling that trigger, but I'm not sure I can make it over this desk in time. But if you're set on doing this, the least I can do is try and bring justice to the person who set it all in motion."

Alex pushed his chair back from the desk as far as the wall of windows behind him would allow, well out of Bill's reach. "The person who put all this in motion is already dead, Chief. Reginald was the architect of his own death, and his cruelty nurtured the dark heart of his killer." He sighed and shook his head. "In my mind, for Reginald, justice has already been served. He got what he deserved. But what happened to Valerie should never have happened. And for that I bear a measure of responsibility. If you promise that you will bring Reginald's son to justice for what he did to Valerie, and promise not to try and stop me, I promise you his name before I pull the trigger."

Bill's heart pounded in his chest, the blood in his ears muddying his hearing. His breath was short. He had to make a choice, or Alex would grow impatient and simply pull the trigger without warning.

"Time grows short, Chief."

Bill took a deep breath and said a quick prayer. Not that he believed much anymore. A few Army tours in the desert and a drowned kid sister had stripped belief from him.

"It's a deal," Bill said.

Alex nodded. A single tear rolled down his cheek.

Chapter Sixty

B ill dialed Ellie's number frantically, but it kept going to voicemail. After the third unsuccessful attempt, he dialed his one and only detective.

"Morning, Chief," Turner answered in his laid-back manner.

"Turner," Bill nearly shouted into the phone. "I need you to get to Ellie Marlowe's house right now!"

"What's happened?" Turner asked, hearing the panic in Bill's voice, suddenly alert, sitting straighter in his chair.

"I'm stuck at Alex Hillman's office. I've got a mess to deal with here. Find Dennis and send him to the theater."

"What's happened?" Turner repeated.

"I know who went after the Thorntons. And he's been in front of us the whole time."

*   *   *

Ellie raced out of the house, into her driveway, trying to call Bill as she fumbled the keys to her car. "Bill, I know who it is. Call me, we need to—"

She cut off abruptly when she saw the gun pointed at her. She looked at the man behind the gun.

"Steve," she said, almost in a whisper. "No."

Steve Walker didn't look at her so much as through her, and she saw he was not the same man she talked to yesterday. Or perhaps he was, and this was a different side of him, a hidden side that neither she, nor anyone, had ever seen. His eyes were dead, his face stony. Ellie swallowed and thought, *Oh my God, I'm going to die today.*

But then she realized Steve's hands were shaking. *There's some humanity in there somewhere,* she thought. *He's not too far gone.*

"Hang up," he said. "And toss the phone into the bushes."

She hung up the phone, her hands shaking badly, her fear making her tics as bad as they had ever been.

"The bushes," Steve said again. She managed a terrible underhand toss, the phone missing the bushes and hitting the asphalt of the driveway and shattering. She flinched.

"Steve," she said, hoping to reach the person she thought she knew, the person inside this man. "Steve, don't do this."

Steve waved the gun at her, saying, "Inside."

She swallowed, grunted, ticced, and shook as she went up the short steps into the kitchen.

"The bag," he said.

"I'm not armed," she said, setting down the bag, hoping this declaration would trigger something in his mind about the wrongness of shooting an unarmed woman. Then again, he'd poisoned his father and clubbed his father's wife with a candlestick, intending to kill her. Perhaps morality had taken leave of Steve a long time ago.

"Steve, you don't need to do this," Ellie said. "We can work this out."

Nod-nod--grunt-sniff. Her tics were out of control. She couldn't calm herself enough to stop moving. *Sniff-grunt-blink-blink.*

"I didn't want to get to this point, but you couldn't leave it alone, could you? You just had to dig and dig, didn't you? You and the Chief."

Ellie swallowed hard. "I know he was your father. I know what happened."

"I was hoping to let all this blow over. Even Valerie. By the time she woke up, I'd be long gone. But"—he waved the gun at her, and Ellie had the sense that Steve was barely holding on—"I realized too late you would connect the dots. Especially once Bill got his warrant for the finances. You took all my options away from me."

"I'm sorry Reginald was so awful to you," Ellie said, and she was. *Nod-nod-blink.*

"I don't care about that. You think I care about how he treated me? Christ, he walked out when I was a kid, turned his back and ignored me the rest of his life."

"Then why . . . ?"

For a moment, Ellie thought he would pull the trigger. His rage bubbled up, then over as he started crying. Not blubbering, not sobbing. A silent sort of crying where the tears run down the face but the vision is still clear. The gun drifted slightly.

"For my mother," he finally choked out. "I killed him for my mother."

"What happened?" Ellie whispered.

"He killed her. He left her on her own, with a kid, no job, and no health insurance. He left her *after* she was diagnosed with cancer. Couldn't be bothered to call as she got sicker, couldn't be bothered to send any money from his supposed career. Did you know he was such a lousy actor he couldn't get a job? I think he had one paying acting gig his entire time in New York. So instead he made porno movies. Did you know that?"

Ellie nodded. "Yes. We found one of Merilyn when we were searching his house the other day."

The gun dipped slightly downward. Ellie dared hope. The way back for Steve was through the memory of Merilyn.

"Merilyn?"

She nodded. "He had a video of Merilyn. She was busted for prostitution in Manhattan in the seventies. That was Reginald's source for the girls he filmed. He'd post their bail, on the condition they perform for him."

Steve's shoulders sagged. The gun dropped to his side. His face fell, his eyes on his shoes, and he began to sob.

Ellie didn't move. She fought her tics, an epic battle of wills. She didn't want to startle him into shooting her and didn't want to disrupt his grief. She figured the best chance of staying alive was to remain still and silent. She didn't speak, barely breathed.

Steve wiped his eyes with the back of his free hand. He sniffled and wiped his nose on the shoulder of his shirt. He looked at Ellie, the gun still at his side.

"I'm sorry, Steve," she said. "I know how much Merilyn meant to you."

"She gave me my first job when I started doing theater work. She was always so kind, so complimentary. She reminded me of—" He hitched a sob but held it together. "Of my mom."

"Don't do this." Ellie indicated the gun. "Merilyn loved us all. Don't damage the memory of her with more killing."

For a moment, Steve looked at Ellie, and she saw those dead eyes again. Then it was gone. "What am I going to do?" he asked. In a single question, she heard the hurt child inside him, the hurt he had been carrying since Reginald left and since Annie died—the voice of a little boy who wanted his mother and father.

The door to the kitchen opened, and Mike entered, carrying his bag in one hand and keys in the other. "Hey, honey, I'm back early. I thought maybe we could go out for—" He stopped mid-sentence, seeing Ellie standing in the kitchen and Steve with the gun in his hand by his side.

"What the—?"

"Mike, don't move," Ellie said. Steve snapped the gun up. Mike froze, eyes wide. Ellie's tics released themselves, and she became a shaking, jerking, grunting mess.

"Close the door," Steve said.

"Close the door, close the door," she repeated under her breath, hating her body at that moment.

"What the hell is this?" Mike said again.

"Close the door," Steve repeated.

"You don't—*grunt-grunt*—have to—*grunt-grunt*—do this," Ellie said, trying to regain some control and failing. The stress was too much, and her body had a mind of its own.

"Shut up," Steve said. He sounded like he was trying to sound cold and hard, but to Ellie he sounded more hurt than anything. He indicated Mike. "You, move over there with her while I figure this out."

Ellie felt Mike's intensity as he stared at Steve. As much as she was ticcing and grunting and sniffing, Mike was as still as a statue. Yet underneath, she realized, his muscles were coiling, tensing, readying to spring.

"They know I did it. They'll go to the police," Steve muttered to himself. "I have to get rid of them and get out of here. I have to hide."

Ellie realized Steve was trying to work up the nerve to do the unthinkable. With Reginald, it probably had been easy. Years of festering rage had boiled over, but even then, he had planned it out, trying to make it look accidental. It wasn't face to face; it wasn't killing someone he had been friends with, someone who had been good to him. He was trying to talk himself into this.

Which is what he did with Valerie, Ellie suddenly realized. She must have known about Steve and Reginald and all the weird family twists that were there. Steve killed Reginald, and Valerie figured it out. Valerie was, after all, his father's wife, someone who in a way replaced his mother. So Steve got himself worked up enough to attack her.

And he was about to do it again.

"Bill will come after you," Ellie said, hoping to throw Steve off balance and keep him from reaching the point of feeling nothing.

"Shit shit shit," he said. "Christ. Bill. What am I going to do about him? I've got to run." He looked Ellie in the eyes. "I've got to take care of business here. Then run."

It happened before Ellie could stop it.

Steve lifted the gun. Mike rushed Steve. Steve fired, as if by reflex. Her tics halted abruptly, as if a plug had been pulled from an outlet. "No!" Ellie shouted, the sound absorbed by the gunshot.

Mike grabbed at his abdomen and fell to his knees.

"Mike!" Ellie shouted and took a step toward him. She looked at Steve.

He lifted the gun again, then looked at her. His eyes changed again, the little-boy look coming back. The little boy, horrified by what he saw in front of him. Horrified by what he had done. He raised the gun, and Ellie shut her eyes just at the moment she saw him shift the gun and turn it toward himself.

A gunshot.

She flinched. She opened her eyes.

Steve lay on the floor, a pool of blood welling beneath him. Ellie turned and saw Turner Milton behind her, standing at the kitchen door, gun out, hand trembling slightly. Turner shook his head in a motion, and Ellie realized that he hadn't had to shoot because Steve had shot himself at the last minute. Turner moved toward Steve on the floor.

Steve, eyes fluttering, mouthed words Ellie couldn't hear. She ran to Mike, who was lying on the floor and holding his stomach. He slumped against Ellie, winced, mumbled something, then passed out.

Turner moved closer, kicked the gun away from Steve's hand, knelt, and felt for a pulse.

From the other side of the kitchen, Ellie cried out for help.

Epilogue

I t rained that Friday.

Ellie and Bill stood side by side in the cemetery, looking down at a grave. It had been twenty years since they first stood there, and there they stood again. Tears ran down Ellie's cheeks, and Bill's face was sad and stony, a deep sense of loss in his eyes. They held hands, not saying anything, holding on to each other as they thought back to a time when Ava was still alive. Ellie thought of that bright sunny day and the illicit swim in the reservoir, watching Ava's head slip under the slate-blue water and never come back up.

Today, after a while, as if they'd planned it, they let go of each other's hand. Ellie moved forward and placed a yellow rose on the ground in front of Ava's grave. Then they turned and started back to Bill's cruiser and got in. He pulled away from the curb, tires squelching on the wet road, both of them dripping on the vinyl seats of the police car.

He drove to Ned's Diner, where they trudged inside and took a booth toward the back. Cheryl brought them both coffee, then left them alone.

"How is the theater doing?" Bill asked with a grimace. "I'm assuming you can't continue the run with both the lead and understudy dead."

Ellie smiled. "You know what I love most about Avalon? That it's a small town."

Bill frowned, perplexed. Ellie continued. "This town is full of characters and gossip and quirkiness. But when the chips are down, it comes through."

"I don't follow," Bill said, puzzled.

"We called everyone who bought tickets for the remaining shows—and they were sold out—to refund their money. Each and every one told us to keep it as a donation."

"Seriously?"

Ellie nodded and smiled, then sipped some coffee. "Looks like the Kaleidoscope will live to put on another show." She put the mug back down. "Did anyone ever figure out how Steve killed Reginald?"

Bill nodded. "After the crap show with Steve, Alice told the lab to rush it. Tox screen came back this morning. Positive for both benzo and opioid. And Merilyn was missing one of her fentanyl patches. As near as we can figure, Steve laced Reginald's drink the night before, during the final dress rehearsal, with some of Reginald's Valium, crushed up. But it didn't kill Reginald, just put him in near OD territory without actually being fatal."

"And Merilyn's patch?"

"Found it in the trash at Kaleidoscope. It had been cut it in half. My best guess is that, after you prepared the teacups, Steve crushed Valium into Reginald's drink and then dropped the cut fen patch to let it steep. As the stage manager, he would have been the one to make sure which actor got which teacup, right?"

"That's right." Ellie sighed, looking sad. "What a waste."

"How's Mike?" Bill asked.

Ellie rubbed her face. She picked up her mug and took a sip. "He's doing okay. Gut-shot is more survivable than a shot to the head or the heart. He's on pain meds still—not fentanyl—and he's going to have someone coming out for some PT every other day. But he'll recover. Should recover fully, if the doctors are right. He's taking high-test Tylenol and some occasional Motrin."

Bill nodded. He cradled his coffee in both hands but didn't take a sip. His sadness washed over him, coming at him from more than one direction. All the death in the Thornton case, topped off by the thirty-second anniversary of his kid sister Ava's birth. Bill felt numb and looked it.

"What did Alice Keaton say?"

"Oh, well, she said congratulations. She's got the box of Polaroids and the catalog of girls we made. She's reaching out to prosecutors in New York."

"That was nearly fifty years ago," Ellie said. "Is there anybody left to prosecute? How would they even find them?"

"No idea. Maybe they can't. But Alice handed it all over to New York, and now it's their mess. Who knows? Maybe with some digging, they'll find something there." Bill shook his head. "Still, it feels like an empty victory. Steve killed one person and nearly killed another, and killed himself before he could be brought to justice. Plus Merilyn. I mean, the body count has been awful."

"By the way, how did you stop Alex from killing himself?"

Bill found his smile, for a moment. "He knew exactly nothing about firearms and loaded the wrong caliber bullet. It was too small, so it slid forward in the chamber. Firing pin couldn't reach it."

Ellie gave a short, small laugh. "That poor man. I liked him. What do you think will happen to him?"

"Not sure how much will come out about the blackmail and the rest of it—or how the public will react—but the fact is, he was trying to protect Merilyn from Reginald's extortion. If there are financial irregularities, well, he did help us solve the case, and he's cooperating fully with the DA's office. With some luck, no jail time."

"Even if he was, um, money laundering?"

Bill smiled at her. "You know, if he hadn't told me it was Steve, I never would have known to send Turner to your house to try to save you."

Ellie smiled back. "How is Turner?"

"He's good. Relieved he didn't have to shoot Steve and relieved he was willing to if it was necessary. I'm glad he didn't have to—killing someone can leave a dark mark on your soul, even if it's justified."

He snapped his fingers. "I nearly forgot to tell you. I got a call from the hospital earlier today. Valerie came out of her coma last night."

Ellie's face brightened. "That's amazing!"

Bill smiled. "She came to, her doctors gave her a going over, and declared she was healing nicely."

"Does she remember what happened?"

Bill nodded. "She does. Confirmed a lot of what we thought. Steve pushed his way in. Seemed agitated and jumpy. Said something about covering his tracks, then brained her. She knows how lucky she is to be alive. You know what's the funniest part?"

"What?"

"She immediately asked if there was a piano in the hospital where she might be able to play."

Ellie smiled, the relief she felt radiating throughout her body, making her feel flush. She reached across the table and squeezed his hand. "Thank you. Without you, there would have been two more bodies."

He smiled weakly and took her hand. "You don't need to thank me. Ever."

Cheryl came over with her check pad out, ready to take their orders. "What'll you have?"

* * *

Six weeks later was the beginning of December, and the New England weather had lived up to its reputation for unpredictability. The

Farmer's Almanac was calling for some heavy snowstorms. Ellie didn't know if she really believed in that, but this was New England after all, and if there wasn't at least one huge snowstorm in winter in New England, then the winter never felt quite right.

On the first of December, nine inches of snow covered the hills of Worcester, helping the almanac live up to its reputation.

Mike had mostly healed, though he would still have the occasional stab of pain, making him double over unexpectedly.

She came in from clearing snow all morning from the driveway, the walk, their section of the sidewalk, and the cars. She and Mike had talked about getting a snowblower one year, but kept putting it off. Now she wished she had one.

She found Mike on the bed upstairs, propped up on pillows, the remote loose in his hand. He was dozing, technically still on disability leave from his job, and had taken to napping in the early afternoon. She joked about him having a rude awakening when he went back to work, and he smiled and said his clients were so boring, he might keep napping and didn't think they'd notice.

Ellie took the remote from his hand and clicked the TV off. Mike snorted and blinked, then yawned.

"I'm sorry. I wasn't trying to wake you," she said.

"No bother," he muttered. "I should probably get up anyway."

"Why? I'm going to shower now."

In the bathroom, Ellie stripped out of her wet clothing, a mix of snow and sweat. She turned the shower on as hot as she could tolerate and let the water warm and cleanse her. After fifteen minutes, she stepped from the shower, wrapped the towel around her, and picked up the pregnancy test.

She turned the box over, reading the instructions. It wasn't the first one she'd used, but she liked to double-check. She unwrapped the test and followed the instructions and came out of the bathroom.

The Last Line

Mike was awake now and she nodded at him, and he understood what she'd just done.

"How long do we have to wait?" Mike asked.

"Five or ten minutes, max."

"Okay." His heart was racing, and hers as well. They tried to make small talk, finding it awkward and strange, even after all these years together. The nervousness of learning whether they were going to have a child together made them so awkward around each other that they were laughing. After all the trying, the not-trying, then the possibility that it happened without the pressure of trying, the tension was almost amusing, and they fought back nervous smiles.

She stood and said, "Okay, that should be enough time."

Mike started to get up but winced, and she gently pushed him back into his pillows, saying, "Sit there. I'll go in, see what it says, and tell you."

Ellie went into the bathroom. The test sat on the sink. She took a deep breath, went over to it, and looked down. She blinked, her breath short.

From the bedroom, Mike called out to her. "Well?"

She came out of the bathroom, looked at Mike, and smiled.

Acknowledgments

This book has taken a long circular route to reach its destination, but it did finally arrive, and had quite a bit of help on the journey.

Many thanks to my agent, Adam Chromy, who took a chance on this book because of his love of theater and was very patient as I worked the kinks out during a number of re-writes.

If you could only see the before and after of this book, you would understand that Sara J. Henry is the most extraordinary of editors. This book would not be what it is without her eagle-eye for details and talent for making it flow smoothly.

Erin Miller provided me with a wealth of state forensic processing info. I may have only used a single piece, but it made the death in this book a murder.

The first responders of the town of Boylston were very patient with my questions. Many thanks to the volunteers at the Fire Department, to Officer Robert Barbato, and especially to police chief John Annunziata who answered email after email (after email).

To my informal writing group, Mikel and Norm: we'll find a new wing place, fellas, I'm sure of it.

My first readers, Abigail Strom, Leslie Lutz, and E.E. Holmes, were the most gracious of readers and offered such wonderful encouragement, advice, and feedback. Particular shoutout to Em, who made

Acknowledgments

me feel that the theater aspects were actually working when she said she could "smell the sawdust and old costumes."

As you doubtlessly realized, local theater plays a big part in this book. The theater community is a group of people like no other. Who else would willingly spend hours several nights a week, eight weeks straight, cramming words and music into their heads, dance moves into the muscle memory of their feet, and battling the stomach-dropping nervousness of opening night to step out on stage and tell a story? For no pay? No one else, that's who. Theater folk are a fun, funny, eccentric, quirky, welcoming group, and I feel blessed to be part of it. Special thanks to the folks at Calliope Productions, my family's second home over the last decade.

And of course to my family, Linnea, Olivia, and Maggie. None of this would have been possible without their love and support, and for that I can never thank them enough.

A couple of final notes that need to be mentioned:

First, some organizations in this novel are disparaged, most notable the Worcester Telegram (the T & G) and the Massachusetts State Police. This is strictly for narrative purposes only. I have no knowledge that the people who work and represent these organizations are anything other than good, hard-working, decent folks.

Second, while some of the technical aspects of police procedure in here are accurate or based on accurate terms, this book is not strictly a police procedural. There may be some "stretching" of the methods, timelines, etcetera. Any errors you find are mine and mine alone.

Lastly, Ellie, the main character of this book, has Tourette syndrome, as I do. And while it was important to me for my lead character to have TS, it was equally important that it be one aspect of who she is, not the all-consuming trait that drives the story. We see a lot of ridiculous portrayals of Tourette syndrome in the media. I wanted to show you a different side of it. I hope I did.

If you'd like more information about Tourette syndrome, please visit https://tourette.org